The Light at the End of the Day.

By Kevin Habekost

DEDICATION

For Jack, Bobby and Jackson. The dearest, sweetest souls.

For Marita, by my side, always.

CONTENTS

1   The Wish Walker .... Pg. 1

2   Jack the Dripper .... Pg. 41

3   The American Home Managers Association .... Pg. 87

4   Buses .... Pg. 109

5   The Best Cobb Salad this Side of Montreal .... Pg. 141

6   Bird Brain Experiment .... Pg. 175

7   Winter Patio .... Pg. 195

8   The Crooked Bank Robber............ Pg. 213

9   The Scarf............................... Pg. 251

10   Google it................................ Pg. 263

11   Main Street.............................. Pg. 287

ACKNOWLEDGMENTS

Thanks to Marita, Graham Averiss, Mark Gilmore, Gail Ainsworth and Paul Jenner for their valuable proof reading. I really appreciate your extra effort in helping edit all these words.

No thanks to Jackson who kept me at the dog park when I should have been writing.

THE WISH WALKER

Conlan had lost hope, his spirits were as low as they had ever been. Thankfully he was on the move again, so there were no eyes watching him. Not like there is when he stays in one place for a long time and people get to know him. While on the road he could afford to be lax with the façade of sleeping and eating. For the time being, as he walked out of Big Piney, Wyoming, which happened to be the town he was passing through, Conlan gave up pretending to be mortal.

He had been warned about losing hope. 'A good Wish Walker never loses hope', his teachers had repeated ad nauseam. He'd been trying his best to honor his training and keep his spirits up, but he was at a breaking point. He recently started questioning everything. Hadn't he been at this for far too long? Surely it shouldn't take a good Wish Walker this long to fulfill his obligation. What kind of Wish Walker was he then? Apparently a poor one. To tell the truth there was no evidence to show he was any kind of Wish Walker at all. Is a mailman the proper title for someone who has yet to deliver any mail? Conlan's obligation remained resolutely unfulfilled. After all this time and despite his so-called training, Conlan was coming to the realization he must not know the first thing about Wish Walking.

He was constantly making mistakes now. For one, thinking a Wish Walker has an *obligation* to fulfill is absolutely the wrong way to look at it, the absolute wrong word to use, and Conlan knew it. He'd been warned about such thoughts, such words. Being a Wish Walker, a WW, is a privilege not a job. He should be using the word honor, not obligation.

Conlan took his first steps upon the earth completely believing in the apotheosis of being a Wish Walker, a miracle maker, an Angel of good fortune, the embodiment of God's grace. To grant one life changing (possibly even world changing) wish to some lucky human soul was a fantastic assignment. Yes, he'd believed in the beginning, but that was a long time ago. Now he couldn't count the calamities, famines, floods, droughts, plagues and wars he'd seen. There were plenty of opportunities to release his wish, but all had ended in failure. In fact there were such multitudes of failed attempts he could scarcely remember a day he'd spent on earth that didn't include one. Humans are lucky in that they can eventually forget things. Angels remember everything, forever.

He had been on the move all morning so when he spotted a patch of forest off of Highway 189, Conlan thought it would be a perfect spot to go and rest for a while, shut his mind off and dismiss the idea of being a WW completely, commit the whole thing to oblivion. A sabbatical would help him get his spirits up again. Conlan promised himself it would only be for a short period of time.

From the beginning Conlan knew the chance of failing was high. He had heard all the rumors about it in WW School. How the stress level is enormous because a Wish Walker has only one single definitive act. One undertaking and the whole job is done, mission accomplished. "One shot! One shot!", the headmaster would say, "so don't rush." All this really meant, Conlan decided, is they expected him to perform perfectly his first and only time at bat. Forget the whole premise that practice makes perfect. At least Conlan had got the not rushing part right - he had been at it for more than four hundred years!

Conlan would never rid himself of the horribleness the plethora of disease, natural disasters and war had bestowed upon him. By far the worst was war. Man's ingenuity in maiming and murdering each other was beyond reproach. He'd been through civil wars, holy wars and world wars, crusades, revolutions, genocides and a holocaust. Not to mention numerous mutilations by automobile, train and airplane. All fundamentally man's doing. He had been trained to accept without repugnance or judgment all humanity's pointless self-imposed misery and suffering. Earth was a world ruled by fates- fates designed with purpose and educational value to human souls. This is why a WW gets only one wish to grant. It would never do to have fate counteracted by a throng of answered wishes. In fact, a WW was really an instrument of fate, conceding they provide a reversal of one fate to be superseded by another. And a Wish Walker was to acknowledge all of this well before setting one foot on Earth. Conlan was supposed to be a professional with stout sentimental detachment. War was just another day at the office to a WW. Getting all emotionally wound up over the woes of humans would cost him, it would degrade his decision making process and he could very well end up walking the earth another four hundred years.

Many times he could have manipulated the gears of fate and prevented some mortal's doom. So many times it was technically within his capabilities to grant a wish to shrivel a brain tumor or prevent a deadly bridge collapse. But he just hadn't felt it. He could still hear his instructors, "It's not an intellectual thing. You must feel it. It's the most important thing of all…the feel".

Conlan was not happy about losing faith in himself, but he understood why. The fact that he had more than a few times come very close to giving away his wish, but in the end he hadn't felt it and therefore failed was discouraging. At the same time the only reason he had any faith left at all was the very fact that he had come close. There was the wish of the parents of a three year old with bone cancer, and the prayers of a little boy whose father was decapitated because he fell asleep at the wheel after driving all night just to make it home for Christmas. The countless young soldiers all wishing the very same desperate wish: to see their homes again. So many wishes came close, but the prize didn't come. The closest of all was the German soldier in WW1 who'd stormed a fox hole in Somme, killing or wounding all the Canadian solders huddled there. With such despair and anguish the young German soldier wished he hadn't used his gun on those poor men. There was no need; the Canadian soldiers would have easily surrendered. They were just as starved, cold and dehydrated as he was. Some were, like a lot of German soldiers, already wounded. So hard the German soldier wished to take his bullets back and still Conlan could not evoke the feel, so his wished remained un-granted. Conlan felt such sympathy for the boy he thought of giving up the whole operation, breaking cover and appearing to him in his true angelic form, telling the young soldier God would know the killings were a product of war and war alone, that he would be absolved. He almost risked everything by exposing the truth to the soldier, but still he could not grant the boy his wish. That was a hundred years ago.

Breaking cover then would have meant instant failure and a quick trip back to heaven, his WW status revoked, busted back down to a mere Prayer Listener again. Which was a noble enough thing, listening to prayers and giving the prayer the feeling they had been heard (even if a lot of the time it was more venting and human hopelessness than real prayer). Another millennia as a PL was not Conlan's idea of moving up the ranks. Doing PL again would be in Conlan's words, and he never liked using the expression, pure hell. Eventually he wanted to work his way up to being a Guardian Angel or possibly even an Archangel. Conlan was serious about being chosen for an Archangel position. It is what drove him initially as a WW. And he was using it now as motivation and a last reason to hang on. He knew there would be no way he'd ever become even a Guardian Angel if he couldn't complete his duties first as a Wish Walker. For a hundred years there had been no more thoughts of breaking cover. Recently, however, it had crept back into his mind. It was, after all, the easiest way to give up, a quick trip home.

He walked down the hill towards the trees, trudging through the February snow with its shrubs and wild grass imprisoned underneath. The bite of the north wind felt good on Conlan's skin. He was under dressed and he didn't care, didn't care to keep up the masquerade of being a fragile human being. It was much easier to simply be the immutable, unchanging, immortal being he was. And anyway there was no one around to wonder why he didn't take care not to freeze or starve to death.

It was accepted by the higher powers that there would be the occasional 'Accidental Exposure'. That was their official name for it. Conlan had had plenty of AE's. Forgetting, for example, to eat and sleep for extraordinary lengths of time, which was easy to do. Eventually people ended up noticing. Going out in freezing weather in a short sleeves shirt and sauntering nonchalantly as if it were the middle of July was his most common blunder -'Excuse me sir but aren't you freezing'. The worst of such AE's was the time he was horrifically run over by a car. The accident was gruesome to onlookers. Of course Conlan received no injury. An Angel cannot obtain so much as a scratch. A policeman had to ask witnesses if they were sure the car had actually struck Conlan. Conlan did his best to act injured, but it was clear to everyone who saw the accident a miracle had taken place. He fled when reporters turned up on the scene.

What was so frustrating about being a WW was the lack of information about the actual experience, the way he was left to discover for himself how to do it. Some things cannot be taught. Conlan understood the practical part of learning by experience, but he thought it unfair when applied to Wish Walkers, as they do their job once and only once, experience simply doesn't come into it.

He made his way to somewhere in the middle of the clump of forest and sat down on a fallen log stretched out under a row of pine trees. He emptied his mind of as much of the last four hundred years as he could and began a form of Angelic meditation. Conlan's body formed the outline of a white Buddha as snow began to accumulate on and around him. He didn't mind the snow; he thought it a good thing, especially if he became completely buried by it. This way, while he forgot about the world, he would be invisible to it as well. He'd be invisible to the world maybe, but not to heaven. Conlan knew this far too well. It was fine he thought, they could all watch him take a break. If they didn't like it they could withdraw him and classify him as a failure. Conlan almost wished they'd pull the plug on the whole affair anyway. He would accept himself as a washout, the entire matter a long drawn out blunder.

As fate would have it, it began to snow heavily.

But try as he might, he couldn't keep his mind from turning to Wish Walker School and what a breeze it had been, how it should have been much harder. Most of what they did was talk about what not to do: absolutely no fraternizing with other WW's while on earth, never discuss heaven or other dimensions with humans. Under no circumstance do you expose yourself ! EVER! Those kinds of things, along with the perpetual 'never lose hope', were beat into WW students ceaselessly. There was also the empathy training to bring up their main Wish Walker skill, which was: to precisely feel what humans feel, but on a much higher energetic plane. This would help WWs feel out who to award their wish to. The actual granting of the wish was easy; they all practiced it on each other with training wishes.

It was the who and why that was the hard part and to this the School Masters would simple say 'you'll have to study'. There was a lot to study, volumes and volumes of verified successful wish granting and the stories surrounding them. But this only served to confuse the students because there was no discerning pattern. Some of the granted wishes were nothing short of epic and probably changed the course of human history. Others seemed trivial, merely heartwarming. Yet both were considered equally successful. 'You have to suspend all judgments and feel, it's all about the feeling' the School Masters would say, over and over. It couldn't be demonstrated because after all how can a feeling be shown. Now, four hundred years later Conlan was struggling with his frustrations over how baffling the 'feel' was.

Conlan and the rest of the students were so blindly optimistic back then, even a little cocky. Only a petit Angel named Nora had any sense of the difficulty that lay ahead. It was only Nora who worried about failing. Conlan remembered Nora being obsessed with failing. 'I'm not sure I'm very confident with the 'feeling' part,' she would say to the instructors at the end of almost every class. Conlan and the rest of the class acted like she was worrying about nothing and attributed her anxiety to a lack of confidence. So self-assured were Conlan and some of the other class mates that they often tried to out brag each other, boasting how influential and legendary their wishes would be. Absolutely sure the most famous and miraculous Wish Walkers, the ones that every wannabe WW read about, would soon be superseded-by them. Only Nora was doubtful and read everything she could get her hands on about the mythical 'feeling' of Wish Walking. Once she confided in Conlan privately saying: 'There is going to be a time down there, something so horrific and sad will happen, and my heart is going to scream to release my wish, but I'm not going to 'feel' it and I'm going to have to walk away. I don't think I'll be able to walk away. I'm going to release my wish without 'the feeling' and I'm going to fail. I just can't get the notion of failing out of my head.' All Conlan could do was tell Nora to be more confident and not to be so adherent to the 'Angelic Code' of human devotion. Try putting herself and her needs before those of the human race for once.

Conlan knew now that was easier said than done. Now it really bothered him he'd been so cavalier with Nora. And it angered him that he didn't wonder, as Nora had, why the statistics on the success rate of a first time WW was kept such a secret at school? Why did Guardian Angels never talk about their prior experience as a WW? It all seemed a dirty, cruel trick now. Maybe the secret was that everybody failed the first time out and he should have given his wish away long ago-feeling or no feeling, to the German soldier or the parents of the baby with cancer. Nora was right to have worried so much. She had probably made out much better than he had.

Now after all these years Conlan realized he was burned out. He decided fatigue must be the root of his lack of confidence. After all who can go four hundred years without a break? Not even an Angel. Merely the thought of being worn out made him wearier still. He had been caught in a downward spiral and he finally hit bottom. He was too tired now to worry about losing hope or about breaking rules. He decided he needed to take a break from the entire ordeal, maybe just a week or two, to re-charge his halo, as Angels often said.

He was so tired he wished for sleep, real sleep, human sleep. It suddenly struck him that he had made his own wish. He wondered if it were possible to grant himself his own wish? That would be a first: a WW granting himself his only wish and ending up the only Angel in heaven who now needed to sleep. That would be certain failure. He forced himself to forget about wishes altogether.

Three days after Conlan began his meditation a mortal named Thomas Grady was walking down the same hill just off of Highway 189, looking for his lost dog. The snow was deep so he took large, strident steps. Eventually the snow was well past his knees, still he pushed on. 'Bailey,' he shouted, 'Bailey, here girl…Bailey!' Thomas walked towards a patch of trees, calling for his dog. Somewhere in the middle of the trees he put his hands up to his mouth to amplify his shout, 'Bailey…come girl.' Thomas listened. Turning his head slightly to the right he caught sight of a strange form within the snow laden trees and bushes. His first thought was that it was a stump buried by snow, which happened to have the outline of a person sitting crossed legged; like one of those statues of Buddha you put in your garden. Thomas considered the irrationality of it being anything other than a stump and put any other idea out of his mind. He continued to scan the oasis of trees for his dog. He took a few long strides forward and called for Bailey again. But something drew his eyes back to the odd pattern in the snow. From this new angle it looked even more like a person. Thomas could see clearly the outline of folded legs within the casing of snow. With trepidation he approached the shape. Thomas was sure if it was a person covered in snow he or she would surely be frozen to death. An even grimmer thought came to him: the person might not only be dead but solid as an ice cube as well. He remembered the time he and his brother had found a frozen frog and how shocked they were when it shattered into a thousand pieces on the frozen pond after they tossed it up in the air.

Thomas was horrified when he got close enough and realized it most certainly was a person under the blanket of snow. Most likely a suicide, Thomas thought. Someone had come out here to a peaceful stretch of woods, sat down on this log and simply waited until hypothermia snuffed out the last embers of life. Thomas was impressed by this in a morbid sort of way; it would have taken a lot of will power to make it past the pain and instinctive fight to conserve life. Once the pain and violent shivering were over, however, it was probably not a bad way to go, at least Thomas reasoned so. It was definitely a peaceful spot to end things.

Thomas wasn't sure if he should go immediately for help or check the body for vital signs. He knew he should be sure, before he went back to the highway to wave someone down, that whoever was under there was in fact dead. He felt sick at the thought of touching a dead, frozen body. He formed the edge of his hand into a wiper blade. Holding his breath and grimacing he cleared the snow from the frozen shape's face with a quick jabbing swipe. Thomas leaped back, an eerie shudder jolting up his spine. He held his breath as he took in the ivory face framed in ice and snow.

For a long moment Thomas couldn't breathe. Finally his lungs made heavy gasps for air as his mind tried to catch up with what was happening. Only moments ago he was merely searching for his lost dog. Now he was staring into the face of a dead person. The tranquility of the forest and the serene expression on the face of the dead man served to help calm Thomas. His fear decreased and soon he felt only vigilant curiosity. The face belonged to a man, a youthful, good looking man, it had small features and there was a slight androgynous look to it. His skin was an ethereal, waxen, pearly white.

Thomas was surprised how the face of a dead person could look so beautiful, celestial even.

For some reason the face drew Thomas in. He knew he should not delay setting off for help, but there was something about this face which fascinated Thomas and made him want to stare, even ponder. It was a surreal moment; the stillness of the forest was palpable. Large flakes of snow floating slowly, dreamlike to the ground. And that beautiful face emanating something Thomas could feel, but didn't understand. He took a few steps toward the frozen man. Removing his glove he stretched out his arm and ever so gently let the tips of two of his fingers touch a pearly cheek. Two eyes jumped open. Thomas screamed. He lost his footing as he reeled backwards in horror. He scampered across the snow on his stomach away from the frozen man. As he struggled to get away he looked over his shoulder. The Frozen statue was standing now, shaking off its blanket of snow. The last thing Thomas could remember was seeing two enormous wings stretch out, wings whiter than the new falling snow. Thomas passed out.

Conlan may have been enjoying his time 'away', but his acute, otherworldly senses were still very much active. He had heard the man's footsteps clomping on the highway a mile away. Then he heard his shuffling down the hill through the thick snow and then his shouts. He was hoping the man wouldn't come through his thicket of trees. Conlan knew he'd been sitting long enough to be fully buried by snow and supposed it would be enough to conceal him if the man did come his way. As his ever-worsening luck on earth would have it the man not only waded through the snow directly towards him, but then stopped very close by.

Conlan was enjoying his break and didn't want it to be interrupted so soon, but he knew already the man had spotted him and was presently trying to make out what would cause such an odd shape in the snow. Conlan was not completely out of his mediation, nevertheless he could easily track the man's every move and thought. He heard shouts of: 'Bailey…come girl', and felt the man's attention turn towards him briefly, then fade, only to fall back again, stronger than before. Conlan tried to will the man to move on, but he knew it was too late. His fear was realized. The man had decided to find out what was under the odd pile of snow. Conlan understood his respite from the world was over.

Conlan's cognizance was coming back. He came dreamily out of his meditation just as the man wiped the snow from his face. Moments later he felt the man's hesitant touch upon his cheek. Warily, he opened his eyes. Conlan saw the poor man almost jump out of his skin and stumbled backwards in fright. After so many days of immobility Conlan needed to stretch. He had an insatiable need to open his wings and relieve the cramping that had been building there for four hundred years.

He stood and shook the covering of snow from his body and despite the fact that it was forbidden to do so upon the earth, especially with a human present, and even though it would rip his shirt to shreds, Conlan spread his wings until they felt like they were going to fly off by themselves.

Now Conlan knelt over Thomas, who lay mumbling in the snow. When Thomas opened his eyes and saw the snow statue was now immediately over top of him, he squirmed with fear and let out a muted cry.

"Easy, easy now," Conlan said, "I'm sorry I gave you such a fright."

Thomas sat up and looked incredulously at the... man?

"The name is Conlan," Conlan said, smiling. He held out his hand. Still laying on his back, Thomas shook Conlan's hand guardedly. "It's a pleasure to meet you Thomas?" Conlan said.

"How...how do you know my name?" Thomas asked.

It was another screw up. Conlan knew he'd have to get back on his game. Get back to playing mortal again and quickly.

"You told me just now," Conlan said, helping Thomas to his feet.

"I did?" asked the man.

"Yes, but I didn't catch your last name," Conlan said, trying to throw Thomas off.

"It's Grady," Thomas said.

"Pleased to meet you Thomas Grady," said Conlan. The two men shook hands again.

Thomas studied Conlan for a long moment. He looked back at the log where Conlan had been sitting and at the jumble of snow that once encased him. He tried but couldn't hide his bafflement over the whole encounter. And there was the lingering vague memory of … wings? Passing out from fright was new to him and he thought the vision was some sort of hallucination. Thomas was feeling the cold now and it brought his attention back to the stranger who might be half frozen to death.

"Well Conlan," said Thomas, "The way I found you I'm surprised you can still walk and talk. How long have you been out here and what in hell were you doing just sitting there like that? You must be freezing to death?"

"Now that you mention it," Conlan said, "I do feel rather cold."

He began the façade of shivering. Despite his time off, Conlan felt instantly tired again. The mere thought of pretending to be a frail mortal was daunting. Thomas believed he saw, if only for a moment, all the will and stature flow out of Conlan, who appeared to want to say something, but changed his mind and instead settled for wearing a forlorn expression on his pale face. His shoulders sagged.

"There is something very odd about you my friend," Thomas said, smiling. He started thinking he had been correct in his earlier assumption that whoever would come out here and just sit in the snow had a death wish. Thomas had compassion for anyone so dispirited that they would consider taking their own life.

"Odd in a good way is what I mean to say," Thomas said. "What you need to do is come home with me. Get some hot food in you and some rest. That is if you have no other place to be." Thomas's gut feeling was this Conlan wasn't a vagrant, more a drifter, a tired, sad, demoralized drifter.

"My wife makes one mean butter squash soup," Thomas continued. "She's making some right about now as a matter of fact."

The thought of having to pretend to eat again did not appeal to Conlan. He knew that it would appear strange if a mortal in a near hypothermic predicament didn't jump at the chance for a hot bowl of soup. Besides he, in fact, had no other place to be. He hadn't made any plans for after his sabbatical. He decided he would accept Thomas's kindness and go with him. After all eating a bowl of soup wouldn't kill him. He thought it best, for now, to continue not caring about being a Wish Walker. He had absolutely no desire to even remember what a wish was, let alone try to grant one.

"That's very kind of you," Conlan said.

"You've stopped shivering," Thomas said, removing his heavy winter coat, "that's a bad sign. It means you are moving into a stage of hypothermia not many people come back from. I don't mean to scare you, but we need to get moving. Here, put this on." He handed Conlan his winter coat.

Conlan realized he had forgotten to maintain his shivering. He put on Thomas's coat and they made their way up the hill towards the highway.

"You were calling for someone...Bailey I think it was?" Conlan asked

Thomas didn't want to burden the stranger with the misfortunate story of why he was calling for his dog, especially a stranger who was half frozen, but the more he thought about it the more he believed keeping a good conversation going would be beneficial to Conlan.

"Bailey is our dog," Thomas said, "a golden retriever. She ran away last November when an autumn thunder storm hit. I know it's been three months now, but I don't have the heart to give up hope. My wife, she's devastated about it. She blames herself because she didn't latch the screen door to the porch..."

"One more heartbreak on an endless road of heartbreaks," Conlan said, softly.

"Pardon," said Thomas.

"It's nothing, please continue," said Conlan.

Thomas looked sideways at Conlan, wondering if it was wise to bring such a strange man to his home. He really had no other option except to drive him straight to the hospital in Big Piney. But the hospital was much further. Besides, the warmth of a real home seemed the more kindly thing to provide a stranger as long as he was not in any immediate life threatening condition. The stranger did seem peculiar, Thomas thought, but he realized it might be the effects of the cold on his brain. Besides there was no indication the man was anything but harmless. In an odd way Thomas found him very interesting. He would take his chances.

"Anyway," Thomas continued, " my wife blames herself because she didn't properly latch the screen door to the porch and that's where we kept Bailey at night. One night we had a freak storm, plenty of thunder. Bailey is absolutely scared to death of thunder. She got out and bolted. We haven't seen her since."

Conlan knew Bailey, the Grady's golden retriever, was dead. He could, with his otherworldly perception see her body, decayed and frozen, lying in an icy ditch under a nestle of wintering cattails, twenty two miles east of where they presently were.

"She may come home yet," Thomas continued, "stranger things have happened. I tell Lisa, that's my wife, and Jessy, that's my daughter, that there are plenty of stories about animals, especially dogs, turning up months or even years later. So when I get the chance I drive a ways in some direction and get out and start calling. No use in losing hope, serves no purpose."

Try looking for your dog for four hundred years then we'll see how your hope is, Conlan thought. Then he wondered what happened to Angels with bad attitudes.

"How old is your daughter?" Conlan asked, but he already knew.

They had made it to the top of the hill and were now walking on the highway towards Thomas truck. Thomas had begun to shiver slightly, being without his jacket. Conlan felt guilty about this, being that he didn't really need Thomas's jacket at all.

"She's six," Thomas said, blowing warm breath into his fists. "Most beautiful thing you'll see this side of heaven, but I'm her father, I'm supposed to say things like that."

Conlan was glad there was a child at the home he was going to. Children have a way of pulling the best out of an Angel. To be around a child would be a good reminder of the good things about mortals and earth. Children always reminded him of what he was supposed to be accomplishing down here.

"Six is a good age," Conlan said.

"You married?" asked Thomas.

"No."

"Children?" asked Thomas.

"None."

They made it to the truck and when Thomas asked how he was holding up; Conlan indicated he was doing much better. Conlan decided to pretend to shiver again and this was a great relief to Thomas. Now he didn't have to worry about warming Conlan up slowly. Thomas cranked the trucks heater to full, which made Conlan feel better, if only for Thomas's sake. It took eighteen minutes to get to the farm where Thomas and his family lived. They had seen no other cars on the highway.

It was five acres of retired farmland with an old, but well kept, farm house hidden from the Highway by a row of poplar trees.

"Every time I pull in here I miss that damn dog," Thomas said, "she'd bark and jump around all excited, tail of hers going a hundred miles a minute. She loved visitors." There was a long, quiet sigh before he cleared the lump in his throat. "Your clothes are frozen now but when they thaw they'll be wet," he continued. "So that's the first thing, change your clothes. You're a bit taller, but not by much. Some of my clothes should fit you. Then we'll warm you up by the fire. We'll have a hot cup of tea before we eat. Or maybe you prefer coffee?"

"Tea will be fine," lied Conlan.

"Come on inside then and meet the wife and kid," Thomas said.

Inside the home Conlan found it surprisingly warm. There were the smells of cooking soup and baking bread from the kitchen. Earthly things that were of no real matter to an Angel, still Conlan found them pleasant. The first to greet the men was Jessy. Thomas found his daughter's reaction to their guest quite out of her character. All she seemed able to do was stare at Conlan and with a grin that was normally reserved for Christmas morning.

"Don't be rude honey," said Thomas, "say hello to our guest."

Jessy said hello with a wild giggle and ran into the kitchen to her mother.

As Thomas began removing his outer wear, he heard his wife, Lisa, talking to Jessy from the kitchen.

"Daddy has brought home a what?" She said. "Oh Honey don't be silly."

Lisa appeared with Jessy peeking out from behind her with the same overgrown smile as before. Thomas did the introductions and explained the story of how he had found Conlan all most frozen to death. Immediately Lisa showed concern, showing her guest to the wash room to change out of the rest of his wet clothes and ordering Thomas to get some dry ones.

After Conlan had changed he and Thomas sat by the fire while Lisa went to finish baking the bread and readying the soup. In the meantime she made a pot of tea and served it to the men warming by the fire. Jessy leaned against the side of her father's chair, showing intense interest in the visitor. In fact she couldn't take her eyes off him.

"This time a year," said Thomas, "with this cold you definitely need to be careful. I don't pretend it's my place to lecture you, but you were hardly dressed for the conditions. The little that you had on was thin at best and of not much protection against mother nature in the raw, or as we like to say around here, in the buff."

Conlan nodded his agreement.

"I'm guessing you're a drifter, passing through. Am I right?" Thomas said.

"I would say a drifter is an adequate word," Conlan said. He took a sip of tea and looked around the room. "You are a very lucky man Thomas to have such a lovely home and family." Conlan then looked at Jessy. "And you young lady, do you know you're lucky to have such a kind father?"

"Yes sir," Jessy said.

It was indeed a very lovely home in the real sense of the word, Conlan thought. He could feel the love they all had for each other. But there was an obvious dark note that rang through their happiness. Conlan could sense everyone was mourning the fourth member of the family, their dog Bailey. But Conlan clearly felt Lisa had more than sadness echoing in her heart over Bailey. She had deep guilt and regret as well. She squarely placed the blame of Bailey's running away on herself. It was unbearable to hear her daughter crying herself to sleep at night over Bailey.

They sat and ate the soup and bread at the dining room table while Jessy asked Conlan silly questions about the sky and the clouds. Conlan was surprised to find he didn't mind any of it. Even eating wasn't the drudgery it usually was. He found he was actually enjoying himself.

After dinner they sat in the living room where the fire place was crackling and hot. Thomas wanted to inspect Conlan's fingers and toes, especially his toes, for damage from frost bite.

"Everything looks fine," Thomas said after his awkward but necessary inspection. He had never seen such fine hands and feet before. They looked more like an artist's rendition than actual human appendages. Jessy lay on the floor coloring in a coloring book she had been given as a Christmas gift. She was coloring the wings of an Angel gold. It was apparent to Conlan that the little girl somehow knew that he was an Angel. How she knew he couldn't guess. He had heard of some humans having extrasensory perceptions that would allow them to identify super-beings such as Angels. Despite all the questions about the sky and clouds and her present attention to the figure in her coloring book, Jessy was behaving admirably –she was keeping her little secret to herself.

"Tomorrow is Sunday," Thomas declared. And after a reasonable pause he added, "Any idea where you might be headed?" Conlan appeared indifferent if not outright indignant to the idea of having to head anywhere.

Lisa caught Thomas's eye with a stern questioning look. He knew she was not going to be comfortable having someone stay in the house overnight. Especially one who didn't know where he might be heading the next day, as if he were some vagrant. Was there any alternative Thomas wondered.

"I was thinking maybe heading out towards California. Shake off this cold." Conlan said, finally.

Thomas looked surprised. "California?" he said. "Well if you left from Big Piney, like you say and judging where I found you, you were going completely in the wrong direction."

Conlan shrugged. "I guess the idea just came to me now," he said.

There was a long pause as the fire crackled.

"In some ways I admire you Conlan," Thomas said. "Having the freedom that you do, being a free man of the road. But on the other hand not having the comforts of a family and a warm home, well, quite frankly that would wear on me."

"You have no children?" Lisa asked Conlan, "No family?"

Conlan saw Jessy look up from her coloring book and grin curiously.

Conlan guessed in reality he had a very large family. All Angels were considered to be brothers and sisters. But as far as here on earth, strictly speaking, he had to say no to having a family. And of course he had no children; Angels couldn't have children.

"Ever thought of settling down?" Lisa asked, "Stick it out somewhere and carve out a life?"

Conlan didn't like these lines of questioning from people. It always caused him to have to lie…a lot. He found, for the most part mortals weren't stupid. They could discern when he was holding back, omitting relevant information. This made him seem elusive, as if he were hiding something. Which was certainly not an enduring trait.

"I'm getting to the point now," Conlan said, "where my need to 'drift' will hopefully come to an end." That's about as honest an answer as I can give Conlan thought. "I do plan on having a family someday, before I get too old," he added, which was not truthful by any stretch of the imagination. Conlan was mad at himself. He had sworn never to bring up a reference to his age. It always resulted in the same question, a question he had to be more than elusive in answering.

"If you don't mind me asking, how old are you?" Lisa asked.

Again Jessy took a keen interest in a question. She stared expectantly at Conlan.

"Let's just say," Conlan said, ambiguously, "that I'm a lot older than I look."

Conlan sensed that Lisa didn't appreciate Conlan's evasiveness. Age was something you didn't ask a woman; men, on the other hand, should have no aversion in discussing the subject.

Thomas, sensing the sudden tension, chimed in, "The reason I asked about your plans is Jess and I will be going to church in the morning and I thought we could drop you off somewhere," he said. "I was thinking maybe the bus station in Big Piney. You can't walk all the way to California. I could lend you a couple bucks for a bus ticket… if needed."

"The bus station in Big Piney will be fine," said Conlan. "I appreciate the offer of the loan but I have money."

Jess giggled at this. Conlan noticed she was now coloring in the outline of a golden retriever, another to add to the multitude of such pieces stuck on the Grady's fridge, all of them with red colored hearts and captions such as 'Bailey, please come home' and 'Daddy will find you '.

"Lisa, you don't go to church?" Conlan asked.

"I've never been theological," she answered, "I was brought up by non-believers. My dad was a scientist, ex-catholic and my mother was a doctor, a definite atheist thru and thru. I've just never had the need for religion."

Jessy was all ears now. She had always been concerned that her mother didn't attend church with her and her dad and wanted to hear what a real live Angel had to say about the matter.

Conlan smile reassuringly at Jessy. "Martin Luther once said, 'no man may reach heaven by any religious effort," he said. "Only by faith and faith alone may one ascend."

Conlan's own words struck him, as if they had been meant for his own ears to hear. 'By faith alone may one ascend'. Or re-ascend, was what Conlan was thinking. It suddenly hit him that he had been feeling sorry for himself. Yes, he was tired. Yes, four hundred years is a long time, even by an Angel's sense of time. But he must go on, he must restore his faith. After all, there were plenty successful Wish Walkers. His own success was possible. Given enough time…

"I'm not certain I understand what dear Mr. King meant by all that," Lisa said.

"Well, I guess," said Conlan, "he meant it is our personal relationship with God that counts. Structured religion is merely an aid to strengthen our personal relationship. You may be involved in the church and be very religious, but your true relationship with God may be neglected."

"Well at least one of those outmoded religious people was making sense," Lisa said. This got an apprehensive look from Thomas. "I'm sorry I don't mean to offend," she said. "Are you a religious man Conlan?"

This got more giggles from Jessy.

"Religious no," said Conlan, "but, I do have a sort of faith in the world and mankind. I guess I believe the world is made up of mostly good people." Conlan directed his words as though he were talking to Jessy. "And I'm a realist. I have faith in the fact that although bad things sometimes happen and we may not understand why, there is a higher purpose to the world. All things, good and bad, happen for a reason."

Conlan knew Jessy was an intelligent girl. It was evident the way she played along when she realized her parents didn't see him for what he was, a real live Angel. But she was only six years old; would she understand what he was trying to tell her? All evening he could feel her getting her hopes up about Bailey. After all he was an Angel and what were Angels to spend their time on other than protecting people and answering prayers, but surely to help lost dogs find their way home as well. Conlan knew it was only a matter of time before Jessy would make a wish: that the real live Angel that came to her house for dinner bring Bailey back home safe and sound. And the pattern of four hundred years would repeat: the all immutable, the all inflexible feeling won't be there and he will fail Jessy. What would be his explanation to her? What would she think of Angels then?

"I think that's a good way of looking at things," said Thomas. "I pretty much feel the same, but I definitely believe in going to church as well."

"Well I know one young girl who has to get up early in the morning if she wants to go with daddy and Conlan into town and then to church," Lisa said.

"Ok mommy," Jessy said. She stood and smiled at Conlan. "I'm going to say my prayers before I go to sleep." She hurried into the kitchen.

Thomas and Lisa exchanged forlorn looks.

"Every night since Baileys been gone," Thomas said, "Jessy says a prayer and lights a candle for her and puts it in the window."

Conlan had just spoke commandingly about religious faith and he could feel the girls faith and knew it to be limitless; even more so since her father had brought home an Angel. What shall be her reward for such loyalty to heaven's grace? He felt his heart sink now and wondered what happened to his own faith. He tried to tell himself things could be different this time. There were so many peculiar details about today, things that could be taken as signs: he'd just come out of a deep, meditative rest, Thomas had accidently seen his wings and Jessy somehow knew he was an Angel. Besides, hadn't they said any wish could be the wish. He had to come across *the* wish at some point. He couldn't go on Wish Walking forever. Or could he? For whatever reason something felt very right about being here with Jessy and Thomas and Lisa. Conlan wanted to take this feeling and expand it. He wanted to stay around the Grady's longer, but he knew it was better not to force things. Things had to come naturally. He would think of a way. Maybe hold up in Big Piney for a while, get to know them a little better.

Jessy brought out a candle in a porcelain holder. Lisa struck a match for Jessy and together they lit the candle and placed it on the window sill. Then Jessy went on her knees and said a silent prayer. Conlan could hear every word as if she were whispering directly into his ear. She wished, very politely and with all her heart for Bailey to come home safe and sound.

Conlan took a deep breath and waited for the feeling to come. He was told he would know it when it came. One more time, it did not come. He filled with despair and sorrow for the little girl and her family. The last hope for Bailey's return had vanished.

Jessy stood and turned and smiled at Conlan. It was a smile full of confidence and knowing and of gratitude and it made Conlan feel ashamed he was a Wish Walker. He wondered what the hell he was good for as an Angel anyway if he couldn't help a little girl as innocent as Jess bring her lost dog home. He felt he had blundered into the worst situation he could imagine. He wondered how it was she could see plain as day he was an Angel. What heavenly or earthly purpose it served? It was as if he had been pinned by his wings to a wall, unable to writhe away from the bright light of a little girl's expectations. A girl who fully expected him to do something, make a miracle happen. Jessy went and hugged her father goodnight. She then went to Conlan with that same smile full of assurance and hugged him as he sat on the sofa.

"I love you," she said to Conlan and kissed his hand.

Thomas was taken aback and looked at Lisa who was equally aghast by Jessy's show of affection to all but a stranger.

"Jessy," Conlan said, and he said it very seriously, "we don't always get what we wish for."

Jessy could not only see that Conlan was an Angel, but she could hear his true Angelic voice as well. It rang out like an entire Christmas choir; and what he had said had a visible effect on her. Her expression became one of puzzlement.

"Hey now," Thomas said. He was upset by the travelers comment. The look he gave Conlan said it clearly: who the hell are you to break my daughters spirit, shatter her faith.

"Alright bed," Lisa said forcefully. She grabbed Jessy by the hand and led her upstairs.

Conlan could hear Lisa at the top of the stairs saying: "Young lady that is not how we behave with strangers. Do you understand me?"

"With strangers, no…but," Jessy said. Hope had returned to her small voice.

"No buts young lady," Lisa said.

Thomas sat staring at Conlan with an annoyed expression. Conlan felt almost as horrible as he did a hundred years ago when consoling the young German soldier. He recalled the old saying shared among Angels: A bad day in heaven is still better than a thousand good days on earth. What about a bad day on earth? What was it worth?

"You know Jessy is only six years old," Thomas said, finally, "plenty of time for her to find out how much life can suck. And if anyone, it'll be me and her mother who explains it to her. You understand me?"

A parent's reprimand will probably not look so great on an Angel's resume Conlan thought. "Fully," he said, "My apologies. It was a…I was merely…ah." Conlan left it at that.

There was a long silence. Thomas recognized it had been a long day for everyone, especially for the frozen stranger. He knew his wife did not particularly approve of the strange drifter. He knew it was up to him to ease the tension that had built up over the evening. This was as good a situation as any to employ the service of a drink or two.

"Scotch?" Thomas asked.

Thinking it may help to smooth things over and ease the tension his comment to Jessy had caused, Conlan accepted. There were no rules for Angels in regards to earthly vices. When it came to mortals and the shepherding of their soul's small vices, such as alcohol or tobacco didn't seem to be high on heaven's list of concerns. Conlan in fact used to pretend to have a smoking habit in the forties and fifties to avoid arousing even minor suspicion. It was an oddity for a man not to smoke in those days. Thomas handed Conlan a fine crystal glass which contained a double portion of superior single-malt whiskey. Once Conlan got through the medicinal burn of alcohol, he quite enjoyed the warming flavors of almonds and apricots. The alcohol itself would have no effect on him. The two men sat in silence in the living room listening to the crackling of the fire. Thomas had nearly dozed off when Lisa, having finished putting Jessy to bed, returned. Conlan could tell that Lisa did not approve of the whisky.

"May I have a word with you in the kitchen?" she said to Thomas.

"Certainly. Can I pour you a drink my dear?" Thomas asked.

Lisa walked straight into the kitchen without a reply. Thomas gave Conlan a wink as if to say not to worry he could handle his wife in these moments. But Conlan couldn't help noticing the tense look that came upon Thomas face just before he entered the kitchen. It was more than just the alcohol that was bothering Lisa. She didn't like the idea of a stranger staying in the house overnight, especially considering Jessy's pull towards him, and now, above all, Thomas was adding

34

alcohol to the mix. Thomas pointed out that they couldn't just send him on his way seeing he had almost froze to death only hours before and it was considerably colder outside now, being late evening. Lisa wondered if it would be best if Thomas drove the stranger into town and rented him a room for the night. Thomas reminded Lisa that the stranger had a name and thought that perhaps she was being a bit too cautious. A compromise was reached: they would make a bed for Conlan in the enclosed porch. Being fully insulated and heated it would be dry and warm; in addition they could lock the inner door and Lisa could feel safe. They agreed to simply go ahead with this arrangement as if it had been the plan all along, this way avoiding the possibility of embarrassing or insulting the stranger. Conlan of course understood he had been downgraded from the spare room to the porch.

Lisa made a comfortable bed in the enclosed porch with a number of sleeping bags and comforters. She threw in an extra fluffy pillow and told herself it was not because she was feeling twinges of guilt, it was strictly for the sake of Conlan's amenity. She was, after all, only thinking of the welfare of her family as any mother and wife would; besides she considered the porch to be better than a motel room.

When it was time for bed Thomas offered Conlan a pair of his winter pajamas, which he politely declined saying the clothes he had borrowed earlier were more than comfortable and loose enough for sleeping. The three made their way to the porch. Conlan commented to Lisa what a fabulous and cozy bed she had made him. He crawled in under the top layer of comforters careful to look as contented as possible for Lisa's sake. Thomas told him to rap on the door if he needed anything during the night. Conlan advised them not to worry he'd sleep as sound as a stone. They said their goodnights. Thomas closed the inner door and de-emphasized its locking as best he could.

Conlan had all night to puzzle over how Jessy would feel when she realized Bailey wouldn't be coming back. He wondered if he should grant her wish regardless of the fact he hadn't felt it. If he intended to give up he might as well do it now and save the reputation of all Angels. How would it help anyone to have a little girl, who could see Angel's, but no longer believed in their powers or kindness? What good would that do for the development of poor Jessy's soul? The thought made Conlan cringe.

He lay remembering Nora's repeated question in WW School: how was it decided, exactly, when a wish would be felt? No one had provided an answer then. Conlan tried to answer for himself now: Was it someone in heaven that decided, possibly a panel of Archangels? Could it be the decision went even higher than Archangels? Or was it simply the product of something in the Wish Walkers themselves. Maybe it came down to destiny? It was possible everything was already written in some book somewhere on high, that he was simply an instrument in the hands of a much superior force, playing a part in a tune that had already been composed. Predetermination, the mortals called it. If this was the case the last four hundred years had nothing to do with him really. He had no personal responsibility in any of it. One part of Conlan liked this idea because it took him off the hook; the other part of him loathed the idea. It made WWs pointless, merely divine puppets.

Somewhere in the distance a dog barked. It brought Conlan's mind back to Jessy and the matter of why he hadn't felt her wish. She was clearly someone who was blessed with heavenly favors, so why hadn't he felt her wish? Conlan had a theory he fell back on whenever the absence of the 'feeling' made no sense. This idea had been at the back of his mind for the entire four hundred years he'd been on earth. A concept that mortals had summed up with a simple adage: 'be careful what you wish for'. The idea was that you never knew what effect getting what you want now could have on the future. One could wish for a trip to Paris and then be killed in a plane crash on the way there. It was this cause and effect, Conlan hypothesized, that was the cause of his failure so far in giving away his wish. But he couldn't help but wonder, as he always did, how adversely it would change the future by bringing someone's dog back, or curing an infant with cancer.

He'd been ruminating over these ideas for a couple hours and it was now very late at night. Again he heard a dog bark, this time from further away. A minute later came the sound of the inner door being quietly unlocked. Conlan knew it was Lisa. The dog barking had awakened her and she had come in hopes it might be Bailey. Conlan closed his eyes and imitated the heavy breathing of a person deep in sleep. Lisa tiptoed on to the enclosed porch, removed her slippers and put on Thomas's heavy winter boots and threw his heavy coat over her housecoat. She slipped out into the winter night. Conlan heard her soft calls for Bailey and felt her desperation. She called a few times more and waited. Conlan could feel she was at the very end of her own faith. She knew too much time had gone by and they would never see Bailey again. Why had she been so careless that evening of the thunderstorm and not properly latched the screen door to the porch? Lisa had asked herself this a million times. There simply was no answer.

In her heart she said goodbye to Bailey. She apologized for not taking better care of her, hoped that she had found another home somewhere and that she was happy and being well cared for. It was fine to hope, but something told Lisa that Bailey was dead. Lisa couldn't hold back her weeping as she went back inside. She did her best to silence her sobs so she wouldn't wake up the traveler sleeping on the floor of the porch. When she closed the outer screen door she made a slow, conscious effort to latch it properly. Silently she wished she had latched the door with as much attention the night Bailey ran away.

Conlan eyes snapped open. He was told he would know the feeling when it came. It had come. There was no doubting it. It was the feeling of having his feet land upon solid ground after swimming in a wild ocean for four hundred years. Conlan granted Lisa's wish with such speed it surprised him. He could not contain his joy and elation. He couldn't keep his wings from expanding the width of the room as he rose to his feet, enveloped by a shimmering white light. Lisa whipped around in surprise, feeling herself about to scream, but no one actually screams when confronted by a real live Angel.

"I have granted you your wish," Conlan said.

Lisa was awestruck and was about to say something when she disappeared. Causes and effects were rearranging themselves to suit a new reality. There was no reason for Lisa to have been on the porch that night in this new reality, she was still in her bed asleep, dreaming of seeing an Angel in the enclosed porch. Conlan's bedding disappeared, it never had been neatly assembled on the floor and neither were his clothes borrowed from Thomas. There was no reason for Thomas to have been searching in the woods. No reason for him to chance upon Conlan meditating in the snow. Conlan felt a cold and wet nose press against his fingers. He bent down and petted Bailey. She wagged her tail cheerfully, oblivious to the heart ache she had caused. Conlan was determined not to have the scenario repeat, so without consultation or permission from his superiors, he removed Bailey's fear of thunder. This was a breach of the rules. Conlan didn't mind, he would deal with the consequences later.

"Take care of yourself girl; take care of your family. They love you very much." Conlan said to Bailey as he patted her on her head. Her ears perked and the Angel was gone.

Conlan was walking in the deep snow now in the yard outside the house. Then he remembered there was no more reason to continue with earthly pretenses. He stretched his wings as wide as he could. In the space of two steps he was walking on top of the deep drifts. He turned to look back at the Grady house. Jessy was peeking out her bedroom window. He waved to her and she gave a cheerful wave in return. Conlan wondered if she was seeing him for the first time or if she somehow remembered the old reality. Either way his work was done.

There was a brilliant flash of light as Conlan ascended back to heaven.

Jack the Dripper

I remember I was on my bicycle heading home when I heard the scream. I had the local paper, The Daily Mule, rolled up in my back pocket. It was my job to fetch it for my father during the summer break. Every morning since school was out I'd ride over to the post office, grab the 'Mule', and take my time getting home. My father didn't really want the paper anyway, he never actually read it. He only thumbed through it with cynicism, ending with his usual condemnation of the silhouetted animal under the main header: "That is not a mule - it's a bloody donkey," he'd say. This particular morning I had just finished a couple of brake slides in the empty school parking lot, which was gravel and perfect for throwing up dust clouds, I then turned my attention to wheelies. I'd got one long one off and then I heard the scream. It was shrill. Definitely a lady's scream, coming from a few blocks over, near the fire station. I spun my bike around and sped towards the woman in distress.

I was hoping the scream meant something exciting was happening, like a fire or a purse snatching, both neat things to a fourteen year old boy. Instead I turned the corner and saw Councilwoman Parksmeyer in an awkward undulation. It took me a moment to realize she was trying to run. At first I assumed she had been stung by a multitude of bees and anaphylactic shock was setting in. I was too young to know this is what happens to someone who hadn't run for decades. Nerve paths fossilize, energetic movements become awkward and spasmodic.

Mr. Parksmeyer was standing next to her. He was clearly dumbfounded, his face red, asking his wife, Ethel, where she was running to.

"I'm fetching Councilwoman Bayweather," Ethel yelled, breathlessly, "Bernard you get Chief Harris and be quick about it. This is outrageous!"

And what she was calling outrageous was outrageous... wondrous too. I looked up and I too became dumbfounded. My eyes were so wide it felt like they had joined each other at the center of my forehead. Bernard tried to move, but eyes are connected directly to legs in cases such as these. This was far too much for Bernard Parkmeyer's eyes and so his legs remained frozen.

What Bernard and I stared at covered the entire east wall of the Whompaton Fire Hall (Whompaton is the actual name of the town in this story). On exhibit before us was a gigantic painting of a partially naked woman. The background was unmistakably a bedroom. She had apparently just taken off her dress and had thrown it over the back of a wooden chair, which she was leaning lithely on with one outstretched arm. There was a gentle lilt to her upper body which gave the impression that further down - if the painting were to continue - her hips would be pleasingly thrust to one side. I noticed these fine points and the overall beauty of the painting only after I took in the pièce de résistance: her magnificent, full breasts and their exquisite honey brown nipples. My fourteen year old loins runneth over. That painting was the beginning of a lot of changes in the Whompaton Macrocosm. By the end it would rock our town out of the rut it had been in for years. And no one saw these transformations coming, except for possibly the creator(s) of the painting itself (one might guess it was their original intent).

It was also the beginning of a lot of changes to my microcosm as well. It was the first time I looked at art as something beyond its elementary form, and the first time (as you shall see why) I looked upon adults with true skepticism. And, of course, it was the first time I realized the power the female form can have on males, as I felt it in myself that morning. One of the great experiences of my life was under way. It was to be my most memorable summer.

"Bernard, get moving!" yelled Ethel.

To tell this story properly I have to think back on that summer of 1969 as accurately as possible. Which, honestly, I've never had difficulty doing; the events seemed stored forever in the circuits of my brain. As all great experiences do, it became a part of who I am. It helps, too, that I have recounted this story many, many times. I've never once felt the need to embellish it. It is absurd enough as it is.

My formative years, ages 4 to 14, took place in the turbulent sixties. Being born in Whompaton I'd missed out on most of the good stuff the sixties had to offer. The only counter revolution in Whompaton at the time was Mr. Peabody's and Phil Philips' crusade to get beer flowing again through the taps at the town bar. The Town Council had voted to make our town 'dry'. The Mayor and Council had pretty much thrown a wet blanket on Whompatonians having any kind of fun. Flower power was non-existent. Rock and Roll was the outright enemy of the people we were told. It is important to note, the first time I heard about the Beatles they had already broken up. Our school's colors, being light brown on dark brown, was the antithesis of the 'hippy movement'; our football uniforms looked like they'd been dipped in dog crap (this fact being pointed out to us by the chants of rival towns).

It's hard to believe our town carried on the way it did, especially in the middle of 60's America. While other places were experiencing the spice of the times Whompatonians were living a bland porridge life. It would be natural to suspect religious zealously was behind such languor and apathy towards the heart and vivacity of life. However, this was not the case in Whompaton. The Mayor and Council Members running the town were moral elitists rather than devout purists. Beneath their elitism, however, at the very core of their motivation, what I see now drove the manner in which the town was being run, was a deep fear of change. Everyone on the Council, including the Mayor abhorred outside influences which in their eyes brought insolence, mockery and frauds. Moreover, the Mayor and Council members were likeminded in their belief that ordinary folk (meaning everyone but themselves) required an overseeing hand. They believed the common people of Whompaton needed order passed down from above. And for this tiny slice of America (population 946), they should be the ones who dispatched it.

You are probably asking by now how such a group got to control our little town in the first place? But, I ask you, who really knows how most politicians get elected? That is a different story. We can leave that to the psychologist and their studies on the workings of the human mind and temperament. This is a story about their ending, not their beginning. This is a story about a Mayor and his undoing, his fall from grace, a story about the Whompaton Town Council getting knocked off their collective high horse by a scandal incurred by art, if you can believe it. In a lot of ways it's a story about art itself.

I recall, that day in the summer of 1969, a crowd had quickly gathered around the east-side of the Whompaton Fire Hall. No one knew quite what to make of the larger than life girl painted on the enormous wall of the fire station, her mammary glands (the anatomical term I recalled from biology class) exposed for all to see.

"When the hell did this get here?" asked Ernie Miller the Fire Chief, scratching his head, "How the hell did this get here?"

"Who would paint a poor girl exposed to such a degree?" asked Rose Pinlap. She was the largest member of the Town Council. I remember she was sweating quite profusely. Which quite frankly was her natural state.

"Someone who knows how to cut to the root of things," said 76 year old Mr. Galsworthy. "Some handy showmanship…knows how to delve into human desires," he added.

"Well," said Rose in her usual lofty, snobbish, damp tone, "we know who ever painted this was a man….it's disgusting."

"Maybe you've never known real passion Rose, never known the pleasure raw human nature affords us," said Mr. Galsworthy, looking wooingly at her.

"Well I never….." Rose huffed, as she walked off.

"I can take care of that," said Mr. Galsworthy, turning and winking at me.

My face turned red.

"Well I think it is absolutely beautiful," said Gilbert Lewis our new, homosexual (Or so my dad said. I barely knew what the word meant at the time) Librarian, "No ordinary graffiti artist painted this, I assure you. This is a work of real refinement. There is a palpable style here. One of the best paintings I've ever seen in such a large format. This is not graffiti. This is art!"

Gilbert Lewis knew a lot about the arts. He talked about them all the time, especially with Mr. Bayweather, who was the husband to Mrs. Bayweather, the head of the town Council.

I was just glad to hear that I wasn't alone in thinking the thing was spectacular. Minister Hayes, our town Preacher, came around the corner of the fire hall at the same time the Police Chief, Bill Harris, rolled up in his squad car with its red gumball light flashing and Mrs. Bayweather in the back seat like it was her own private limousine.

"Vagrants!" roared Mrs. Bayweather, getting out of the squad car. "Transient guttersnipes... just wait until Mr. Coombs sees this filth!" Her eyes prowled the area, no doubt she was making note of who was there. Her attention turned to me

"What are you gawking at boy?" she hissed.

"The…nipples…." I said, hesitantly, and pointed at the wall. She had taken me off guard and I couldn't formulate a lie quick enough.

"Well don't just stand there scratching your head over it Ernie, get a ladder and some paint and get rid of this thing before it corrupts the entire town," yelled Mrs. Bayweather.

"Let us not act fearful," said Minister Hayes, "Knee jerk reactions never prove to win the day." He stood back next to me to get a better look. "Well now, it's not that bad, not that bad at all. A trifle bit animated, if not a scant erotic, but I dare say it is quite lovely over all – the colors and style, quite engaging."

"My vote is we get rid of it," said Council Member Bernard Parksmeyer.

"Your vote!?", snickered Mrs. Bayweather, haughtily. "There'll be no vote. Minister Hayes can practice pornography at his church if he likes, but this smut will be removed from public at once."

The Minister looked scorned and sheepish.

Soon old Fire Chief Miller was up on a big wooden fire ladder with a bucket of white wash.

"Start there, at the audacious bits," said Mrs. Bayweather, pointing.

"At the which bits?" asked Ernie. He was too close to get a proper perspective now. He couldn't make out what blur belonged to where. He leaned back on his ladder to get a wider view.

"The offending parts first," said Mrs. Bayweather.

"The whole thing is offensive," said Rose Pinlap.

"Here?" asked the Fire Chief.

"To the left"

"Here?"

"Left"

"Here?"

"For God sakes, someone hold the ladder!" yelled Mrs. Bayweather.

"Here?"

"Yes Mr. Miller, right there," answered Mrs. Bayweather.

"Now to the right, you say?"

"No there-there!"

And with a swipe of his scraggy brush Fire Chief Miller white washed out of existence a brown and beautiful left nipple.

Ewan Billforth rolled up in his black 57' Cadillac and immediately Mrs. Bayweather, Rose Pinlap and Mrs. Parksmeyer, all the members of Council, began to sneer. Ewan Billforth was the biggest opposition to the Mayor's and the Council's hold over the town. Time and time again Ewan called for a new election, but no one else in town had the courage to run. He showed up at every town meeting and a few times brought with him a lawyer from the big city to thwart some ambitious plan or other the Council slithered out from their collective sleeve.

Mr. Billforth waved me over and spoke to me through a half rolled down window.

"What's happening son?" Ewan Billforth asked.

I filled him in on what I knew.

"Did Herman get a picture for the Mule?" he asked. He meant Herman Eckstein, the reporter, photographer, editor, writer and the guy who cleaned the toilets for The Daily Mule. He did all those jobs because he was the only one who worked there. As a matter of fact he owned it too.

"I didn't see him," I said.

"You there" yelled Mrs. Bayweather, pointing at me. Anyone talking to Ewan Billforth was the enemy. "HOME!" She motioned down the street towards my house.

"You better go son. No sense bringing heat to your family by fraternizing with old Ewan," Mr. Billforth said, in his usual kind, gentlemanly manner.

The council held an emergency town hall meeting at four o'clock that day. My dad had gone to hear about the painting and the fuss it had kicked up. At dinner that evening my parents and I talked about the meeting and the mystery painting.

"How was the meeting?" my Mother asked.

"Same old crap," my Father said. "The Council was there talking about town security, bustin' old Chief Harris' chops over what he gets paid for and where he was when the fire hall got painted."

"Well, where was he?" asked my Mother.

"He said he was where everybody else in town was: in bed sleeping. They want to raise taxes and hire a deputy and start policing at night."

"I'm sure what old Mayor Coombs and Mrs. Bayweather really want is to surround the town with a wall" Mother said.

"What they can't figure out," my Dad continued, "was where they, or whoever, got a big enough ladder to do a giant painting like that. They think whoever it is, is most likely from out of town. But, to haul a big ladder like that you'd need a truck and someone would have heard it in the middle of the night."

"Couldn't they have used the ladders from the Fire Station?" my mother asked.

I'd already had that same thought.

"No, Ernie says all the ladders were still on the fire truck which was locked in the station. There is no sign of a break in," my Dad said. "I think they might have used the old scaffolding behind the church," he continued. " It would be a better way to paint. Much more stable. With a ladder you always need one hand to hold on."

"Did you tell them that?" asked my Mother.

"Not on your life," scoffed my Dad. "I'm not doing a thing to help that damn Council. Not after that fine of yours! —Imagine, five bucks for having empty milk bottles out on the steps a day early, it's thievery." His forehead crinkled heavily.

"I hear it was quite the painting," my Mother said, moving the conversation off the milk bottle scandal. At the time I remember her being more upset about having her name on the 'culpable' list outside the post office than my father's five dollars. He talked about those five dollars for the next thirty years.

"Well you saw it son, so tell us, was it as indecent as they say?" asked my Dad, as he got a can of beer from the fridge; contraband that he'd smuggled from two towns over.

"Well," I said, "basically it was a picture of a pretty lady and the lady had her boobs out and she was smiling at someone that was in the room with her, but you had to imagine that because you couldn't see any one, only her."

"Young man we don't say boobs in this house," My mother said.

"Sorry," I said, "her tits were out I meant."

"David!" My mother yelled, "We say breasts! And it's a painting not a picture." My Dad tried to hide his amusement, but his grin was too wide to conceal. My mother shot darts at him with her eyes.

"That's all?" asked my Dad.

"Ya that's it I guess," I said. "It wasn't all that smutty. But, it was....I don't know how to describe what I really liked about it. The colors and everything looked real great. I wanted to keep looking at it. It was like it was alive and a real place I was peeking into. You know the picture...or...painting (my mother appeared satisfied) on the billboard on the highway of the lady holding a Coke bottle? Well that looks more like a real lady and all, but the painting on the fire station was a lot nicer to look at for some reason. Gilbert Lewis said it was real art and had what's called artistic style."

"I'll bet he did," said my Dad.

"Now don't you start ," said Mother. She was referring to how my Dad made little comments about Gilbert being gay.

"Mr. Billforth showed up in his Cadillac and when I went to talk to him Mrs. Bayweather yelled at me to go home," I said.

"There's a real pair for you," my Dad said, after finishing his first beer in almost one gulp. He was getting up to grab another. "On one hand we have our idiot mayor and the dragon lady, old wicked witch of the west lording over everybody like she is queen of America and on the other we have secret agent man, do-gooder, millionaire Ewan Billforth trying to make us all feel guilty about the state of things around this town."

"I think Ewan's got a point," said my Mother and I knew the fireworks were about to begin. "Everybody complains about the Council, but no one tries to do anything about it. Ewan tries his best to get an election going, but not one of you big talkers ever wants to run."

"Why doesn't Ewan Billforth, ol' E.B. run himself, if he's so great?" my Dad asked.

"You know he does try to run, but when no one else joins him he backs out. Would you want to bump one of them off the Council and be left to deal with the rest of those vipers on your own? I think not." Mother said.

"Gee Dad you could be Mayor," I joked. I imagined my dad in a big top hat like the guy from Monopoly.

"That'd be something," Dad said, "I'd bring back the liquor and buy some real uniforms for that sorry football team of yours, son. Tell ya what else I'd do. I'd get my five dollars back form the damn milk bottle Mafia!" He was heading for the fridge to get his third beer.

"Oh, you're not getting drunk tonight and starting up with your Buck Owens records blaring away on the stereo," yelled Mother, slapping her hands on her thighs the way she does when she means business. "Not," she said, "with the Council all worked up over what happened at the fire station. You keep sneaking the volume up 'til they can hear it in Springfield. It'll be your turn for a fine along with your name out there at the post office!"

"Jeez, everybody's a dictator in this town," Dad said. Then he raised his empty beer can and shouted, "Screw old Billforth – Buck Owens for Mayor!"

I laughed. Mother did not.

That night I dreamt of beautiful breasts with honey brown nipples.

The next morning was Saturday morning. I got up early to go fishing at a nearby stream. My folks were still sleeping as I rode off on my bike with my rod in hand. I peddled down 'Fool' Street (Or so my Dad re-named it. It was actually School Street.) towards the highway where I would cross onto the county lane that led to the stream. As I crossed 'Shame' Street (actually Main Street) out of the corner of my eye I caught a flash of a black and grey swirl on the upper portion of the bank building. The colors were just peeking out over the shorter buildings directly in front of it.

I had spent my entire life in Whompaton. Consciously or subconsciously, I knew every slab of concrete, every fine detail and nuance of every building, as every kid does who spends their summers just kicking around their home town. I turned my bike in eager hopes of another scandalous painting. Why did I so badly want another painting? I guess I enjoyed the upheaval the first painting caused. Maybe, like my father, I took pleasure in watching the Whompaton Town Council writhe in uncertainty. I think my intuition, young as it was, knew something big and important was brewing, some kind of force, benevolent or otherwise, was at work. And I had listened to my father and my mother, but mostly my father, talk every night in a way that told me something was terribly wrong with our town. My father would say the Council and the Mayor had slowly turned up the burner on us Whompatons, one little change at a time. Now we were all like a bunch of apathetic frogs in a boiling pot.

I stopped my bike at the side of the bank building. The early morning air was heavy with dew. The sun's first rays were beginning to expel the cool and damp of night. The town may have been sleeping, but I was wide awake staring up at two familiar, brown nipples. Only, this time my focus wasn't solely fixed on the woman's breasts. My eyes flitted towards the patch of hair between her legs with equal vivacity.

This second painting was a full three stories. It was undoubtedly the same woman as before. She still had that swaying lilt to her hips, although this time she was seated on a sofa. Her arms were stretched along the top of the sofa; her legs were extended and loosely crossed. I could see the upside down pyramid of pubic hair covering her pudendum (I knew that word because the boys joked about all the girl parts in biology class). Both breasts, full and shapely, were beaming outward. I felt my groin come alive and remove itself from my control. A swirl of energy hovered just below my zipper. She was looking and smiling at the man in the room. You couldn't see this man, but the expression on the girls face and the angle of her stare made you feel certain he was there, just out of sight. She was looking up at him with mostly her eyes, her head only tilted slightly. The smile on her face was a type I was unfamiliar with at my age. But, even at fourteen, I knew what that look meant. As every young man eventually does, I suddenly realized I wanted to be the recipient of such a look, and even more yearningly to be the reason for it. This was my inauguration into the primeval male motivation, the impetus, some argue, behind all human motivation: the pursuit of procreation. Not everyone remembers the day their hormones kicked in. I have mine tied to an unforgettable incident involving a naked woman three stories high and newspaper clippings to boot.

Once I got beyond my adolescent arousal, I realized Gilbert Lewis was right: this was no graffiti hack job; here was another work of authentic art. Even I, having no official artistic training, could appreciate its magnificence. As an adult I am one who feels art school is not going to give anyone a monopoly on recognizing or appreciating 'true art'. Just as no one has to teach a baby how to dance to the beat of a song. What individuals feel is 'Art' might be subjective, but it's intrinsic. It's inherent value, I believe, is already inside of us. This painting on the bank wall vibrated at the same frequency as some chromosomal sequence in my DNA. I felt an affiliation of life looking at it. It was the same feeling I had when I found a Nautilus shell at the beach when I was six: millions of years of life on earth expressed in that swirling pattern I held in my hand. The more one analyzes the less is understood because 'art' has nothing to do with the brain.

The way the texture of the bank's cement wall showed through the paint, how one color augmented and improved every other color. That day I became an enthusiastic adherent of the female form and true art. Now, all these years later, I can't fathom why people sneer at the millions of dollars something like an original Van Gogh auctions for. Myself, I wonder if there is enough money in the world to equal its true value. And it's not only the 'classical establishment' art such as Van Gogh's and the like, which has the rights to the term 'real art'. In college my art professors were snobbish about art. They had no right to be. My first experience with art was an exhibition of soft porn on the sides of buildings. It's ludicrous to think some authority out there gets to decide what is considered art and what is not. One man's Warhol can be another's waste of perfectly good soup cans. I had a college roommate who majored in art; he played Pink Floyd's Dark Side of the Moon twenty four hours a day. To him that music was just as sophisticated and important as anything Jackson Pollock ever did.

More people showed up to a campus reading of The Lord of the Rings by one of J.R.R. Tolkien's sons then to a performance of the London Royal Ballet. Art truly is in the eye of the beholder, it vibrates in unison with something inside us. At best it can expand and enrich our outlook of life on this planet. I'm not trying to give an art lesson here. I guess I'm trying to explain how discovering art changed me, how my world expanded the morning I got art, staring at the naked girl on the bank building.

I knew how upset I would be if I had to witness this second composition being destroyed. I had to think fast. I rode my bike with lightning speed as every fourteen year old boy can. Over sidewalks, across lawns, through yards, every short cut I knew all the way to Herman Eckstein's house. Because the first thing I thought was this time a photograph of the painting was needed for the Daily Mule. At least that way it could live on in some capacity, diminished as it may be. I knew the council would get its way, as it usually did, and this painting would also be destroyed.

I pounded on the door of the Daily Mule with urgency. I knew this wasn't a time for social grace.

"Hang on for craps sakes," I heard Herman say from inside. "Oh it's you kid," he said as he opened the door. I explained the situation. He bolted awake and grabbed his camera and stepped out the door with only his housecoat and slippers on.

"Hop on," I said, "I know a short cut."

"You're joking kid," Eckstein said.

I wasn't joking. "What's the matter, you never been doubled before?" I asked.

Off we went, his camera rattling from around his neck as he yelled "F-o-r-f-u-c-k-s-s-a-k-e-s" every time we went over a curb or up onto lumpy grass.

"Jesus kid, that's some short cut," Herman Eckstein said, as we arrived at the bank. He stared at the painting, motionless, for a moment.

"See what I mean," I said, more statement than question.

"Was the first one this…this…..was it like this?" He asked.

"Her dress is all the way off now," I said. "Do you think she took it off for the person she's smiling at?"

"It's hard to say…." Mr. Eckstein suddenly stopped speaking and looked at me, as if he all at once remembered I was far too young to continue this line of conversation.

"I like how it looks as if she's right inside the building," I said.

"That's called perspective kid," he said, "if the lines of perspective are all just right it will give you a 3 dimensional look even though it's painted on a flat 2 dimensional surface."

I remember pretending to know what he was talking about.

"But, the overall style,' he continued, "really blows me away. It's really powerful, remarkable. The sexual overtones are secondary." He then started clicking off picture after picture.

Suddenly I had it in my mind that I wanted to share the outrageousness and beauty of this new painting with my parents.

"I'm going to wake my Mom and Dad," I said, "My Dad will want to see this."

"I bet he will." Herman Eckstein said. "I hope he will be on the side of trying to save it," It was an odd sight Herman in his housecoat and slippers clicking furiously away with his camera. "We're going to need all the help we can get!"

"I know he will, my Mother too." I said, over the whirl of his camera. I turned my bike towards home.

By the time I got back to the bank with my parents there was a small crowd gathered in the street. Minister Hayes was there, Police Chief Harris and old Mr. Galsworthy.

"What ya think about this one, boy?" Mr. Galsworthy said. "It gets better all the time. Couple more and we'll be right down to the good stuff." Again he winked at me.

I looked at the ground because I could feel my Mother glaring first at me and then Mr. Galsworthy.

"Well, isn't this something" said my Dad. He was gleaming like it was Christmas day.

More and more people were showing up, but so far there were no Council members present.

"It's really quite striking to tell you the truth," my Mother said, "But why does it have to be smutty like that. Why can't it be a painting of cows or something?"

"Cows!" said my Dad; he almost seemed startled by the idea. "For plum sakes, all you have to do is go to the edge of town and you'd see all the cows you'll ever need to see for a life time."

"Well something else besides nudity is what I mean?" my Mother said.

We all stood admiring the side of the bank as more people gathered. Ewan Billforth rolled up in his Cadillac and my Dad started sneering and making comments under his breath, like "here comes Mr. Money bags," and "Every town needs a hero." My mother ordered him to behave. From around the corner came Mayor Combs and Mrs. Bayweather and along the adjacent street came Mr. Bayweather and Gilbert Lewis.

"Isn't it strange," Mother said, "that you never see Mr. and Mrs. Bayweather together anymore? Mr. Bayweather seems to be constantly in the company of Gilbert Lewis."

"Maybe they're friends," my Dad said. He made a gesture with his hand and said the word 'friends' in such a peculiar manner. At the time the gesture and its meaning was beyond my understanding. My Mother hummed softly, as if agreeing that there could be truth to whatever my Dad was implying. All the while I stared at the marvelous woman who seemed to be sitting right inside the bank building on a sofa, and tried to solidify it in my memory forever. I knew its continuation in the world was going to be brief at best.

"Well this just has me stumped," said Police Chief Harris, scratching his head. "We'll have to do an investigation, forensics and all that."

"Is this your nefarious handy work?" sneered Mayor Coombs. He was addressing Mr. Billforth.

"I dare say I only wish I possessed such an artistic talent! It's marvelous!" said Mr. Billforth.

"With enough money I'm certain one could make anything happen to any building," said Mr. Coombs. "Oh but, I guess I should watch my tongue or Mr. Billforth here might sic one of his high powered lawyer dogs from the city on me."

"Or possibly an entire pack," said Mr. Billforth.

"Now before we start drawing lines and pointing fingers," interjected the Minister, "and accusing and threatening each other, I want to put forth a proposition I think the entire town can benefit from," he said pointing at the painting. "If I may have a moment of your time?"

For the most part he had the crowds attention.

"I believe," the Minister continued, "beyond the infringement upon our moral sense, this painting is a true work of art and is of such a monumental scale that it will no doubt be an attraction, a reason for folks to come visit our town. Visiting people mean commerce. Every business will benefit if not directly than indirectly. So in light of this benefit and in acknowledging the painting is a tad brash, I (here he cleared his throat)… propose we paint undergarments of some fashion on the woman and then leave the painting as a town attraction."

"What!" Gilbert Lewis cried. "You mean paint a bra and panties onto her. Why, that would be like slapping some clay 'fruit of the loom' onto Michelangelo's David!"

"Even being a man of the cloth I can tell you I have no problem with Michelangelo's David, but this painting has a little more than simple nudity going on. There is a lot of suggestion in her face and the positions the artist chose to paint her in……I'm only suggesting we soften it a little. I'm not sure exposed breasts would be a proper statement….from a commercial aspect."

"That's the problem I see with your plan," Gilbert Lewis said, "True art and commerce can never be mutually beneficial."

"I can't say I agree with you there Gilbert," said Ewan Billforth. "I like the idea the Minister has put forth. Compromise can often be the thing that pulls us out of the fire. But, is there anyone we know that could do a proper job of it?"

"This is outrageous!" yelled Mrs. Bayweather, "there will be no compromise. Whompaton will never be known as a town of fools and clowns and immoral paintings. People will come and contribute to the town's industry on the account we act good and proper here. They may think of Whompaton as a stronghold against the vile, reprobated attitude that has swept this nation. And that is fair trade by any possible estimation."

"I currently don't see a line up to get in the place," said Herman Eckstein.

"You watch it or that little paper of yours will see its final edition," scathed Mrs. Bayweather.

"Freedom of speech is something this nation was founded on," Herman shot back. "That is if this town is still part of the nation, which I truly wonder sometimes."

Mrs. Bayweather ignored him and went on, "We can certainly assume that the intention of the deviant painter or painters, whomever they maybe, has a bias that is not of goodwill or charity towards this town. Hence these lewd murals happening under cover of night."

"Yes, yes," Old man Galsworthy interjected, "this whole affair is quite the mystery, quite the mystery indeed. I'm certainly up for it especially if there are naked girls involved, hey boy!"

I smiled sheepishly and this time even my dad glared at the old man.

"Well since I own the building," interrupted Mr. Billforth, "I would say it's my choice whether we slap a bra on this here lady or not."

"Well now that would be quite the boon to the town's commerce after all," Mayor Coombs said, "I couldn't begin to count the fines this piece of trash would procure for you Mr. Billforth, if it were left purposely on a building here in Whompaton, such as the one the Bank is currently leasing. I'd certainly be sorry for your loss of rental income once the Whompaton Credit Union was forced to find residence elsewhere, seeing that it couldn't be associated with vile wickedness as would be displayed on the side of this soon to be vacant building."

"But, we can tone it down," yelled Minister Hayes from the sidelines.

Mr. Billforth looked shot down. He knew he'd been pushed into a tight corner which often accompanies matters of finance.

"You know what they say," crowed Mr. Coombs. "Money can't buy everything. Oh, and they also say you can't fight city hall." He gave an abrupt snicker. "But, I guess you know that by now Mr. Billforth, you and your hounds from the city."

And with that, right on cue, came the howl of the Fire Engine as it turned the corner onto Shame Street, with all the ladders and white wash Mr. Coombs and Mrs. Bayweather could wish for.

"Jack the Dripper Strikes Again" – read the head line of the Saturday evening special edition of the Daily Mule. It was the first time the artist (or artists) was referred to as 'Jack the Dripper' and the name stuck. It was certainly quite the tag line and it summed things up pretty well. The 'Dripper' part referring to dripping paint of course. It was a hell of a mystery to everyone how two such grandiose paintings could be completed right under all our noses. I was lying on the living room floor reading the article (the first news article I had ever read from start to finish). It talked about the theories going around town about who was responsible and what their motives were. The biggest questions: was the Artist(s) someone from Whompaton or an outsider? And was this the work of a lone wolf or was a conspiracy in play? The article also had a lot of interesting things to say about art and art styles over the years. To tie everything together it included a few facts about the original Jack the Ripper of London, England, 1888, who was attributed to performing 'extreme works' under the cover of night and essentially under everybody's noses as well. The best part was the pictures of the bank building. Even in black and white and 1/1000th of its original size the painting looked good.

"I think old Billforth hired some art students from Springfield" said my Dad, from his arm chair looking at his copy. I had grabbed three copies of the Mule. My mother had put hers in a keepsake and was busy in the kitchen.

"I'm not so sure," said my Mother, now standing in the threshold of the living room. "He seemed as mystified as the rest of us."

My Dad made a huffing sound. "Good acting maybe." Then after a pause, "But I have to admit it's a bona fide mystery."

"I'm glad for it," Mother said, "I like to see the Mayor and the Council in such a snit."

That evening we illegally watched I Love Lucy with the sound low and curtains drawn. I was in my usual spot on the floor, half watching the television and half looking at the newspaper and the black and white photos. There was a good one of Mayor Coombs and Ewan Billforth staring each other down with Mrs. Bayweather right there as the Mayor's back up. All the while painting number two loomed in the back ground.

After a while I stood up and holding out the newspaper I said, "See how the lady looks like she's right in the bank building?" My parents nodded slightly. "That's called perspective," I said, remembering what Mr. Eckstein had explained to me. I then went to bed thinking about the lady and the expression upon her face. Imagining I was the one she was smiling at.

The next morning I got up early, but with no intentions of going fishing. I left the house silently. I found my bike on the back lawn where I had left it, or as my mother says 'dumped' it. I wiped the morning dew off the seat and proceeded to ride all over town looking for painting number three. I was certain it was to be found. I had once read an archeology adventure book and my young imagination had now put me in the plot looking for the lost painting of the Kama sutra. Everywhere I looked I saw only lifeless fading walls with crumbling bricks trying to hold up weather worn roofs. I scoured the usual fossilized structures, bathed in their venerable shadows as I glided along 100 year old sidewalks. The only paint I saw was either flaking or peeling. The faded advertising signs that were so familiar and routine my eyes didn't bother to register their colors or words any longer, mocked me.

Off course there was nothing really wrong with all the time weariness of my town. Whompaton was handsome enough in a nostalgic way. However, the disappointment of not finding another painting made me feel contemptuous towards our little boring town that morning and all its perpetual sameness. In fact it appeared quite deplorable to me. I was maddened by the prospect of another usual dull day, with no painting to stir up a hornets nests. Worst of all it was

Sunday so I would have to give up my search and get back home and ready for church.

Actually, there were worse things than church. Minister Hayes did a fairly good job of keeping the sermons down to earth (if it's appropriate to use that expression when talking about sermons). He was much better than the previous minister who would often get my Father whispering – "What the hell is he talking about?" This would get an elbow from my Mother and her angry whispered reply of -" he's talking about you!". Minster Hayes at least used modern language and paced around the room see-sawing his arms, attempting to keep us all awake. He would often talk about things in a way that would make me ponder long after church was over. Like the time he talked about gossip being the devils assistant and how quiet my parents were that evening, but the next evening they were loud as ever talking about Rose Pinlap and the man who came to visit her one weekend.

The entire town knew Minster Hayes would talk about the paintings and their subsequent destruction. You don't often hear a sermon on the morality of three story nudes. There was an enormous turn out. The Church hadn't held that many people since the last bingo night .

"Fear," began Minister Hayes, "fear is one of the two prime forces of the human heart, second only to love."

Even as a kid I remember thinking our dear Minister had peeled back all the layers and got right to the core of the whole thing.

"If we get fixated on our fears they become phobias. Then no matter where we look in the world our fears will be realized, because we, ourselves have projected them onto the world. We become suspicious and filled with hate, crazed with spite. He with burning eyes sees only fire. Now, consider the saying, which I think is very true: 'Beauty is in the eye of the beholder.' Do you see the angle I'm working here?" asked the Minister, pacing up and down. "Where some find love and beauty others find vileness and evil.........."

"Light!" yelled Rose Pinlap, struggling to raise her large frame out of the narrow pew, her loud voice startling the hell out of everyone. "Light!' She was perspiring.

"Do you mean the light of God, my child?" asked Minister Hayes looking pleased, yet perplexed at her explosive enthusiasm.

"Don't be stupid," Rose said, looking annoyed. Which, thinking back now, demonstrated a lot of nerve given she was in church during sermon.

"Whoever perpetrated those disgusting paintings during the night had to have had a light, lots of lights." said Rose.

There was a silence as everyone took in what she was saying.

"Well don't you see?" Rose continued, "The light would be spotted from anywhere in town. If one of us (she looked at police Chief Harris) were to do a stake out during the night there could be no conceivable way the bright light would go un-noticed."

"You are quite right Rose and good thinking," said Mr. Coombs, "but say no more as you could be tipping off the enemy here and now as you speak. Let the town Council, Chief Harris and I convene at the court house."

And with that all the Council members got up, even though our poor Minister had barely begun his sermon, and marched out. Mr. Coombs motioned to his house keeper Maria Gomez to come along, but she held her rosary with one hand and crossed herself with the other (which wasn't anything our church was accustomed to as we were protestant) and said "I stay, I stay".

Mrs. Bayweather stood and addressed the minister, who was reeling at his sudden loss of control over the congregation. "Minister Hayes," she said firmly. Everyone froze so we could hear the exchange. "As for your scarcely veiled insinuation that somehow we had brought this on ourselves," she said, fiercely, "I, for one certainly did not contribute to smut being plastered on the Fire Hall or the Bank Building - Good day! " She turned to scold her husband who had remained seated, "Hurry up you imbecile, we're leaving!"

"I believe I would like to stay," said Mr. Bayweather, " hear what the Minister has to say."

Of course most of the town's people left along with the members of the Council. My guess was most had come only for the spectacle of the Minister confronting the Council with a rebuking disguised as a sermon, and it had all quickly reached an anticlimax. My father stood, but my mother pulled him back down and we sat through to the end. The Minister finished his sermon half-heartedly, wounded, as if someone had punched him in the gut. My dad fidgeted until the end.

For whatever reason after that Sunday, there was a loosening of the grip the Mayor and the Council had over the town, and however slight this loosening was, it was perceptible. The volunteer firemen, who counted for the entire department except for Fire Chief Ernie Miller, declared that, if the matter were to arise again, their services would no longer be available for removing paintings off the sides of buildings. Of course, the Mayor and the Council tried to intimidate the volunteers into obedience, but when Ernie Miller made it clear that there was nothing even the council, or the mayor for that matter, could do to force volunteers to volunteer. The Mayor and Council backed down. No doubt they were thinking of the potential danger to their own properties if a fire broke out and no volunteer fireman showed up. Police Chief Harris, as well, informed the Council that he would not be spending sleepless nights looking all over town for the hue of unusual lights. He would require a volunteer or the budget would have to be expanded to allow for the hiring of a trained deputy. The council again tried intimidation, threatening to fire Harris and hire a law man who was more obliging. Once Chief Harris informed them they would have to go through the Police Chief's Association of Missouri to do so, the Council again backed down, not wanting to deal with an established organization on matters of contractual agreements and fairness.

Sunday night and much to my chagrin Monday night as well went without a painting. Both nights Mr. Lambert the school custodian kept watch from the water tower. He had wanted to fulfill a childhood fantasy and be officially deputized, but had to settle for overtime pay. I was beginning to feel indignation towards Jack the Dripper. Had he or she or they abandoned their effort so easily? It seemed to me there was a lack of resolve to continue what had been started. Was one school custodian on a water tower such an insurmountable roadblock? Knowing Mr. Lambert he was probably drunk and sound asleep most of the night anyway. Maybe keeping a low profile was the right idea. Was it possible the two paintings were the complete exposition? Maybe the woman and the man were destined to merely stare at each other for eternity.

Being a 14 year old boy on summer holiday and therefore having all the resourcefulness, energy and time in the world, I promptly opened my own investigation. By Tuesday afternoon I uncovered a considerable lead. Behind the church under a haphazard pile of scaffolding I had discovered recently used painting materials wrapped and hidden in an old canvas. It was a good thing my father had not mentioned his idea about Jack the Dripper using scaffolding instead of ladders, they certainly would have found the cans and brushes and trays. I had the urge to tell someone what I'd found. I considered my parents, but I could not trust my dad not to let the cat out of the bag with his idle chit-chat to gas station attendants and store clerks. My mother would never keep a secret from my father. The only other person I considered was Herman Eckstein. But even a kid knows not to give a burning secret to a newspaperman. It was difficult, but I kept my discovery too myself. I wasn't going to accidently help the Council in anyway. This made me feel like an agent to Jack the Dripper, an ally.

I continued my grid pattern search of the town. On Wednesday I turned up something odd. On the sidewalk outside of Mr. Coombs' house I notice a bit of brown paint. I knew I had seen that shade before, on the fire hall and the bank building. Suddenly it came to me- the wooden chair! I was sure of it. I got right down on my hands and knees to have a look when Maria Gomez came out of nowhere holding grocery bags and shooed me away in Spanish. Her vigor in doing so surprised me. In fact I recall her kicking at me. Despite those grocery bags and the fact that I was an agile teen she nearly landed a good one on my butt.

Outside of Mr. Coombs house was not one of the places I expected to find a clue as to who Jack the Dripper was. What it meant I had not the faintest idea. Was it possible the Council its self was responsible for the paintings? Was it some kind of stunt on behalf of the Council and Mayor to gain even more power? Why did Mrs. Gomez react that way? I could barely fathom such questions let alone answer them. I needed to tell someone, an adult. Possibly an adult could help in figuring out what I'd found and what it meant.

I decided to let Herman Eckstein in on what I knew even though he likely couldn't help putting it in The Daily Mule. I thought there was a chance I could convince him that doing so would only help the Council and Mayor Coombs. When I arrived at his place he had a visitor, a reporter from a big time New York magazine. Herman and the reporter were sitting at a picnic table on the front lawn looking at the photos the reporter from New York had just had developed at the local drugs store. There were photos of the signs at either end of the highway heading into town: Welcome to Whompaton – population 946. Here we fly straight. If you want to stay you must do the same. That was the side of the sign heading into town. The side heading out read: You are now leaving Whompaton. Please take your high jinx with you.

"That is some real weird, Orwellian shit man," said the New York reporter, whose name was Brian (I don't remember his last name).

"Ya we're real proud of our chunk of the twilight zone here aren't we kid," Herman said, addressing me as I sat down at the picnic table. I nodded. I didn't know what Orwellian meant but the sound of the word seemed to fit our town. Herman and Brian had a long, wide-ranging and sophisticated conversation about the state of our town and the right of an individual versus a community. My young mind was overwhelmed. They both had a lot of patience with my constant questions. Brian wanted a look at the rule board and shame list outside of the post office.

'Guidelines for a Better Township by your Whompaton Town Council', was the official name of the rule board. It read as follows:

Radio and TV are reserved for educational and news purposes only. No playing of music of any kind in public unless authorized by Whompaton Council. No holding hands or any other public shows of affection. No crowds larger than five persons shall gather anywhere unless sanctioned by the Whompaton Council. No unapproved costumes or clothing. Bell bottoms are not approved. Mini-skirts are not approved. We do not celebrate Halloween in Whompaton. . (It went on like this until the end, where it read) No dancing and empty Milk bottles must be put out the day of pickup-not before.

We had a look at the shame list. There were five names on it. I'm happy to report my mother was not one of them.

"I doubt this is even legal," said Brian. He was snapping pictures. "It's a simple case of abuse of power."

"It's a bit more complicated than that Brian," said Herman. "The Council was given the mandate by voters, therefore the authority to pass By- Laws. They are also very knowledgeable when it comes to understanding what their limits are, and very good at finding slippery ways around things. That's probably the reason they call it a list of suggestions and not actual rules or laws."

"I think if we can get a picture of your Jack the Dripper's next exhibit," said Brian, "We'll have a decent story for my bosses in New York."

Brian left us to buy some essentials at the grocery store. He was scheduled to stay in Whompaton for a week. Herman had invited him to stay at the Daily Mule's headquarters. I took this opportunity to tell Herman what I found on the sidewalk outside of Mayor Coombs place. He was as perplexed as I was. He agreed we should keep it quiet until we understood what, if anything, it meant.

Three more days went by with no painting. Friday night seemed to go by uneventfully as well. That is until Saturday morning when a traveler passing through informed the clerk at the gas station that he was no prude, but the painting on the grain elevator just outside of town was a bit risky for his small children and that his wife was surely not impressed.

It's a Whompaton historical fact now that if Mr. Lambert the school custodian had turned his head 40 degrees to his right sometime Friday night while he was perched high up on the water tower he would have seen bright lights splashed against the grain elevator located just outside of town. He could have alerted Chief Harris and something could have been done about these lights. Instead, he kept his eyes fixed forward and mostly shut and as a result a huge painting of a naked lady sprawled on the floor hugging a naked man's leg came into the world uninterrupted. It was painting number three in all its glory. The same beautiful unabashedly naked woman lay sprawled out on the floor. The man in the room was visible this time and he too was naked. She was hugging his leg and looking up at his penis and testicles, which looked gigantic there on the entire side of the grain elevator . Jack the Dripper had struck again!!

The upheaval it caused the town was beyond explosive. I wasn't allowed to go near the part of Whompaton that bordered the grain elevator . It was rumored the Mayor had called the state police and the FBI. Of course these were only rumors. The FBI and the State Police don't care about crimes involving graffiti, even as enormous and bawdy as theses were. It was a full on crime scene, but one the local police were left to solve. My parents ordered me to stay away. But I got a good look at the painting from the hill across the highway, a spot I showed Brian and Herman and they took all their pictures of the third painting from there using telephoto lenses.

"Stick and berries," said Brian.

"Parsnip and taters," said Herman.

"Two plums and a banana," I said. They laughed.

I continued with my own investigation and rode over to the church and found the scaffolding stacked differently than before. At least I thought so. Then I went by Mayor Comb's house and the dash of paint had been removed from the side walk. I beat it out of there. I didn't want another encounter with Maria Gomez.

I went back to headquarters, so to speak, The Daily Mule, to talk to Herman and Brian. I was just in time to say good bye to Brian. His New York bosses had sent him to Woodstock to cover the developing story of the free concert there. In the end Brian and the New York magazine never did publish the story of our odd ball little town. The Woodstock concert got all the national attention.

Of course the Mayor and the Council had plenty of emergency closed door meetings about painting number three. Police Chief Harris was at his absolute wits end. Curiously, in the midst of all this turmoil, Gilbert Lewis, our new, homosexual (or so my dad said) Librarian and Mr. Bayweather decided to put on an art exposition. Once the Council and the Mayor heard about this they tried to block it at every turn. It was Ewan Billforth who saved the day by hiring a high priced and rather eager lawyer, who in turn pointed out it was legally impossible for the Council to discriminate and prevent the art exhibition from taking place at the community center which was built and maintained for by tax payers, and finding a county judge who would agree would be easy.

So the exhibition entitled: "The Appreciation of Art in all its Forms", took place in the Whompaton Community center on the last Saturday of July, 1969.

Because it was such a hot bed of contention, and given recent artistic events, it was natural the entire population of Whompaton attended.

Gilbert Lewis and Mr. Bayweather sat at the front and gave their lecture on art. They had borrowed a slide projector from the library and were showing slides on art history. I'm sure what they were explaining was interesting. I remember the keenness in which they tried to educate us about art. No one, however, was listening. No one could take their attention away from Maria Gomez, who was up front painting on an easel just to the right of Gilbert and Mr. Bayweather. She had been hired by Gilbert to do a live representation of art. Painting on the canvas wildly as the men gave their presentation. We were all surprised as no one knew Maria Gomez was an artist in the first place.

And what struck us all was what Maria was putting on the canvas. The style was familiar, to say the least. In fact it was unmistakable. It was Jack the Dripper's! And the more she filled in the canvas the more we couldn't look away. The mystery of who the painter was had been solved and yet everyone knew there was a lot more of the story to come. Gilbert and Mr. Bayweather had made sure everyone in town had a seat with a view to its dramatic conclusion.

We could all feel the tension building . Mayor Coombs' own house keeper was Jack the Dripper! Wasn't he the self-proclaimed vestige of morality? And furthermore she was painting number four right before the towns eyes. Mrs. Bayweather seemed especially disconcerted. She was poking the Mayor, prodding him to get over his shock and get up and say something, put a stop to his own employee making a mockery of the council, making a mockery out of all the invaluable things she and the Mayor had done together for the town. Finally he stood.

"Maria," he shouted, "I order you to stop this at once!"

Maria stood, her brush gracefully finishing a few broad strokes before saying, "Have you forgotten it is my day off Mr. Coombs."

"Your day off!" Mayor Coombs shouted, "Your day off! Have you forgotten you live in my home? I hate to say this, but if you don't stop this at once you are fired!"

"Fired?" Maria scoffed. Then she smiled the way one smiles when one is eternally sure of something. She had something over the Mayor and the Council, some secret that had elevated her above a mere subordinate. "Why, Harvey (which was apparently the Mayor's first name. I don't believe anyone knew it, but Maria and maybe Mrs. Bayweather) instead of threatening me you should be offering me a raise. After all I clean that extra room you keep hidden upstairs." Her accent was strong but her English was definitely understandable..

To this Harvey Coombs' face turned first red and then an eerie shade of pale. Mrs. Bayweather looked at him with surprise and bewilderment. Her face was distorted with confusion.

"Any room, even a well-hidden one, will collect dust," continued Maria. "All those magazines, all those pictures, the film strips, quite a collection. I have to admit they have influenced my latest works. "

The Mayor slunk back in his seat as if his knees could no longer support his weight. Maria made a few quick, broad strokes with her brush. She had painted the rough outline of a woman's face including her greying hair. With the skill of a caricaturist Maria had outlined in rudimental form Mrs. Bayweather. Unmistakable! The room gasped. Mrs. Bayweather let out a breathy cry. The Mayor moaned. His head rolled back, and he looked as though he had fallen unconscious. It was all too much.

"In fact," Maria went on, "it is one of the photos hidden in that room that I'm reproducing on this canvas today. Of course I'm taking artistic liberty and making things appear as pleasing as I can. You know, tighten things up. Smoothing out a few wrinkles here and there." Maria said this and winked at Mrs. Bayweather.

"Herbert! You took pictures?!" shrieked Mrs. Bayweather. "How could you?!-How could you?!"

The Mayor could only groan and let his head flop back again. People began to also look at Mr. Bayweather now. I remember he wore a fixed, unfaltering smirk through it all.

As the painting came closer to completion it was clear it was the Mayor and Mrs. Bayweather in a compromising position. I was well pleased that everyone was so caught up in the drama, including my parents, they forgot there were children present. I shrunk down in my chair hoping I wouldn't be ushered out.

"There are many more like this," said Maria, "many, many more!"

It was clear even to my adolescent brain that there had been a conspiracy at work. Gilbert Lewis, Mr. Bayweather and Maria had all schemed to expose what the Mayor and Mrs. Bayweather had been up to behind closed doors. But, what was exposed was so explosive and shocking, it let the conspirators off the hook instantly. There was a collective cringe in the silence. No one seemed able to crack the awkward hush. Then the mighty Rose Pinlap rose to her feet.

"This is a bloody outrage," she said. "I cannot allow myself to be associated any further with a pair of frauds. I hereby officially resign my position as a member of the Whompaton Town Council."

One by one the remaining members of the Council followed Rose Pinlap's example and publically broke ties with the Mayor and Mrs. Bayweather. Then they all followed Rose out the door. The last Council member to leave the community center was Mrs. Bayweather herself.

Before she walked out she said two things. The first was to Harvey (I think it is safe to say at this point in the story he was no longer the Mayor of Whompaton.) She said: "I trusted you. I trusted you, you sick twisted pervert." She said this in a hushed tone, but everyone had heard perfectly. The second thing she said was to her husband: "Come along. Let's go home." She spoke as if she was ordering a dog.

To this Mr. Bayweather said, "I'll never set foot in that... house again. It certainly is no home. From now on I'll be staying with Gilbert." To my dad's credit he didn't make any jokes.

I remember I felt sorry for Mrs. Bayweather as she slinked her way out past the painting of herself left on the easel and the town's fixed, glaring eyes. She was a mean woman, but I felt in return life had been a bit too harsh on her that day. Or maybe not.

Soon everyone was leaving the community center. Gilbert and Mr. Bayweather didn't bother to finish their presentation. It had only been a ruse anyway, a set-up to expose Mr. Bayweather's wife and the Mayor as secret lovers. And by the look of Maria's finished painting they were both quite keen at playing the role.

My parents got up to leave and I went to talk to Maria. She was packing up her paints and brushes. It was obvious she had had Gilbert's and Mr. Bayweather's help while painting the large murals, but it was clear who the actual creator was. I wanted to ask her why she wasn't a famous artist. Her answer has always stayed with me. "Because," she said, in a way that was scolding. As if I should have already known the answer. "I am a woman."

And that was the end of the Whompaton Town Council and its Mayor. The fraudulent moral high ground on which they stood sifted away like loose beach sand right before our eyes. The next day Mr. Billforth put a notice of elections in the Daily Mule. Candidates for the position of Mayor and Councilmembers were sought.

Wednesday evening there was a meeting at the town hall. People were asked to stand if they wanted to run for Councilmember or Mayor. When the call came for candidates for the Mayor's office there were a few people who stood. Old Mr. Galsworthy winked at me as he rose to stand with the others. To the surprise of both myself and my father, when the call came for councilmembers, my mother stood up. There was exactly seven who stood, which was the number needed. Whompaton had a new Council. In a few months, after an election, old Mr. Galsworthy became our new Mayor.

The highway signs came down along with the notices at the post office, the shame list and 'Guidelines for a Better Township'. The entire previous regime's twaddle disappeared almost overnight. Which made me wonder, even at my young age, how something so fleeting ever had such a hold over the town in the first place?

In the end my Father never got his five dollars back for the milk bottle incident even though my Mother was to be a Councilmember for the next twenty years. As for myself I learned to be suspicious of people who claim to have some moral authority over others, whether in government or elsewhere. I learned to be educated about who I vote for. I teach my kids these things. But the thing that most stuck with me from that summer was my appreciation for art. My wife and I have an original Maria Gomez hanging in our bedroom, although it is signed… Jack the Dripper.

The American Home
Managers Association

It is past dinner time. I've come home late again, which is happening more and more due to my work load being insane lately. My wife is all excited about something she'd found on the internet. As it happens, when my wife gets fixated on one thing, everything else suffers. She must have been exceptionally fixated today because I sit down to one sorry looking late dinner.

"You know the association you belong to - for Notaries?" My wife says, beaming from across the table.

"Yes," I say, chewing a mouth full of rice with something in it that has the texture of wet cotton. I am trying not to imagine all the things she could have, through lack of attention, accidently thrown in the slow cooker. Whatever it is, it is oozing through my back molars, almost making me gag. 'Beans,' I say to myself, 'let's just pretend it's beans.'

"Well I found an association," my wife says, "for someone like me." She can't contain that smile of hers, the one that spills out the sides of her mouth when she thinks something is going her way.

Alarm bells immediately go off in my head. What the hell does she mean by 'someone like her'?

My wife believes I should know exactly what she is talking about at all times. In her mind she has clear, invented ideas about how a spouse should behave. A good husband, for instance, who pays attention to his wife, should be able to fill in huge gaps of missing information in order to immediately understand what point said wife is trying to make. It's a matrimonial psychic power I have yet to develop. I have to think quick to fill in the missing info or dinner will be the least of my problems. I employ a technique I call 'The Cluster Bomb', in which I lavish copious amounts of compliments upon her (Yes, it could be simply considered as ass kissing…but it's an advanced form).

And so I begin the Cluster Bomb: "People like you, meaning beautiful and sexy and…"

"No,' she interrupts.

"Intelligent, witty and funny..."

"No."

I have the feeling dark clouds of marital disharmony are forming over our house. A tornado is in the works. In her highchair our daughter, whom we'd affectionately nicked named Zuzu Petals is staring blankly at me while sucking on a crust of bread. She senses my fear.

As usual my wife sees right through my Cluster Bomb. I have begun to question its effectiveness. Lately it only makes things worse. Maybe I've used it too many times, giving my wife opportunity to develop an early warning system with counter measures. I am reluctant to admit my self-acclaimed Cluster Bomb has become an obsolete strategy all too soon, a misadventure in the effort to keep the peace.

'I had a child with this idiot and he doesn't understand me at all', is what I know my wife is thinking. It has written its self all over the contorted muscles around her eyes and the corners of her mouth.

Hoping to lighten the mood I take a chance with a bit of banter, which I think my wife might appreciate since she is an aficionado in all matters of ribbing and razzing, as in: honey I'm just kidding around don't get so mad.

Note: I don't think one should banter about male pattern balding or erectile difficulty. One arises from a man having too much testosterone and the other from a man having too little. I happen to suffer from both ailments at once. My wife finds this endlessly funny. I, however, do not.

"A native Californian relocated to the mid-west?" I banter. I know instantly I've fallen short of my wife's wise cracking standards.

"No!" she says.

I can tell by the tone of her voice she is close to the point where her mood will be permanently set for the evening. Diplomacy will no longer be possible.

Somewhere in a man's chromosomes there is a default mechanism, telling him no matter how bad it gets he should just keep cluster bombing.

"A great Mom?" I say.

"That's only part of it," she says.

Taking a fork full of …salad?...I pretend to like the way she must have forgotten she had already added the tarragon to the slushy vegetables and heaped in a shovel full more. After chewing (and barely being able to swallow) I say, "I give up. What kind of an association?"

"You're such an asshole," my wife says.

I guess I had that coming, after all I had just called my wife: beautiful, sexy, intelligent, witty, funny and a great mom. (And for the record I don't think relocated Californians are that bad either.)

The baby, sensing the darker turn our dinner is taking, begins to fuss.

"Now you've made the baby cry!" she says.

"Ya I made the baby cry?" I say, astonished. I reach for Zuzu Petals, saying, "I am completely lost at how we got to a point in our conversation where you felt the need to call me an asshole."

"Shhhh! Watch your language in front of the baby," my wife says. "Don't' listen to the Daddy. He doesn't mean it," Zuzu immediately goes right for my glasses; something she recently discovered was a fun thing to put in her mouth.

"I said asshole because I shouldn't have to tell you what association I would belong to," my wife says. Her voice has risen to a shout; signifying we may have passed the point of no return for this evening.

From my experience with our 'domestics' (my term for these little flare-ups of ours) I've found it necessary to develop another technique which I call the 'turtle', whereby I relinquish all my points of contention and remove myself from the argument. I close my mouth and keep it that way. The logic being: it is hard for even my wife to continue an argument all by herself for very long.

Recently, though, it has become more difficult to remain quiet. I think my wife has also figured out this stratagem. She tries to penetrate my 'turtle'. Hoping I'll react as she picks away again at the emotional sore spots of old exhausted arguments. The ones she knows so well. Nothing is off limits. It's a shower of venom much like an evil version of my 'Cluster Bomb'.

I've learned to parry her counter to my 'turtle' with an upgrade which I call the 'super turtle', (a recent addition to our nuptial arms race) in which I add continual and sympathetic eye contact; a sort of 'yes dear' look. This negates her ability to accuse me of ignoring her. Because that's when things go really bad, if she feels ignored. I will generally super turtle until there are irrefutable signs that she has cooled down –i.e. her grimace eases, she discontinues the stomping of her feet, her body is free of the forward lean it has when she walks around full of anger.

Note: Her entire family walks leaning forward when they are mad. I remember a big family argument one Christmas; I thought the entire house had tilted.

"Where is it that I work?" she asks. "What do I do with my day? Where are my energies and talents spent?"

Note (to self): These are all rhetorical questions. No need to break the silence. Maintain the Super Turtle.

"You know what this is?" she says, leaning forward, "full-on-ungratefulness!"

'God help us all!' echoes in my turtle shell.

"You just don't appreciate me!" my wife continues, "Sometimes I think you take me totally for granted, as if everything freezes here when you walk out that door! Like taking care of Zuzu and the house and dinner is like being on one giant long weekend," she says.

I swallow hard.

I find it odd that my wife should make out that I don't appreciate her. Only last weekend, for no occasion, I had given my wife flowers. The card read- I appreciate you! Could it be in some paradoxical way I had given her this angle of attack?

Note: I'm starting to believe there is a paradoxical under tow prevalent in all marriages.

A short lull in our dinner time 'domestic' occurs when my wife takes Zuzu Petals away to change her. I make the most of this time by rearranging the food on my plate to make it look as if I have eaten more than I have. I even slide some food from my plate to my wife's plate.

My wife comes back into the dining room with our daughter, who is smiling - in love with the feeling of fresh clean clothes.

"Finished with your dinner dear?' she asks.

Unbelievably she has come down from Mt. Ever-un-rest and I can come safely out of the Super Turtle.

"Yes dear, thank you," I say. She takes my plate and I avert my eyes, never wanting to look upon it again.

"You know my friend Cindy (rhetorical)? Well she sent me a link to 'The American Home Managers Association's home page," my wife says, looking at me, waiting for my reaction.

I dissect those words in my mind. *American Home* —this of course was obvious. *Manager* - can my wife be considered the manager of our home? I think of all the things a manager does and of all the things my wife does. Yes, I think it's a fair assessment.

"That's essentially what I am," my wife says.

"Yes," I say, "it is a fair assessment." And I smile and she smiles and the baby reaches for my glasses.

"Well I checked it out and you know I think I want to join," my wife says. "I think it will be important for me. I feel like I want the support of other home managers and I want to give my support to them. I think it's about time something like this happened. I think of my poor mother and all the…..all the …I think of my mother and she could have used the support of an official association."

Note: I don't know if an association, professional or otherwise, could have kept my wife's father out of the neighbor's bedroom, which is the only way anyone really could have helped my poor mother in-law. And no association would have been there after to help de-scandalize the whole well publicized affair (the neighbor lady also happened to be the principal of my wife's school). But I wasn't about to share my thoughts and light a match in that fireworks factory again. Given the right influence - i.e. an extra glass of wine or a movie with some womanizing asshole in it, my wife can become a hater of all men, projecting the blunders and indiscretions of her father onto men in general, which in general, out of convenience, means me.

"I think it sounds great," I say encouragingly, "it is about time too."

She gives me a look which means it isn't my place to say that. As if I were Hitler remarking on how long the war was taking.

"What kind of support?" I ask, flatly. I decide I better take any false inflections of enthusiasm and sympathy out of my voice and go with the even tone of something like a farmer assessing the weather.

"Well once a member of the American Home Managers Association's you get full access to the online open discussion forum and a lot of ladies have ongoing blogs and there are articles about home managing techniques," my wife says.

Note: Last mother's day I had given my wife a large bouquet of flowers and a year's subscription to 'Good Housekeeping' magazine. She seemed a little miffed about the subscription, finally remarking coldly in bed "I guess a season's pass to the opera would've been too fancy for this stay at home mom."

Further note: 'Good Housekeeping' should change their name to 'Good Home managing'.

"I think you'd be a great blogger,' I say. I mean it too.

"I guess," she says, putting Zuzu Petals on the floor with some of her toys.

"Cindy and I really want to get involved in this and help it expand," my wife says while clearing the table. "I mean why haven't I heard about this before? They obviously need someone to help with PR. Can you imagine if every housewife in America joined, that would be incredible. We could really get our voices heard. It would be the biggest voting bloc in the country. I mean can you imagine?"

I can imagine and I see the first woman President of the United States walking down the steps of Air Force One and the 'First Man' following a few steps behind her. I think how hard it would be to be the first - First Man - in the White house.

Then I say something stupid.

"You mean 'if every Home Manager in America joined'" I say.

"What?" she asks.

"You said: 'Can you imagine if every housewife in America joined.' You meant: 'if every Home Manager in America joined,' I say.

There is a moment of non-reaction and then I get the cold pissed-off stare she frequently gives me. Every time I get that look I can't help but imagine her doing something to get even like sneaking into the living room at night and deleting things I've recorded on our PVR. Like that season finale of Dexter that somehow went missing.

Note: I promised not to bring this Dexter thing up again so please ignore what I just said. Even though I had to wait and borrow a DVD from a guy at work in order to watch said episode (by the time the DVD had come out I'd heard all about what happened so it was all very anti-climactic).

"Myself, I was all for belonging to an association at first," I say, breaking the frosty silence. "Now it's just a big pain in the ass. I told you about the forms they changed last year, remember? There was nothing wrong with the old forms, but they came up with new ones that weren't thought out and it was such a cluster fuck. We all went back to the old forms and those idiots threatened to fine us if we didn't use the new, useless ones."

"Watch your language," she says pointing to our daughter playing, then she asks, "What happened with that?"

"We're still using the old forms and they're still threating to fine us. If it ain't broke don't fix it, that's what I say. But, that's not what associations say. They love to tinker with shi... (I look at Zuzu)....stuff just to justify their jobs and make us all think we are getting our money's worth," I say.

"Hmm," my wife says.

The evening progresses and I wait until we put Zuzu Petals to bed before I have an extra scotch to try to disinfect my mouth of the aftertaste of dinner. She reads and I watch my shows and then I read and she watches her shows. We don't like each other's shows or each other's books or magazines. I read somewhere this is ok, but she saw a TV program that said it isn't ok. We are working on it.

Before bed my wife shows me the American Home Managers Association's website. It is what I expect: slick packaging without a lot of real content.

"Are you sure this is an official association?" I ask. "I mean have you checked it with the registry of American associations?"

"Thanks for looking out for us halfwits," she says, with her front teeth pushed out, buck tooth fashion, ala Goofy, along with the voice and stupid chuckle.

I love my wife no doubt, but as a lot of spouses can attest- you can only take so much shit. And by trying to keep the peace at all costs you start to feel a trifle diminished.

"Listen," I say, "your attitude tonight is a bit caustic and it's wearing on my nerves. There is one thing you are forgetting."

"What's that?" my wife says, all tough, as if I was about to let loose with some kind of verbal threat.

"We are on the same side," I say, "We are partners." This I hope would hammer some perspective back into her bird house.

I look up at her from the chair in front of the computer desk. She stands next to me staring at the A H M A's website. Suddenly her face fills with an expression that surprises me and quite frankly scares me at the same time. It is the look of discontentment and unhappiness that has appeared on my wife's face. And what is worse it seems to have been triggered by my saying we are on the same side, that we are partners.

My wife is a whiz in all things mathematical, a real marvel with numbers. She had a promising career at a large logistics firm. When Zuzu came along we made the decision together that she would put her career on hold, and become a stay at home mom to raise our daughter with the possibility of her going back when Zuzu is in her teens. I would financially support our family. Certainly it is the most important job in the world: being a Mom. However, I realize now maybe I've been insensitive to the possibility such an intelligent woman may find it, from time to time, quite unstimulating to entertain a toddler with large brightly colored plastic blocks and do laundry all day. Now I wonder if she resents the choice we made together about sidelining her career. I kiss her hand and hold it to my cheek.

"We are partners honey," I say, and I mean it. I was in the middle of saying, "if you're not happy we can…" when she pulled her hand away.

"I want to show you the blogs," she interrupted.

"I guess sometimes it's hard to see what the other side is going through," I say. "I guess I could do a better job at understanding what it's like to stay…"

"Don't placate me," my wife says.

"That's it, I'm done with this now," I say, and I very much mean it. I was at the point where I felt I couldn't say or do anything my wife would find correct.

I walk out of the spare bedroom we use as our computer room and I feel her eyes follow me. Good, I think. My wife knows when she has pushed me too far. It is only Wednesday so there isn't any chance of sex tonight (we don't really have mid-week sex anymore), but at least we might have a peaceful time in bed before we turn out the lights.

We keep a respectable distance from one another until it's time to laze about in bed for another half hour or so before we turn the lights out (the time we once used to have sex). She climbs into her side and I open the bedroom window a few inches before getting in on my side. She browses the web with her iPad and I read a book. After a while I lay my book on my chest, and I don't know what possesses me to focus again on the subject that has robbed us of a harmonious evening.

"I don't know, I mean most of the people in my association think it isn't worth the money you spend on the monthly dues to justify what you get back," I say.

"Really?" my wife says.

"How much money are we talking about for this thing of yours and Cindy's?" I ask.

"For Cindy's and my *thing* it is a little over a hundred dollars a month," she says, a little too huffy in my opinion. She doesn't bother looking up from her iPad.

"Good god!" I say, "That's nearly what it costs for mine!"

"Your point?" she snaps.

"Well, I mean I'm a bloody Notary!" I say.

"Well I'm a bloody Home Engineer," she says.

"Manager you mean" I say.

"What?" she says.

"Well which is it, Engineer or Manager?" I ask.

"Both!" she shouts. "Maybe I'll join two Associations!" She thunders up out of bed.

"Where are you going?" I ask rather sweetly, trying to undo what I've just done, which was poke a sore gorilla with a stick.

"I'm going to check on Zuzu Petals," she says.

"The baby is fine," I say.

"How the hell do you know," she says and stomps out, leaning.

One might think things are really bad now. It could be for someone with less experience and skill in handling these types of 'domestics'. As I've demonstrated I'd become proficient at reading the lay of the land, tasting the air and dialing up some defensive strategies. I knew I'd have to withstand one more barrage and then the lights would be turned off and our night time rules of respectful silence until morning would be in effect- (Re: a book my wife read on relationship communication endorsed by Oprah Winfrey herself).

She stomps back in the room and crashes into bed.

"How is the baby," I ask.

"You know damn well she's fine," my wife says.

She is heated enough that I consider the Super Turtle again, wondering if it would even work in bed.

"Honey let's work all this out tomorrow," I say, thinking the best strategy would be the old tried and true 'giving her a bit of time to cool down' maneuver. "Let's go to sleep."

"I can't believe it all comes down to money," she says.

"I didn't exactly say that," I say.

"You exactly said that. You got all excited about a hundred dollars a month," my wife says.

"No, what I meant was value for money. I mean I'm a professional; most professionals almost need to belong to an association. We don't belong to unions, so if the shit hits the fan we have someone to back us up," I say.

"Well who backs me up when the shit hits the fan here?" she asks.

"Well I like to think I do.....wait...what do you mean 'when shit hits the fan'? When has the shit ever hit the fan here?" I say.

"Last year with the fire in the kitchen," she says.

"Honey you caught an oven mitt on fire that's hardly the shit hitting the fan," I tell her. "That could happen to anyone. I went right out and bought you a new set of oven mitts."

Note: I realize this might have come out sounding condescending or demeaning, but it is not intended that way. And I certainly don't think my wife is reckless or clumsy or a threat to our little girl or our home. I believe anyone could catch an oven mitt on fire. I honestly think this.

"Let's go to sleep," she says.

I turn off the lamp. The silence is infused with her anger. I can feel it radiate throughout the bed.

"It's a great idea and it is about time," I say, ass-kissing shamelessly one last time into the darkness.

There is a long moment of stillness. I can feel sleep pulling down the blinds on my consciousness. Dreamy like, I say, "I love you." There was another long moment of silence. It is her rule that we have to tell each other this every night before we go to sleep. Another moment goes by before I turn over to face her.

"I love you too," she says, weakly attempting to hide the resentment in her voice, to hide her leaning words.

I am near comatose and at the point where I don't have it in me to bullshit anymore, not even to myself. I'm at that semi-dream state when all there is left is how you truly feel.

"Listen," I say, all drowsy, "remember when your boss cried, you know when you left the logistics firm to have our baby. Your boss cried because she knew she'd never replace you. That's like how me and Zuzu would cry, the house it's self would cry if we ever lost you.

Who gives…shit….association…love… you." I don't know if she answered me, I fall asleep.

The next morning I wake to the smell of bacon. Thursday morning and my wife is already up and at 'em.

"Honey time to get up," she says all sweet and melodic. She comes in the room and kisses me. "Ewww! Brush your teeth." she says.

Honestly, not a bad way to wake up, better than the clock radio.

"You're up early," I say, sitting down at the table.

"Yep, don't know why," she says.

"Zuzu good?" I ask.

"Still sleeping like an angel," my wife says. She sits a plate, piled with bacon and eggs and hash browns, in front of me.

"Wow!" I say, "Sunday morning breakfast on a Thursday - livin' the high life."

She smiles and pours me a cup of coffee. We sit and eat breakfast swapping sections of the paper and taking our time with our second cups of coffee.

"You better get dressed honey," my wife says, finally.

"Ya...I guess. Well good luck with your association thing," I say. "When you sign up use the American Express card, so we get the points."

"Oh, I decided I'm not going to bother," she says, putting the dishes in the sink.

"No?" I ask, trying to conceal my utter bewilderment.

"Nah...I can't see what I'd really get from it," she says. "Hundred dollars a month to read some blogs seems a little steep to me."

All I can do is sit there and stare at her as she glides in and out of the fridge and cupboards putting breakfast things logistically away. There is no sarcasm in her movements, not the slightest hint of a lean. It's as if all of last night hadn't happened

"I still think you should do a blog on your own," I say, "why not a video blog on YouTube, that would be awesome,"

She smiles and shrugs her shoulders. "Could do I guess."

I get dressed and play with Zuzu for a few minutes.

"Do you want last night's left overs for lunch?" my wife asks.

"No!" I say, worried the word might have sprung from my mouth too eagerly. "Actually, sure," I say, in a feat of incredible acting, "that'll be great."

This way, I realize, I can simply throw it in the trash at work and grab a sandwich somewhere for lunch. Taking it now would eliminate the risk of having it for leftovers tonight. Instead, for this evening, I would be assured one of my wife's attentive, appetizing meals. Genius!

Buses

They say when you are Ernest Feldman's age any day you wake up is a good day. For Ernest it was true; every day was good. With one exception: Tuesdays. He hated Tuesdays. It was the day he visited his doctor. He didn't care much for his doctor. It was precisely because of his doctor and his reports that Ernest had lost his driver's license. Now he had one thing he detested more than visiting his doctor's office and that was taking all those damn buses to get there. Ernest Feldman loathed buses. Buses, to him, were for old women and school kids.

Ernest's wife, Nell, woke Ernest a half hour early as she did every Tuesday. She smiled her especially abetting smile she reserved for the second day of the week. He was about to smile back at her, but remembered what day it was and frowned instead.

"Now dear," Nell said, sitting on the edge of the bed, "it's only until they get your medication sorted then we can have our Tuesdays back."

"I just hate missing so much work," Ernest said, shutting his eyes tightly.

"Come get your breakfast," Nell said. She stood and went to the kitchen. She had that strange feeling in her stomach she got whenever Ernest acted confused about things, like saying he hated missing work when he'd been retired for twelve years.

Nell couldn't put her finger on exactly what emotions were intermingling in her stomach - fear, sadness and anger all mixed up together. It troubled her deeply what was happening to her husband. To her it was a damn shame such an intelligent, vigorous man was ending up in such a state. 'Diminished' was the word Nell liked to use. She didn't care that eventually everyone got old, it was an unbreakable law of nature she knew, but old age had no right to steal the sharp mind of her husband's. He of all people didn't deserve to be 'diminished'. This was why she pushed him to see the doctor once a week, to get his medications and their dosages exactly right. She wanted Ernest to be able to fight the bully thief senility right to the bitter end. She wanted him to go kicking and screaming and Nell was determined to be right by his side. It didn't matter that she had her own health problems to deal with: an atrocious case of edema in both legs which had resulted in open ulcers. She was determined, no matter how swollen and sore her legs and feet got, she would stand by her husband to the bitter end.

Nell's legs were worse than ever lately. She'd been up less than an hour and already she was hobbling. Her calves and feet were swollen and red. Her kneecaps felt like any moment they were going to pop off and fly across the kitchen onto the linoleum.

"Nell, you should let me fix my own breakfast," Ernest said, standing in the kitchen now. He could see she was suffering. He grabbed her arm and helped her to her chair at the kitchen table.

"It's better I let you relax before you go off to the doctor's," Nell said trying to hide her pain. She dare not look at her swollen ankles. Ernest brought a pillow from the living room and placed it on one of the dinette chairs.

"Nell put your feet up and I'll go get your grandma socks and Tiger Balm," Ernest said.

The grandma socks were what their granddaughter called her prescription pressure socks that helped relieve some of Nell's pain and swelling. The Tiger Balm was a suggestion from a neighbor when Nell complained the other ointments didn't work. She rubbed it in all the places where there was no bandage.

"The least I can do," said Nell, "is make you breakfast. I just wish I could go with you. I can't bear the thought of you on all those buses by yourself. I know how irritated you get. It's a wife's duty to be there to calm her husband when he starts seeing red."

"Here you go my dear," Ernest said, handing her the socks and balm. "Well it's a husband's duty," he said, "to make sure his wife stays off her feet and doesn't inflict herself with pain needlessly. A little frustration on a few buses is nothing compared to the hell your legs will give you my dear, if you tried to go with me. Now I don't want to hear any more of this silliness."

He poured her a cup of coffee and put a slice of raisin bread, her favorite, into the toaster.

"Oh Ernest would you please just take a cab, you know plenty well we can afford it," Nell pleaded, as she did every Tuesday. "Or call Kevin. You know he doesn't mind driving you."

Ernest sat down awkwardly in his chair; his face had taken on a faraway expression.

"Are your legs bothering you Nell?" he asked.

Nell nodded glumly. Her stomach filled with the uneasiness.

"I'll get your grandma socks and your balm," Ernest said, rising from his chair.

"I've got them here," said Nell.

"You should really let me make my own breakfast," Ernest said.

"I know," said Nell.

She was still not sure exactly what to do when her husband's mind jaunted off like this. Up until now she found it best to simply go along with it, agreeing with what he said, answering his questions and simply wait until his mind recovered. She did her best not to show that his episodes, which were becoming more frequent, distressed her. Sometimes it was all she could do to fight back her tears.

"What day is it?" asked Ernest.

"It's Tuesday," Nell said.

Ernest frowned.

"It's only until they get your medicines sorted," Nell said, once more. There was a pause while Nell studied Ernest to see if he was hearing her. "I want you to take a cab to the doctor's office Ernest...please."

"I won't have it," Ernest said. His mind had come back to him, "We didn't work hard all our lives and manage our money so we could throw it all away on cab fare. And besides I'm not helpless you know. I can manage a few lousy buses."

Nell continued to study Ernest. She knew her husband, every mole on his body and every thought in his head. They had become extensions of each other. It amazed their children that she would suddenly blurt out exactly where Ernest had left his reading glasses before he'd even asked about them. There were countless similar instances; it was like they could read each other's mind. Now, at the kitchen table this Tuesday morning, Nell looked behind her husband's aging features, and saw he was frightened. Nell panicked, her stomach rolled.

"I'm going with you. I don't give a damn about my bloody legs," she said. She began to cry. "If you don't take a cab to the doctor's or get Kevin to drive you then I'm going with you!" The last four words ascended into a shout.

"I won't allow any of it," Ernest shouted back. There was a stunned pause. Even at the worst of times they rarely if ever shouted. "Now Nell," Ernest's tone had turned soothing, "I know you're upset and you worry about me. You always have worried about me and I've always been just fine." He stood behind her and began to rub her shoulders. "Shhhh - Shhhh," he brushed away her tears. "I don't want you to cry Nell. I'll take the buses to the doctor and he'll fix my medicines and I'll be back in no time. In the mean time I want you to rest your feet."

"You've always been a stubborn old mule," Nell said.

"Yes, but with the good sense of a horse," Ernest added. They both laughed.

"I'm beginning to hate Tuesdays more than you do," sighed Nell.

"They'll soon have my medication right. Then Tuesdays will be ours again. In fact it may turn out to be our favorite day because we'll appreciate it more when I'm through with these damn doctor's visits," Ernest said. "Anyway I'm more concerned about your legs than my medication or those bloody daft buses."

"My legs will be fine. The ointment and the socks are enough," Nell said. She glanced at the clock on the stove. "My dear, you've got to get moving now to catch the 107." She shuffled to her feet. Ernest sighed and went to the bedroom to change.

Naturally, because it was Tuesday it was raining. Nell handed Ernest his umbrella, one more thing to add to his frustration. She pulled open his jacket and placed the bus passes she had purchased at the grocery store (being sure to get the seniors discount) into his breast pocket. Nell did up his jacket and patted his chest where the passes sat safely underneath his jacket and overcoat.

"I've given you extra passes in case something goes wrong," she said. "Hang onto your umbrella this time."

Ernest grimaced at the thought of the ordeal he was about to face. The worst part was the downtown central exchange: so many school kids, so many bloody identical buses. Why was it they were all 1-0-something? 107, 109, 101, and 104- what happened to the 5-0's or the 7-0's? What would be wrong with a bus numbered 708 for instance? The school children were another matter. Did they not have actual school buses anymore? At the central exchange there was always a river of school children flooding the sidewalks, coursing this way and that, making a simple bus transfer not only a mental feat but a physical one as well.

It was all very confusing for someone relatively new to the game. Two Tuesdays ago he got on the 103 instead of the 105 by forgetting to cross the street at his next transfer after the central exchange. Only after the bus had gone by the mall again did he realize something was wrong and dinged the bell to get off. Ernest suddenly found himself standing on the side of the road and couldn't remember why. He was at a loss at what to do and stood there for a long while before he heard someone say, "Dad?" It was his son-in-law Kevin on a work delivery. Seeing Ernest standing there he had pulled over. Kevin coaxed his father-in-law into his truck and drove him to his doctor's appointment. Much to Ernest's chagrin Kevin waited and gave him a ride home as well. Ernest swore to himself this blunder was an anomaly, that that kind of ridiculousness would never happen again. He would rather call a cab himself and hide his mistakes and confusion then be an embarrassment to his family again.

At the front door Nell kissed Ernest goodbye. He stepped out into the gloom of the morning rain. Nell reluctantly closed the door behind him. As he descended the steps his mind stumbled. He had the feeling he had forgotten something. Confused, he turned and went back up the steps and tapped on the door. Nell hobbled back as quickly as possible to open it.

"Did you change your mind about the cab?" she asked, hopefully.

"What cab?" he said, he was clearly discombobulated. "Nell, the bus passes, I've forgotten them."

"Ernest they're here in your breast pocket," she said, patting his chest again.

"Ah," he said trying to put a brave face on his disorientation. "Don't you worry Nell I haven't forgotten Todd's wrestling practice. I'll have him there on time." He kissed her and went out the door. Nell began to panic again; she could not allow him to go off on those buses by himself in such a confused state; Todd, their son, hadn't had a wrestling practice in 30 years. She was momentarily dazed, trying to decide what action she should take. She turned to go to the kitchen and call Kevin, but then she thought it better to call Ernest back and use the veto power of a wife and outright order him, no matter how mad he got, to accept a ride from Kevin or take a cab.

Her anxiety made her move too quickly which put more stress on her already swollen legs. Her ankles burned wildly; shafts of pain zig-zagged up and down her thighs like lightning as she fumbled at the door lock. She flung the door open and called for Ernest. She was surprised at the frenzy in her voice. Ernest had already turned the corner and was too far down the street to hear her. The large hedge that surrounded the front yard was not only blocking her view it would also be stifling her voice as well. Nell leaned all her weight against the outside step railing. It was slippery from the rain and she half stumbled down the steps as she yelled out to Ernest once more, hoping for the slim chance that he would hear her. She waited, but he didn't re-appear at the front gate. Nell knew Ernest hadn't got very far; there was still a chance to catch him. If she could make it out to the front sidewalk there would be a better possibility that he would hear her shouts or see her waving. The rain had started to seep through her house coat and her slippers were already soaked through. She took a few steps and began to weep. The pain was immeasurable. Her tears were wild with panic. An implacable dread filled her body convincing her something terrible was going to happen to Earnest. She was convinced Tuesday had yet to show its worst. Without the railings to hang on to she could only manage a few feeble steps. 'Ernest,' she called again, but it was more of a frail whimper than a shout. The idea came to her that she could crawl to the front gate. She would probably be able to make if she went on all fours. Nell was so worried about Ernest that crawling along a rain pooled sidewalk seemed a completely reasonable thing to do. The only thing that stopped her was that it would take too long and Earnest would certainly get away. She didn't care how furious Ernest would have been seeing his wife dragging herself along the ground in the rain, only for his sake, only to force him to take a cab or wait for a ride. Her urgent concern for her husband was what gave her the strength to overcome her pain and heave herself back up the steps and inside to call Kevin.

Ernest popped his umbrella and walked towards the end of the street where he'd make a left and walk a couple blocks to the bus stop. He paused when he thought he'd heard Nell call his name. He considered going back to make sure, but after a moment of listening and hearing nothing more, his urge to get the day over with pushed him on. He couldn't help feeling angry and ashamed as he walked past his perfectly good Jeep Wagoneer parked in his garage only to line up with a bunch of school children to board a bus.

Ernest was a modest, reserved man. He was certainly not prone to boasting, but he knew that in his day he could manage and coordinate the equivalent of a hundred buses. For him having to take a bus was tantamount to the President of the United States having to stand in line at the White House cafeteria. He didn't feel that people who took buses were lesser than him by any means. He just felt he was more than capable of driving his own damn self to the doctor's office. No time schedules, no senior seating, no bells to make you stop every few blocks and no loud, obnoxious children required. Ernest's and his partner Clive Woodcock's civic engineering firm had helped build entire cities. Now, thanks to his doctor, he wasn't even allowed to sit behind the wheel of a car.

Speaking of Clive, where they hell was he, Ernest wondered? Clive was never late. Ernest found himself befuddled. Just the thought of his old partner Clive now had his thoughts mixed up again, the past infiltrating the present.

This was how Ernest's disorientations invariably arose: one minute the entire weight of his mind would be resting on a coherent thought and he would be very much present, oriented and cognizant of the world around him, the next minute and for no apparent reason (which was what the medicine was supposed to prevent) that thought would get pulled out from under him, evaporate, leaving his mind to stumble into a disoriented state, a maze of lost times, places and people.

Presently Ernest was standing motionless while he attempted to remember why he was out walking in the rain. He searched his memory, but events had stepped out of line and rambled into disorder. Recent memories, even the conversations with Nell only minutes ago, seemed distant. All his prevailing thoughts were of his long ago partner Clive. His mind had disarranged these memories and he believed they were recent and not from years ago.

Clive? Was Clive coming to pick him up? For some reason the idea of a doctor flashed in his mind. He must be heading to see poor sick Clive in the hospital.

Just then a bus pulled up alongside Ernest. With a hiss the door opened.

"Good morning," said the bus driver, "are you off to see the doctor this morning sir?"

Ernest's thoughts began to grip. It was Tuesday! Of course the doctor, he remembered now. He boarded the bus not realizing he was still a block away from the actual bus stop. Ernest would be on time for his transfer at the central exchange thanks to the kind consideration of the bus driver and his knowledge of his route, where people got on and off, what days and the fact he had stopped to pick Ernest up a block from the actual bus stop, even though it was against the rules.

"Clive has been dead seven years now," Ernest said to the bus driver as he sat down.

"Pardon me," said the bus driver, puzzled.

"Nothing," Ernest said, shifting in his seat.

As the bus pulled away the din of the school children suddenly rose up, as if they had been waiting for Ernest to settle in his seat before assaulting him with their unruly clamor. The bus had just gained full momentum when a bell rang and it began to decelerate again, pulling at Ernest's stomach. The noise of the children and the constant acceleration and deceleration nauseated Ernest. He believed he'd underestimated how much he hated buses, and how much he hated the reason he had to use them now. He cursed the fact that he had become an old man.

Ernest knew too well the indignities that came with old age. For him losing his self-reliance was the worst part of all. He had always been known to family, friends and colleagues as proudly independent and capable. If there was a complicated job to be done and it seemed the fate of the human race hung in the balance, everybody knew you were a fool if you didn't get Ernest Feldman on it. He was a tenacious bulldog when it came to work and you best stay out of his way. Now he had to ask a stranger with younger eyes to read the labels at the supermarket (he swore the printing on the packages were getting smaller). He had to ask the neighbor for help if there was any heavy lifting in the yard. Nell had to point out where he left things and even remind him what day it was. The worst insult of all was the bastards wouldn't let him drive anymore.

Ernest once thought that old people shouldn't complain. That setting off towards the sunset of your years was a noble thing. He used to think it was the only acceptable time to rest on one's laurels. He remembered years before being perplexed by a colleague's emotional turmoil over retiring. It was as if the man was being forced to march out in front of a firing squad. Ernest now understood. Retiring wasn't just golf during the week and lingering at the breakfast table in your house coat, it was also a leap off the edge of relevancy into obsolescence. After his own retirement the sudden feeling of irrelevancy had hit Ernest hard. He knew plenty of people who retired gracefully. He, however, didn't suit retirement. It had only served to make him miserable. Watching the game from the side lines, all the while having age plunder away at his health, was not Ernest's idea of fun. He had heard it said so many times, sometimes as a joke and sometimes seriously, that after retirement the next big thing to look forward to in life was death. Whichever way it was put, in jest or otherwise, Ernest hated that saying.

Retirement robbed from Ernest the thing he was most good at: the daily slog. He had an aphorism for it: success is the sum of small efforts repeated day in and day out. He lived by those words because he saw firsthand the truth in them. Ernest was an unfaltering worker. In the world of hares and tortoise's, Ernest was a tortoise, a tortoise that whopped the ass off of every flash-in-the-pan hare he ever went up against. He knew the steady, deliberate, day after day approach worked with everything in life, from financial success to physical health to family happiness. Earnest did his best to instill this value into his son and daughter by repeatedly telling them: "If you want to be good at something you've got to do that something every day. You carry pebbles consistently day after day and one day you'll look up and you'll realize you have just accomplished what everyone said couldn't be done - you moved a mountain".

Ernest was seventy when he retired. He had watched friends try to hang on even longer. There was always an air of sadness surrounding such drawn out situations, such inability to let go. He didn't want to be like an old suit worn long after its lapels had gone out of style. His partner, Clive had already sold out his shares in their company. Finally Ernest did the same. When they asked if they should keep an office for him, Ernest politely, (although deep down reluctantly) declined.

He found ways to stay busy. He had, by leaps and bounds, the best lawn in the neighborhood. The house and his vehicles received daily up keep, whether they needed it or not, and hours and hours were spent in volunteer service for the community. But all these things couldn't give Ernest the feeling of being genuinely needed like going to the office every day and commanding his own business had.

Now Ernest had been retired for over a decade. The added years brought new struggles of crumbling health for both he and Nell. Now his daily efforts were taking care of his wife and her failing legs and getting his medicines sorted, because he knew his mind was developing a habit of abandoning him throughout the day. He didn't want to put that burden on his wife. He needed to be there, really there, for Nell and her legs.

Presently, someone rang the bell and the bus began its deceleration. More school children got on, gleefully greeting their friends. They were followed by two elderly ladies, well into their pension years. All smiles and no hurry the ladies poked their way onto the bus. Ernest was about to become impatient, and then he thought of his Nell and the effort it took her to climb those high steps the last time they took a bus together, before her legs got so bad accompanying him became impossible. Suddenly Earnest had all the patience in the world for the ladies. The bus driver made doubly sure the elderly pair were safely seated before he accelerated towards the viaduct that would take them to the central exchange.

At home Nell had reached her son-in-law Kevin before he had left for work. Initially Nell's daughter answered the phone and she told her mother she was 'worrying too much about dad again. The man used to design cities for crying out loud.' Nell knew her daughter was referring to her former father, the strong and capable one of years ago. It pained Nell to have to convince her daughter that her father was failing now; that he was merely a shadow of the man he was. Now he needed to be doted over and worried about. Nell wasn't going to argue the point. So when her daughter said, "oh mom it's just a couple of buses", she demanded to speak to Kevin.

Kevin was more understanding. He recognized his father-in-law had been slipping these last few years. He recalled the lost look in Ernest's eyes that day he stopped and picked him up near the mall. Nell asked Kevin if he wouldn't mind driving to the central bus exchange and possibly along the bus route to the doctor's office to make sure Ernest hadn't become confused and bungled his transfer and was now wandering around like he'd done before. Kevin didn't need convincing. He heard the fear and worry in his mother-in-law's voice. Without finishing his breakfast he was out the door. Once Nell hung up she immediately called the doctor's office to ask them to call her when Ernest showed up or more importantly if he didn't show up on time. She wanted to know, as soon as possible, if she should stop worrying or become absolutely frantic.

The 107 pulled into the central exchange right on time. Ernest knew once the buses stopped it would detonate an explosion of children onto the sidewalks. They swarmed out of all the buses at the exchange like bees out of busted hives. Most of the adults knew to wait in their current seats as long as possible. By leaving just enough time to get to their connecting bus they could avoid most of the rush of school children. Ernest looked out the window at the river of brightly colored raincoats and lunch boxes. The raincoats made him think about his own umbrella, which he was surprised to realize, was nowhere in sight. Damn! Another umbrella lost on these god forsaken buses. He imagined some defrauder, some dark vagrant riding the buses all day, profiting from honest people's honest mistakes, gathering umbrellas and other misplaced items to sell at a flea market. He looked suspiciously at the woman across the aisle. She, in turn, smiled politely.

Turning to look out the window again it suddenly dawned on Ernest that he could make his next doctor's appointment later in the day. There was no shame in not being the very first patient. This way he could avoid the Niagara of school children. Not that Ernest hated children, on the contrary. He had a little granddaughter who he adored. He loved the little games they would play together. 'Grampy will you buy something from my store,' she would say and he would pretend to buy whatever she was pretending to sell that day and then try to return it sighting all sorts of problems. She would come up with a range of options to satisfy him; it always ended with a few hugs and kisses being enough to keep him a happy customer. There were all the years of driving his daughter, Nadine, and her fellow Brownies and Girl Guides around. He was a reliable chaperon at all the school dances. He took school buses all over the state with his son Todd's wrestling team. He enjoyed all of it. He loved to engage in young minds, hear them talk with their friends. No, the children themselves weren't the problem. It was the sheer number of them that served up the difficulty on Tuesday mornings, and their knack of getting in the way and under-foot without meaning to, this was the problem.

Ernest felt he had waited long enough. The tide of children had subsided. The majority were now energetically buzzing in the buses that would take them to their prospective schools. It was time he made his way to the 101 waiting around the corner at the top of Ross Avenue hill. The 101 would be filled with kids of its own on their way to St. Mary's Middle School. Ernest had to concede one good thing about being old: no matter how full a bus was there was always senior seating. He stepped on board the 101 and a middle aged woman, sitting alone in the front section where the school kids were not allowed to sit, immediately gave up her seat to him, moving across the aisle to an empty seat there. She looked at him with an accomplished smile. Ernest was instantly put off. Did this woman think he would not be able to make his way across the aisle and sit in the seat she now occupied? There was no real difference in the seats save for a few feet. It was another display of exaggerated mollycoddling of the elderly, Ernest thought. There were people out there that couldn't wait to treat old people like they might collapse if someone didn't help them to press the damn elevator button. If Moses was alive today, with his gray hair, there would be someone out there rushing to help him across the Red Sea. Ernest hated being treated as if he was helpless. It would come unexpectedly; like the girl at the grocery store who asked if he needed help counting out his change. It so infuriated him that his answer - "you think I don't know the difference between a quarter and a god damn dime" flew out of his mouth before he could edit himself.

The worst part was he hadn't added correctly and she had to ask him for another quarter.

It bothered him that all the things he'd done, all the things that he once was, how capable he had been, didn't show anymore. There was no certificate of a viral, productive life. People only saw an old pair of veined hands fumble with coins or a slow gait up the steps on a bus. Ernest thought it was arrogant and presumptuous of young people to look on the elderly and forget or discount all the change counting and stair climbing that went on beforehand, in more formidable years. Worn out bodies are worn out for a reason damn it!

"That's why in the army they hand out ribbons and medals as proof of past accomplishments so people like you won't be so quick to forget and judge when they see a little grey hair," Ernest said, as he sat down in the seat the lady had vacated for him.

The lady didn't understand and took it that Ernest thought she should get a medal for her kindness. "It's the least I can do," she said.

As gruff as he wanted to treat this lady and people like the change counting girl at the grocery store he tried to remind himself that underneath it all their intentions were for the most part good. At least they were showing respect, even if a little of it was back handed.

It was always a long wait at the exchange. The bus drivers took their breaks clustered together; the smokers all huddled unitedly, banished from the main group. Ernest waited impatiently for the buses to start moving again. Undetected by Ernest and with no reason his mind had slipped silently into disarray again. He felt the bus was moving finally and he confirmed it by watching the ground out the window creep along. He wondered, though, why he happened to be on a bus in the first place. Not knowing his faculties were false and beguiling, Ernest reasoned he must be with Todd's wrestling team on their way to another meet. He heard commotion in the seats behind him. Some school kids were yelling about something and he heard a girl scream.

"You kids settle down or we'll stop this bus right now and forfeit the match!" Ernest yelled. He saw, in the seat directly behind him, a small boy. "You look awfully skinny to be on the wrestling team," Ernest said.

"I dunno," the boy said, weakly.

Ernest thought the expression on the boy's face was strange, as though he was frightened and about to cry. Ernest looked at the lady who had given him her seat. She was hanging on for dear life to the vertical hand-hold bars beside her seat, with a dreadful expression on her face, as if she was expecting the worst of something. Ernest wondered who this lady was or what her association with Todd's wrestling team was. He was about to ask her but was distracted by a heavy bump and the shuddering of the bus. There were more screams from behind him. Ernest looked out the window and saw the bus driver. It was about time he thought, but then thought it odd he'd be running alongside his own bus.

A lot of things were not making sense to Ernest now, for instance the bus was picking up speed despite the fact there was no one in the driver's seat. Ernest looked out the window again. The driver was now in frantic pursuit of his bus, running downhill faster than his legs could carry him. Soon he was scraping and tumbling along the side walk.

Ernest was used to the fact there were always shenanigans when high school kids got together, especially the wrestling team. He and the coaches and the other parents had come to the conclusion that a little blowing off steam was probably a good thing when it came to adolescent boys, as long as no one got hurt. But this little joke, Ernest thought, had gotten out of hand. He stood and walked towards the driver's seat. He took wide staggered steps to keep his equilibrium as the bus gained speed.

"Careful, careful now," said the woman who had given up her seat.

"Oh go tell it to Moses!" Ernest said to the lady. "You boys stop this fooling around," Ernest yelled, to the back of the bus. "Todd get your butt up here!"

Ernest plunked himself in the driver's seat. He grabbed the large steering wheel in time to see the immense garbage truck stopped on the right shoulder of the road, directly in the path of the bus. The bus's engine wasn't running which meant there was no power steering. It took all of Ernest's strength to yank the bus to the left. He saw a garbage man leap towards the sidewalk seconds before he heard the sound of tearing metal along the right hand panels of the bus. There was a plethora of screams from the children.

"A joke is one thing," Ernest yelled, "But you boys have gone over the line. Stop these antics at once!"

"Oh lordy me!" yelled the lady who had given up her seat.

"Nell hang on to something," Ernest shouted, as he gripped the steering wheel harder. "I'll get your grandma socks in a jiffy!"

The bus shook with another loud bang causing an adrenaline surge in Ernest's blood stream which in turn caused his confusion to clear. The seriousness of the situation did not afford him the time to question why on earth he was in the driver's seat of a runaway bus careening down Ross Street during the morning rush. There were fading thoughts of Todd and his old high school wrestling team, which didn't make any sense. That was so many years ago.

Ernest realized his foot had been pressing hard against the large brake pedal of the bus all the while he had been struggling with the steering wheel. He knew enough about air brakes to know they should be locked on, what they call 'dynamited', when the engine wasn't running. There was obviously a mechanical failure. Still, by sheer instincts, he furiously pumped the brake pedal anyway. Through the rain streaked widow he realized the bus was gaining on the car ahead. Ernest hit the horn and, to his surprise, it sounded loud and clear. It was one thing he and his unwilling passengers had going for them. Ernest noticed the driver of the car ahead had taken notice of the blaring horn and was now looking in his review mirror and waving his hand in objection to the impatient bus driver. A twenty foot gap between the bus and the car became ten feet and then five feet. The driver of the car began to honk his own horn in fits of violent protest. Almost at the point of impact the car finally swerved to the right. At the same time Ernest pulled the bus to the left causing it to ride up on the center median. The combined maneuvering of the bus to the left and the car to the right was enough to avert a collision. The bus merely ripped off the back bumper of the car. However, the left side of the bus was now demolishing the green iron fencing that ran along the median. Green iron bars were razed over like exploding dominos. Ernest felt the bus slow slightly as it bulldozed the fence.

Down the road on the right hand side of the street, there were people waiting at the next bus stop. Incredibly, despite the horrific sound of the fence being plowed down and the fact the bus was presently driving half on the median, the waiting commuters began to form a line. As if the bus was still somehow going to make its stop.

Further ahead there were real problems. The bus was looming closer to the busy intersection at the bottom of the hill. To make matters worse it was a T intersection. There was no possibility of making a sharp 90 degree turn either left or right at such a speed.

Ernest knew he would have to keep the bus moving straight, which meant smashing through another metal fence and then up onto a greenway and then a park with a playground. There was no possible alternative; this part of Ross Avenue dead ended at the bottom of the hill.

Ernest knew the city well; he and Clive had helped design parts of it. He couldn't see what was beyond the park because it sloped upwards at the far end, but he was sure he once knew. Was it the river or the highway or something else? It seemed to have escaped his mind at the moment. Whatever it was, something told Ernest, it was not good. He would have to stop the bus from making it over the far slope of the park or it would be disastrous. Despite the struggle to see clearly out the windshield he was now glad it was raining; the park would almost certainly be empty of mothers entertaining their pre-school children. His plan was to run the bus into the playground equipment. Their steel construction was strong, but at the same time they would also bend and twist which would help absorb energy and make the impact less severe. If plowing over the swing sets and teeter-totters didn't extinguish the buses momentum he would have to let the bus drift into the heavy clusters of large trees a little further on. He knew hitting the stout, unyielding trunks would result in many injuries or worse.

The median had run out of fence. The bus was gaining speed again at a grim rate. As Ernest struggled to see through the streaks of rain on the windshield, he realized that if there were no fatalities here on Ross Avenue this morning, it would be a miracle.

To Ernest things seemed to be moving in slow motion. But in actual fact, everything was happening very fast; he had only been in the hot seat for a little more than ninety seconds. His old heart was pumping adrenaline to his muscles as fast as it could, giving Ernest the strength he needed to steer the fugitive bus. He knew the climax of this charming little adventure was approaching rapidly. No matter how unstoppable the bus seemed at the moment, it couldn't go on forever. He thought about trying to find the windshield wiper switch. He doubted the wipers would work without power, but the horn seemed to. He also thought about securing himself against the approaching impact by putting on his seat belt. But he didn't dare take one hand off the wheel, not even for a second. His attention shifted to the timing of the lights at the T intersection. It was currently green for the traffic on Ross Avenue, which now consisted of a lone runaway bus. Aware of the unfolding crisis most of the traffic had pulled off to the side and out of the way, thanks to the bus's working horn.

Ernest had the sinking feeling the timing of the traffic light would not be in his favor and a rush of cars would stream into the path of the out of control bus at the last second. Ernest laid on the horn again, mixing long and short blasts in an erratic pattern hoping to alert the drivers waiting at the intersection to the oncoming danger. He could see, refracted all over his windshield in the beading pearls of rain, the light had turned yellow - a forewarning. In seconds the next color

Ernest would see would be red. Even the youngest children on the bus knew that red meant stop. Stop! He frantically pumped on the brake pedal and wildly pounded on the horn.

Circumstances had led Ernest to this exact point in his life where one could argue his age was actually an advantage. Yes, he was an old man stuck in a disastrous situation, operating on adrenaline and nearing a state of exhaustion. True, the young, vigorous Ernest would certainly be better in this circumstance physically. But, what age had taken away from him in strength and swiftness it had made up for in experience and composure. Ernest knew that panic never solved any problem and a cool head can prevail in the most drastic of situations. He knew also that extreme situations called for extreme measures; driving a twenty ton city bus over some playground equipment, he hoped would be extreme enough.

Just as Ernest feared, the traffic light turned red for him and his passengers and green for the line of cars waiting to cross Ross Avenue.

"Oh good lordy!" said the woman, who had given up her seat. "Careful now!"

The bus blazed onward. Hearing the sound of the panicked horn and realizing it was coming from the bus plummeting down Ross Avenue, going too fast to be able to brake; most of the cars at the intersection had remained stopped. As much as Ernest had honked out his warning, two oblivious drivers in the front of the line on each side of the street, moved forward anyway. Ernest pulled hard to the left and narrowly missed the first car. He pulled back to the right, but couldn't avoid hitting the second car. The bus slammed the back of it and spun it violently. The driver of the car was shaken and shocked, but luckily unharmed.

With a thundering crash the bus blasted through the fence at the edge of the park and onto grass that was slick with rain. Ernest rocked violently in his seat. His head jolted forward then back then forward again causing him to catch sight of a lever he had not noticed. It was very low to the floor on his left side. He recognized it immediately as the emergency brake handle.

"You kids hang on to something," Ernest shouted.

"Oh good lordy! Gooood looorrrrdy!" The woman who had given up her seat, wailed.

Ernest steadied himself in his seat the best he could as he steered the bus towards the swings and slides. He grabbed the handle with his left hand and held the yellow button on the top down with his thumb. Keeping the button down, Ernest knew, would keep the brakes from locking which might send the bus into an unmanageable sideways skid, and that would mean disaster. With all his might he pulled the handle up just as he felt the bus wheels lock and begin to slide on the wet grass he released it again. His arms were numb with exhaustion, but he continued to pump the brakes this way. On the sixth pull he released the yellow button and let the wheels lock. The bus came to a tender stop. Through the rain beaded windshield Ernest could just make out the playground equipment he had intended to use to stop the bus. Three feet in front of the bus was a swing set recently painted with a shiny coat of bright blue paint.

"Oh good lord," the woman cried.

There was an eerie silence except for the sound of the rain pattering against the bus. The woman rose and stepped to the front of the bus; standing beside Ernest she pulled out a small round button on the dash board. The windshield wipers began to flap furiously. She smiled at Ernest who stared blankly in return.

At home the phone rang. It was the doctor's office notifying Nell that Ernest had missed his appointment. Nell looked at the clock; it was thirty two minutes past his appointment time. Sick with worry Nell phoned her daughter. There was no answer. All she could do now was wait to hear from Kevin. She sat on the couch with her head back and her eyes closed. She was furious with herself for letting him go. She put the TV on to help calm herself. It was all silly pre-school shows and annoying celebrity panel talk shows at this time of the morning. She lay on the couch staring at the ceiling, trying to let the TV distract her from the guilty voices in her head which were making up horrible things that could have happened to her poor husband. She waited to hear something...anything.

Suddenly there was an anchorwoman on TV saying: "Breaking news - runaway bus careens through the heart of down town - coming up we go live at the scene."

Nell shot up and glared at the TV. She knew; call it a wife's intuition, but she knew that Ernest had been on that bus. There was a series of commercials: dish soap, breakfast cereal and juice boxes. Finally the news lady was back live from downtown, at what looked to be a park. Nell was shocked to see Kevin standing in the back ground.

It had stopped raining. The anchorwoman raised the microphone, "We're live with breaking news from the downtown core. If you can see Ross avenue behind me (she pivoted and the camera followed her) you can see all the way up the hill. Now if you look over this way (she pivoted again) you can see this city bus parked almost on top of this little playground here in Mason Park. About twenty minutes ago, we're told, this bus, the 101, full of school children, rolled down that hill out of control and without its driver.

"Authorities say this incident had the potential to be disastrous due to the amount of commuters heading to work and children on their way to school at this time in the morning. It was a miracle no one was injured or killed. Firsthand accounts say it was a miracle due to this man standing next to me, Ernest Feldman, who jumped into the driver's seat of the 101 without hesitation, and with no power steering or brakes, somehow guided the bus away from disaster and into the relative safety of the park, finally being able to stop it where it sits now."

It took a few seconds for Nell to believe and understand what she was seeing and hearing from her TV. But there he was, her Ernest, standing unassuming, wearing his usual stern expression.

"Sir, they are calling you a Hero," the anchorwoman said to Ernest. Kevin stood proudly next to his father in-law.

"He is a hero, a true blue hero," said the woman, who had given up her seat to Ernest. She put her arm in his arm and leaned her head against his shoulder. "Oh lordy this man saved us all, is what he did."

Ernest, looking uncomfortable, said, "Well I guess if I was a real hero I would have made that stop back there." He flicked his thumb up towards Ross Avenue. There was laughter and cheers from the crowd.

At home Nell laughed too. "This man of mine," she said out loud, "what am I going to do with him."

From off camera a reporter asked, "This was a harrowing situation. What were your thoughts as the bus careened down the hill?"

"About the time we hit the fence along the median," replied Ernest, "I started to worry I wasn't going to make my doctor's appointment on time."

There was more laughter and cheers, then a tangle of questions from the gathering reporters. They all spoke at once. Ernest's face took on a faraway expression. He looked down in surprise at what he was holding.

"Well would you look at this," Ernest said, "my umbrella. I thought for sure I'd lost it."

Ernest didn't know why, but there was more laughter. So Ernest laughed too, until he remembered it was Tuesday.

The Best Cobb Salad this side of Montreal

All week Mrs. Ebersmann had been thinking about how she would kill herself and her cat. What complicated the matter was the cat. She needed to arrange it so her cat would die at precisely the same time or very shortly after she did. Not before. Before would be an atrocity. It would mean Mrs. Ebersmann's last seconds on earth would be spent watching herself murder her own cat. No, it would be a simultaneous death, or at the very least Mrs. Ebersmann would expire slightly before her cat Smoky. The timing was settled. The method, however, was still very much undetermined.

Suicide had only recently come to Mrs. Ebersmann's mind. She had struggled so long with the complications following the death of her husband Morty, and now her Smoky was sick. Bravely she came to the conclusion that suicide was her final and only solution. Before that, like most people, offing herself was simply not part of life's equation; it was something the news informed her other people did.

Self-annihilation (a word she found in the thesaurus) seemed simple enough at the outset, but when she started looking into the subject in earnest she realized it was more complicated than she ever would have guessed. There were not as many options as Mrs. Ebersmann had hoped and her inflexible stipulations surrounding Smoky only restricted matters further. She knew there would need to be considerable planning or she could make hers and Smoky's situation a whole lot worse. Rather than killing herself and her cat, for instance, she could merely inflict grievous harm instead. She had discovered this very thing, the botching of a suicide, happened more often than one would think (failed suicides never make the news). This was the reason she was learning as much as she could about her final solution and considering all her options.

For instance one who is uninformed in the matter might assume a bullet through the head would, by nature, produce a certain and definite outcome. However, as statistics bear out such is not always the case. In Mrs. Ebersmann's case, as she learned, she could never be sure the bullet would pass through her brain and then into Smoky's. Sure she would hold Smoky's head tightly up against hers, but what if the bullet, after going through her head, didn't have enough power left to actually be fatal to Smoky? As evidence indicates the bullet could ricochet within Mrs. Ebersmann skull and exit at some tangent of the original trajectory, missing Smoky's skull completely? The bones of the skull are tough; it was very possible for a bullet to be redirected. She needed to be analytical about everything. Besides she didn't own a gun and had no idea how to get one in a hurry, not legally anyway. She had no intention of breaking the law, except of course the one law about suicide. There was also the chance Smoky might move at the moment she pulled the trigger. She could of course put the gun to Smoky's head while holding her head against his. This arrangement was something Mrs. Ebersmann couldn't conceive of doing. It seemed too horrible and cruel to put a gun directly to Smoky's poor little head.

Naturally, because of the ease and simplicity, the first method Mrs. Ebersmann thought of for ending it all for Smoky and herself was an overdose of some kind. But she once had a neighbor who attempted suicide by taking a handful of pills and never died. The woman writhed in pain for days in the hospital. It would make everything a whole lot worse if she didn't take the right type of medicine or a large enough dose. Waking in the hospital to find she had merely succeeded in killing Smoky and giving herself irreparable brain damage. Besides, Smoky was too good at avoiding pills. He could eat around them. Even when she snuck them in his favorite treats he would swallow the treat then spit out the pill.

In an odd, macabre way Mrs. Ebersmann was enjoying her research. Of course the internet was a great source of information, but her main resource was a book she had taken out of the library entitled: 'The history of Suicide and its Impact on Modern Society' (she reminded herself she must return the book to the library before she…). While reading through its pages she had picked up a collection of wonderful euphemisms for suicide: 'Snipping the primordial cord' was one she preferred over 'topping oneself'. There was much to learn and she found many useful facts. For instance she now wished she still had her deceased husband Morty's car. She could then settle for the easy-peasy, no fuss-no muss, 'carbon monoxide nap'. In her opinion 'letting the car run' should be the go- to method for all people looking to 'call home on their own dime'. CO poisoning is easier on surviving family and friends, because, except for a slight discoloration of the skin, it leaves the body intact. It is far better for the first person on scene to find someone who appears to be sleeping in a running car, rather than the spaghetti thrown against the wall shock of finding a loved one who has swallowed a shot gun blast. It is the difference between an open casket and a closed one. When a death comes suddenly and dubiously followed by a closed casket funeral it is a sure give away the death had been by a violent suicide. This deduction supported by a sad but telling request in the obituary: 'In lieu of flowers, donations can be made to the American Mental Health Association'. You couldn't get any more obvious. All that was left was the gossip at the burial luncheon as to what mutilations were being hidden under that closed lid; "I heard she swallowed acid…oh her poor mother." …etc.

Mrs. Ebersmann imagined herself sitting in Morty's old Oldsmobile with Smoky on her lap, stroking his soft fur while listening to something soothing on the radio, all the while the car idling and doling out its invisible, odorless death. Before either one of them knew it they'd be sound asleep. Forever.

She had thought about renting a car, but she felt it rude to kill herself and her cat in a car that wasn't hers. That would be unfair to the rental company. Besides she would need a garage and she no longer had one. If she had known how badly everything was going to turn out she would have ended it for herself and Smoky while she still lived in the big house Morty had bought for them two years before he died. It had a perfect garage for a suicide.

But, Mrs. Ebersmann had had to sell the house and the Oldsmobile to help pay legal bills. Poor Morty would roll over in his grave if he knew how things had turned out, if he knew he had sold everything he had worked for, his beloved diamond and gem business, to two cold hearted con men. He had worked relentlessly to include, as part of the deal, a measure that would ensure his wife and her beloved cat would be well cared for after he was gone. Morty had signed the final deal with the buyers when he was so sick he could barely stand on his feet. Now he was gone and the agreement he had worked so hard for was being reneged. As a consequence Mrs. Ebersmann was so broke she couldn't even euthanize her sick cat, which was, according to the vet, suffering!

The two cold hearted con men were the Chamberlain brothers. They were well known diamond merchants from California, notorious for running annoying radio ads directed towards men's insecurities. A sexy female voice would whisper: 'My man has a big...BIG...diamond to put on my finger'. Another ad told ladies to keep their options open if their man hadn't put a diamond on their finger at least as big as a carat. If a man had good credit the Chamberlain Brothers had easy payment plans. A fella could go all out and buy his manhood and his woman's love by getting a beast of a diamond and take ten years to pay for it, as long as he didn't mind borderline illegal interest rates. The brothers were vile, slimy and their business practices were barely legal, and therefore they were very successful.

The Chamberlain's first contacted Morty Ebersmann's lawyer when they heard he was selling. Morty had wished there had been another buyer, one of his business associates from New York for instance. He would have sold 'Morty's Certified Diamond and Gem Stones' to any one of them. But the only offer that came from his New York diamond dealing colleagues was one of advice, which was: Morty, for the love of god close the doors; do anything but sell to the Chamberlains. The New York diamond community was competitive, but they were also close-knit. They had worked together for years to keep the Chamberlain Brothers and their shady, over aggressive selling tactics away from the east coast, where it definitely did not belong. But the Chamberlains waited patiently in the shadows for their opportunity to break into the lucrative Big Apple diamond market. That opportunity came in the form of pancreatic cancer. Morty of 'Morty's Certified Diamond and Gem Stones' was dying they had heard.

Morty's New York diamond pals pleaded with him to simply close up shop and he pleaded with them to simply buy him out. Morty could not afford to merely close his doors, which would leave no income or security for his wife. Mrs. Ebersmann's welfare (and by extension her cat's) was his absolute top priority. No one but the Chamberlains seemed to come close to what Morty was asking.

There was a plan devised by four of the bigger New York diamond dealers: The Saul Brothers, Finkelstein and Sons, the Roth's and Frieda Blumbaum would collectively buy Morty's business. The lawyers quickly pulled the plug on that idea saying the Trades Commission would never let a sale like that go through; there would be too big of a concern over future price fixing. The next plan was for the big four to secretly pay Mrs. Ebersmann a 'pension' after Morty passed on if he simply closed down. The lawyers were even more skeptical about this plan. Their concern was that the Chamberlain Brothers were sniffing around now. Their lawyers, along with any federal judge, would see right through the little trick of bribing Morty to close instead of sell. Under the laws of fair and free competition it would mean prosecution for all, including Mrs. Ebersmann. Trying to keep the Chamberlain Brothers out of New York by paying Mrs. Ebersmann a 'salary' after Morty died, simply wouldn't work.

It was a moot point anyway. Morty was offended by the big four's 'pension' offer. He considered the idea a hand out and Morty Ebersmann did not take hand outs and neither did his wife. Besides it added up to a pittance when compared to what the Chamberlains were offering.

Wearing his best suit, now, thanks to his cancer, looking three sizes too large, Morty signed a deal with the Chamberlain Brothers. Mrs. Ebersmann would remain a twenty percent shareholder of 'Morty's Certified Diamond and Gem Stones' for life. The biggest sticking point of the deal was the Brothers would not be allowed to change the business model (which was decisively laid out) or the name for ten years. Even in his weakened state Morty was a hard nut to crack. The Chamberlains tried everything, but they could not budge Morty off this condition. This was much to the satisfaction of the New York diamond retailers because it would make it much harder for the Brothers to use their shady promotions and tactics while using a name and business model that had for years stood as a pinnacle of business ethics. The Chamberlains had to capitulate.

A week later the Chamber of Commerce held a dinner to honor Morty's contribution to the city's business community. There were so many people in attendance they were seating guests at folding tables in the hallways. Two days later Morty's cancer struck its death blow. The Saul Brothers, Finkelstein and Sons, the Roth family and Frieda Blumbaum arranged and paid for the funeral. Mrs. Ebersmann along with her cat, mourned inconsolably.

The first two years the Chamberlain Brothers honored the deal. Mrs. Ebersmann's twenty percent was more than enough to live comfortably. However there were grim forces at work. In Los Angeles an entire office of lawyers were forging a plan that would allow the Chamberlain Brothers to climb out from under their restrictions in New York.

The third year the Brothers began running their shady advertisements advising potential customers to come see the deals at "The Chamberlain Brother's, located in the building 'Formerly known as Morty's Certified Diamond and Gem Stones'. This bothered Mrs. Ebersmann more than the fact that she was no longer receiving any checks from the Brothers in the mail.

So was born the litigation machine that would devour all the things Morty had left behind for his wife. The New York community rallied behind Mrs. Ebersmann and helped her secure the best lawyers at discounted prices. But the writing was on the wall: this was going to be a battle of attrition and the Chamberlains had deep pockets. To feed the law machine the car and the house and everything in it had to be sacrificed. When that money was used up and there was nothing left for the battle, the matter was settled out of court. Mrs. Ebersmann was informed of the new strategy by her lawyers (used for clients who have run out of money): a judge still needed to sign off on any new deal and no judge in his or her right mind would sign a deal that fleeced an elderly widow. The case would stall and the longer it took the more it would pain The Brothers. Her lawyers could then get an injunction to honor the old contract until the stale mate was settled and that could take years. It wasn't exactly a victory, but it wasn't exactly a loss either.

The case must have been put before a judge who was out of his or her mind because, despite her lawyer's confidence of the contrary, the new deal was promptly approved and signed off on. Mrs. Ebersmann, with no car and no home, had to settle for pittance in royalties in lieu of a seven percent share of profits if and when the Chamberlain's ever sold the New York business, which was obviously likely to be never. As well, should the Chamberlain Brothers both become deceased Mrs. Ebersmann would acquire one hundred percent ownership of the New York branch of the Business (the Chamberlain brothers both being much younger than Mrs. Ebersmann, it was more likely she would die long before them). That same day the Chamberlains removed the sign that read: 'Morty's Certified Diamond and Gem Stones'. The Brothers had finally succeeded in putting their crooked teeth into the Big Apple.

Now, after a year under the new conditions Mrs. Ebersmann was barely getting by. Smoky the cat was sick and needed either to be euthanized or to undergo an expensive operation followed by a myriad of medications for the rest of his life. Mrs. Ebersmann couldn't afford either one. It was the final push over the edge. She made her decision to end hers and Smoky's life, to call home on her own dime, as she liked to put it now. She knew she could go back to the Finkelstein's or to Frieda Blumbaum and borrow the money for Smoky's operation, but she had gone to them all already. She had, as of now, many loans she had no way of paying back. She knew Morty wouldn't approve of her borrowing from their old business associates. She would feel embarrassed about borrowing money for her cat; and if anyone asked what the money was for she could never lie about it. It was this and the fact for the last three years life had not offered up one happy moment. Mrs. Ebersmann had grown tired of the world.

Finally, she had made up her mind as to the method of her demise: a leap from the George Washington Bridge with Smoky tucked away inside her jacket. This would be the best thing for all concerned. Curled up in her jacket sound asleep was one of Smoky's favorite places to be. They often took walks together that way. He would at least be relaxed for his final minutes of life, unless he sensed Mrs. Ebersmann's anxiety before or during the leap into the dark waters of Hudson River. If Smoky happened to wake up at the last moment she would accept his panicked clawing as a final sacrifice, her final testimony of love towards her cat before the impact with the water below ended everything.

Presently it was mid-morning on a Wednesday. She set the date of her and Smoky's suicide for the following Friday, for no other reason than she didn't want to die on a weekend. She deemed it necessary to take a preliminary, investigative visit to the GW Bridge. If there was one thing Mrs. Ebersmann learned from her husband it was to be thorough. She had been across it hundreds of times; always admiring the beauty of the city from it. Never once thinking she would one day jump to her death from its height's. Funny how life can change, she thought.

She took a bus to the foot of the bridge along Hudson Terrace and walked the rest of the way to the bridge deck. She instantly knew the reason so many people had committed suicide from the George Washington over the years: convenience. All along its length it was relatively easy to hop the rails of the walk way. After hopping the rails there wasn't much effort required to manage a one on one with the Hudson River; past the rails gravity would do the rest of the work.

Vaulting the rails might be easy for those with youthful dexterity, but for Mrs. Ebersmann it seemed daunting. She would have to wear comfortable shoes and functional, loose fitting pants. This was exactly why she had made this precursory trip to the bridge, all these little surprises had to be discovered and ironed out before game day. The real thing would have to be quick and easy and... final.

A quarter way in from each end of the bridge were giant arched pillars. It was here that Mrs. Ebersmann found a place to climb over the rails. She did a trial run to make sure it would be doable with a cat tucked inside her jacket. She stepped around to the open side of the pillar and looked at the black water below. Although it was perfectly safe where she now stood, surrounded by the crisscrossing steel joisting of the pillars, Mrs. Ebersmann felt a whirl in her stomach and a jolt of fear, like electricity, shoot up her spine. She turned to go back when she felt a wave of dizziness. She was struggling to climb back over onto the walk way when a hand grabbed her arm to give assistance. It was a young woman. She looked not much more than twenty years old.

"Thank you," said Mrs. Ebersmann.

"Are you thinking of killing yourself too?" the young woman promptly asked.

Mrs. Ebersmann was shocked. For a moment there was awkward silence.

"Too?" Mrs. Ebersmann asked. "Surely, you can't be thinking of suicide?"

"Why not?" asked the young woman.

"Why, you're far too young for such a thing," said Mrs. Ebersmann, "What real problems could there be in such a young life as yours? Seems to me at your stage in life any difficulties would have ample time to work themselves out."

The young woman made a disparaged face. "…and what could be the problem in yours?" she asked. "Seems to me at your stage in life nothing should be capable of making you unhappy anymore." she said.

They stared at each other in more awkward silence.

"I'm just here to check things out. I wasn't planning on jumping today or anything," said the young woman.

"Yes, it's good to know what to expect," said Mrs. Ebersmann. "Have you had a look over the edge? It's a frightful way down."

"I guess in our case that is a good thing," said the young woman.

Mrs. Ebersmann chuckled. "Point well taken," she said. She studied the adolescent woman's face; there were hard angular lines inexplicable for such a young person to exhibit. "Whatever your problems are, my dear, I think you should consider waiting a while before you go and throw yourself into the Hudson River. And if in a year, say, you still feel the same, may I suggest you try a nap in a running car in the garage. This way, having a body and all to bury, your family would have a better chance of closure. It's a much more peaceful exit you know. You simply fall asleep."

"I thought of that," said the young woman, "the car thing I mean, but I don't have a car and I kind of wanted to go out with a splash. No pun intended. And I don't have a family, so it's ok if there's nothing of me to leave behind."

Mrs. Ebersmann looked at the young woman. She didn't look sad or depressed, only very tired. She started thinking of ways she could talk the young woman out of her suicide. She thought it sad that the poor thing didn't have a family; maybe she only needed a friend. Mrs. Ebersmann was about to invite the girl for dinner, but realized she wouldn't be around after Friday so there would be no purpose in offering the young woman her friendship. She also realized it was hypocritical for her to be trying to talk the young woman out of jumping to her death. The young woman probably had just as good a reason as she, herself, had. Who was Mrs. Ebersmann to judge?

"I'm thinking this Friday," said Mrs. Ebersmann. "I hope that won't conflict with your schedule?"

"I can wait for a few days if you want," said the young woman. "Maybe Monday, that will leave a bit of space in the papers for you before I take my turn. That's if someone happens to even notice. It might not matter; the way it's been lately there could be half a dozen suicides between Friday and Monday."

"It's alright," said Mrs. Ebersmann, "I'm not looking to get in the papers, and besides it's a big river, she can take as many people as the bridge wants to give her." She looked out over the dark water. "I wonder how many people have jumped without a living soul knowing about it. It's a sad thing to think about."

"I always thought," said the young woman, "when they talk about a missing person on the news, that it's just another unobserved jumper. Dying like they lived... alone. They should put video cameras under all these bridges." After a pause she said, "If it's alright with you I'll take the Jersey side."

"That's fine I was planning on the New York side. This pillar here should do just fine," said Mrs. Ebersmann.

"Alright it's all settled. Good luck with your demise," said the young woman, smiling.

"Good luck to you my dear," said Mrs. Ebersmann.

They each went their separate way.

Mrs. Ebersmann had decided on eight in the evening to jump. By then rush hour traffic would have certainly wound down. Mrs. Ebersmann had always been considerate this way. She knew she might need a bit of time to get her nerve up and if someone happened to notice her up over the rail and called it in, she wouldn't want to cause a traffic jam like so many of the jumpers off the George Washington had. The police would always come and close both ends of the bridge, then try to talk the jumper back over the rail. Sometimes the police would suddenly snatch the person and yank them over the rail and back on the bridge deck by force. She'd seen it many times on the news. She'd also seen impatient people, stuck on the bridge deck, encouraging the jumper to 'jump!' and get it over with and get the traffic moving again so they could go home. Mrs. Ebersmann did not want any such drama.

On the day, she planned to have a meal in hers and Morty's favorite restaurant, then retrieve Smoky and take a taxi to the foot of the bridge. This was the time that Mrs. Ebersmann and Smoky would normally take their walk so Smoky would feel that things were business as usual. He'd been sleeping a lot more lately due to his illness, but when the time came Mrs. Ebersmann was going to give poor Smoky a sedative for caution's sake.

Friday came and despite the day's looming event Mrs. Ebersmann was in a fair mood. The one misfortunate thing was that Smoky was feeling especially ill. She could tell because he didn't get out of his bed, didn't eat and wore an anguished, fed-up grimace on his little face.

"There, there," said Mrs. Ebersmann, "I know how you feel. We'll soon feel right as rain my little man." She kissed his head and felt hot tears running down her face. "If Morty was here he'd have had you at the vets for your operation long before now." Smoky purred and closed his eyes, enjoying Mrs. Ebersmann's gentle strokes. "But Morty is not here is he," she continued, "He's not here and everything has gone to h…" She didn't bother to go on, there was no point.

In preparation of her and Smoky's departure she had decided not to dispose of her belongings. Choosing instead to tidy, as well as she could, everything in the little apartment where Smoky and she had been living since the house was sold. She alternated final touches of cleaning with holding Smoky in her lap and listening to him purr until it was time for her to take a taxi to her favorite restaurant. Although it was well after lunch and a good deal before dinner, a slow time for the restaurant, Mrs. Ebersmann had made a reservation just in case.

She arrived early and the hostess ushered her straight in. The hostess, who knew Mrs. Ebersmann as a regular, enquired about Mr. Ebersmann's whereabouts and was told curtly by Mrs. Ebersmann that he was deceased. Normally, Mrs. Ebersmann wouldn't be bothered by the question, but since this was the third time this particular hostess had been told of Morty's death, she felt her reaction justified. The hostess partially redeemed herself by seating Mrs. Ebersmann at a marvelous seat in the raised section next to the window and near the fire place. Morty and Mrs. Ebersmann had sat at this very table together many times. It was well past lunch so the restaurant was nearly empty. A few lingering business people and others with no real schedule to adhere to were scattered throughout the restaurant at cozy tables of their own. Mrs. Ebersmann looked out the window and watched thick bands of clouds moving across a bright blue sky, their shadows rambling against the tall buildings that lined the streets. She sighed.

She missed Morty horribly when she came to this restaurant, but she remembered him well here also. She recalled his scent, his leathery-musk cologne, so vividly that it actually seemed to be in the atmosphere surrounding the table. She remembered how he would sit across from her looking gratified and content, with a smile that said all his hard work had been a success, if only because he had the time now to spend with his wife in their favorite restaurant. He made her feel like the queen of the world when they were out. She would talk and talk and he would listen quietly and when she thought he had become bored with her chatter and she stopped talking he would say "come dear you haven't finished what you were saying ..." and make her go on. At all the places he was supposed to laugh he laughed. Once you heard Morty's laugh you would never forget it. It was one of the things she missed most about him, his strident, bellowing laugh that seemed to tear right through life's miseries, if only for an instance. It had been hard to live without his laugh these last few years. She remembered once more that she would never ever hear his laugh again. The thought struck her as surely as if someone had stepped up and punched her in the stomach. She fought her need to cry out by biting her bottom lip. She sometimes wondered if it was normal to still mourn so intensely after so long.

The last time she was at this restaurant she played a game with herself by closing her eyes and believing with all her might that Morty hadn't died and praying that when she opened them he would be sitting across from her. But he never was, no matter how hard she believed. It was a painful game and she didn't want to play it today. Instead she thought about how Morty would always remember to take a little something home for Smoky. "A doggy bag for a cat - only in New York," he would say and then laugh, "this damn cat of yours lives better than we do." Morty wasn't fooling anyone with his wisecracks; he loved Smoky and it wasn't only because his wife loved him. If he were alive he would spare no expense in getting Smoky his operation and the medications. People could say what they wanted about Morty, thought Mrs. Ebersmann. He was stubborn and shrewd when it came to business, but no one would ever say he wasn't kind. He once gave away his two hundred dollar leather gloves to a homeless man because his hands looked frozen and red. Now look what fate had given Morty and his kind heart in return: a bamboozling by a couple of confidence men from California. Mrs. Ebersmann wished that Morty would have had the chance to really take those rats, the Chamberlain brothers, on. He would have enjoyed the contest, sent those charlatans back to California with their hairless tails between their legs. It was only Morty's desperation to have his wife's needs taken care of and his debilitating illness that allowed for some hidden loop hole to slip by him. She tried not to think of the painful and obvious fact: she and Smoky would have been far better off if Morty had closed down and sold off the inventory after all. She could have sold the house and kept the money to use to live more than comfortably for the rest of her life. There would have been more than enough to tend to Smoky's medical needs. Hindsight can be an instrument of self-torture. Mrs. Ebersmann was more heartbroken over the way poor Morty's well-meaning plans had been ravaged so cold-bloodedly than she was over her own dismal state of affairs. She closed her eyes and imagined again the scent of his cologne. She imagined herself hugging him and telling him how proud she was of him and that she wanted him to rest in peace, not upset over the Chamberlain Brothers and their cunning.

A familiar waitress came and greeted Mrs. Ebersmann like an old friend. She didn't need to be reminded of Morty's passing. On the contrary, she put her hand warmly on Mrs. Ebersmann's shoulder, asked how she was holding up then remarked sweetly how a table with Mrs. Ebersmann and no Morty seemed impossible. It had come to the point with this particular waitress that Mrs. Ebersmann didn't need to order, the waitress simply asked if she was having the usual: ice tea and a Cobb salad. Mrs. Ebersmann would smile and hand over the menu as confirmation. Then the waitress said the same thing she always said since Morty's passing: 'oh how Morty loved his Cobb salad.' Each time Mrs. Ebersmann heard this it made her feel better, knowing others remembered real things about Morty, everyday things.

The Cobb salad was Morty's favorite, especially this restaurant's version. 'Best Cobb salad this side of Montreal,' he would say. As homage to Morty, Mrs. Ebersmann had adopted it as her favorite. She never thought she would be a fan of anything that had blue cheese made from sheep's milk in it, but she could see now why Morty liked it so much. Each fork full was a diverse, delicious experience. Her order came quickly. She took her time eating even though she felt anxious to get back to Smoky. She wondered if her decision not to give him a sedative before she left was the right one. He had looked so sickly she didn't have the heart to try and stuff a pill down his throat. Although Mrs. Ebersmann had barely touched it, the waitress came and refilled her ice tea. She liked this waitress very much and didn't mind her doting or her kindness, it felt soothing, a brief respite from her on going misery.

And there had been years of misery. She knew all the anguish had taken its toll on her and Smoky. This was why, given what was to come later in the day, she was remarkably calm. She was ready to be finished with it all. She guessed the old saying was true: when you've had enough you've had enough. She was sure Smoky felt the same.

Mrs. Ebersmann had only a few bites of her salad left when suddenly she felt something very hard between her tongue and the roof of her mouth. She quickly spit it into her napkin. Luckily it was as large as it was; if it had been smaller Mrs. Ebersmann was sure she wouldn't have noticed it and swallowed, possibly she would have choked on it. Who would have remembered Smoky? The thought made her anxious and angry. It must be a carelessly left olive pit she surmised. She was about to be thankful she hadn't broken or cracked her dentures, but remembered it wouldn't matter after today if she had. When she looked into her napkin she was sure her mind was playing tricks. It sparkled brilliantly even under the low lights of the restaurant. It was a diamond, about the size of an olive pit or a small grape. Or so Mrs. Ebersmann thought at first, but the color and clarity were both too perfect, more likely it was glass cut to look like a diamond. Yet, it had the unmistakable qualities of a real diamond. It had to be more than four carats, which was outrageous and reinforced the idea that it was not real. She went back and forth like this: one minute thinking it had to be a real diamond, then not believing it possible. It had to be merely an elegant hunk of costume jewelry. Mrs. Ebersmann had held many a diamond in her hands. Morty had taught her all about diamonds and gems before they were married. Right up until he died Mort would hand her a diamond and get her to grade it on all its qualities: color, clarity, cut and shape and carat weight. It was the way Morty kept his wife involved in the business.

But it had been such a long time since she had last looked at a diamond. Getting her wits about her Mrs. Ebersmann began to really examine the thing in her palm, this time with a calm trained eye: The color was a perfect D. The Clarity was stunningly flawless. The cut was without a doubt Asscher and of the highest quality. The carat weight was certainly over 4 carats. Truly it was the most beautiful diamond she had ever seen and worth well over two hundred thousand dollars. There was no wonder she barely believed it was real.

Morty would be truly impressed by such a gem. And he would be the first one to insist the rightful owner be found. Mrs. Ebersmann waved the waitress over.

"Everything alright with the salad?" the waitress asked.

"I'm not sure if you can call this alright or not," Mrs. Ebersmann said, showing the waitress the large sparkling stone.

"You found that in your salad?" said the waitress, looking perplexed.

"Yes. It almost went down the hatch. I thought it was a pit of some kind," Mrs. Ebersmann said.

"Dear lord you could have choked on that thing," said the waitress.

"Or broken my teeth," Mrs. Ebersmann added.

"I'm so sorry about this. Let me get you a new salad on the house," said the waitress, grabbing for the bowl.

"I'm fine," said Mrs. Ebersmann. "What I would really like is to find its owner. It looks like it is from a very expensive piece of jewelry."

"It's the Maître d's day off. The hostess is in charge today, I'll get her at once," the waitress said, dutifully.

Mrs. Ebersmann grimaced. The thought of dealing with the hostess again was not the least bit appealing. A moment later the waitress returned with the hostess.

"Mrs. Ebersmann," said the hostess, "I'm so sorry about your salad. Is there anything we can do to make it up to you?"

"I'm not particularly fussed about it," said Mrs. Ebersmann. "I would just like to see to it that whomever this belongs to gets it back. It looks awfully expensive."

"May I have a look?" asked the hostess.

"Certainly," Mrs. Ebersmann said, handing the large diamond over.

The hostess looked the stone over, flipping it this way and that. The hostess's face filled with amusement and this told Mrs. Ebersmann exactly what the hostess had surmised.

"I wouldn't worry about it Mrs. Ebersmann," said the hostess, "this is nothing but a cut piece of glass, costume jewelry. It's so large and gaudy it's quite possibly from a child's play set."

Mrs. Ebersmann's face was already flushed with anger. "Is that your expert opinion," she said, dryly.

The waitress, being completely aware of how empty-headed the hostess could be, began clearing Mrs. Ebersmann's table in an attempt to ease the awkwardness. "Let me get these things out of your way," said the waitress, "get you a fresh ice tea and bring your favorite dessert. Peach cheese cake on the house."

"Why Mrs. Ebersmann," the hostess said, speaking over the waitress, "if this were a real diamond it would be worth a million dollars. It's far too large. It would be the Queen of England who'd lose a diamond like this."

"I'm quite certain,' said Mrs. Ebersmann, caustically, " you are far more qualified than I to assess such matters, however, I would like very much if you would check with the kitchen to be sure no one there is presently missing a diamond from an expensive piece of jewelry."

"Mrs. Ebersmann," said the hostess with faked goodwill, "could we not call on your husband to give us his expert opinion. If anyone would know if this is a real diamond it would be Morty Ebersmann."

The waitress looked horrified at what the hostess had just said. Red faced, she barely trembled the words, "I'll be right back with your dessert." She left with the dirty dishes to get the cheese cake.

Mrs. Ebersmann sat stunned. The red in her face turned pallor. "Morty would most certainly be the first person I would consult," she snapped, "if he was not currently dead! Did you hear me you stupid ninny?... DEAD!"

There was a hush throughout the restaurant. The hostess, bugged eyed and open mouthed, was frozen with shock.

"Don't just stand there you silly goat," continued Mrs. Ebersmann, slapping the table and causing the remaining plates and utensils to jump vigorously, "get your skinny ass in the kitchen and find out."

The hostess jumped. She could not move fast enough towards the kitchen. A moment later she reappeared.

"I've spoken with the chef who made your salad," the hostess said, her insolence restored. "He insists that, being a large and burly Lebanese man, he never wears little girls costume jewelry."

Suddenly Mrs. Ebersmann's rage left her. All at once she realized she was interacting with a hapless imbecile who was void of the slightest shred of couth. She began to feel a bit sorry for the hostess. After all life must be incredible difficult for such a coarse, boorish person, who was, in Mrs. Ebersmann's estimation, far too skinny.

"That's fine," said Mrs. Ebersmann. She motioned for the hostess to return the diamond to her by matter of fact-ly holding her hand out for it.

The hostess stood pouting for a few seconds then placed the stone in Mrs. Ebersmann's hand.

"What about the suppliers of your restaurants?" Mrs. Ebersmann said, flatly. "It is possible it could have come from an employee at any one of those establishments."

"I guess anything is possible, really," said the hostess, haughtily. "For all I know it could have fallen out of the sky and right into your bowl. Maybe somebody up there likes you," the hostess said, snickering, and then adding under her breath, "God knows no one down here does."

Mrs. Ebersmann had heard the last part of the hostess's snide comment, but it didn't bother her. Her mind was focused on what she had said immediately before, that it had fallen out of the sky. She hadn't arrived at that idea yet, but now that it was presented to her, albeit in a rather crude, insincere fashion, the thought didn't easily want to go away.

"That will be fine," Mrs. Ebersmann said, looking at the diamond in her hand and waving the hostess away with her other. The hostess huffed and slinked away.

The tenacity of the idea fit Morty to the T. If those bastard Chamberlain brothers could cheat in life then why the hell couldn't he cheat in death, break a few rules, reach beyond a few boundaries. Morty had always taken care of her, hadn't he? Now, when she needed him more than ever, maybe he was still taking care of her... and Smoky. It was all too ridiculous, she thought. She didn't believe in such things. When she got home she would place an ad in the paper to try and find the rightful owner, who would surely be frantic over such an enormous loss. Suddenly it came to her that finding the diamond's rightful owner would delay her suicide, possibly for weeks.

The waitress appeared with the peach cheese cake. "I'm so sorry about that obnoxious woman," she said.

"I'm not bothered to tell the truth," said Mrs. Ebersmann, "I'm more worried about trying to find the owner of this immense diamond." She held it up to show the waitress again.

"I think the diamond has found its own rightful owner and that's why it ended up in your salad," the waitress said, "Good things happen to good people. To me it's like a gift from Morty. It's all too coincidental that you of all people should find a diamond in your salad and right here at this table, where you and Morty dined so often, and in his beloved Cobb salad to top it off. If ever there was a no brainer…"

"Well that thought had crossed my mind, but I don't fully believe in such fantastical things," said Mrs. Ebersmann. "I'm planning on placing an ad in the lost and found section of the papers. Whoever lost it must be checking such things, bulletin boards and such."

"I'll tell you what I can do," said the waitress, "most of the ingredients came from a wholesaler just down the street. Let me call over there and see if anyone is frantic about losing a diamond."

"That would make me feel better for the time being," said Mrs. Ebersmann.

Several moments later the waitress returned and with her she brought a very large cappuccino which she placed on the table for Mrs. Ebersmann. "I thought you might like this to go with the last of your cheese cake. All on the house of course, after the ordeal you've suffered today," said the waitress.

"Thank you," said Mrs. Ebersmann, looking anxious to hear what she had found out about the diamond.

"Well it's what I thought," said the waitress, "Seven people over there all claimed to have lost a very large expensive diamond. Once one said she'd lost one they all seemed to discover they too were missing a diamond. This is exactly what is going to happen when you put the ad in the paper. Every shyster and con-man will come out of the woods with a sob story of how they lost it and how much it means to them, how their withered mother had given it to them on her death bed."

Mrs. Ebersmann thought of the Chamberlain brothers and their trickery. She sighed and said, "I thought of that also."

"Listen if it were me and I'd found a diamond in my Cobb salad, I'd keep it," said the waitress. "But, that's me, I believe in signs and angels and all that stuff."

"Thank you, I'll think about it," Mrs. Ebersmann said.

The waitress went to attend other patrons. Mrs. Ebersmann looked across the table where Morty would be seated if he were here now and wondered what he would say about it all. 'The waitress is right you know, go on keep it, it's meant for you,' she heard his voice clear as if he were whispering in her ear, 'Get that damn cat of yours fixed up and live out your day's happy - to hell with those Chamberlains.' She hadn't thought about that at all; she could sell the diamond and pay for Smoky's operation and medication, pay all the nice people back who had helped her. And there was something else she knew Morty would say and that was: 'don't let those bastards beat us like this'. It was true; her committing suicide would be just what they would want. For her to disappear into the Hudson would be a total victory for the Chamberlains. Why not stick around and be a thorn in their side as long as she could. She took the diamond and put it in the safest pocket of her jacket. She finished the last of her cheesecake and sipped her cappuccino. She couldn't remember when the combination had tasted so heavenly.

Mrs. Ebersmann paid her bill and left all the money she had as a tip, only keeping enough for cab fare home. She was just outside the front doors when she heard the waitress call her.

"You forgot Smoky's doggy bag," the waitress said, walking outside to meet Mrs. Ebersmann. "It's liver pate. It's from the chef and I."

"It's so sweet of you to remember," said Mrs. Ebersmann, "he's been feeling rough lately and this will cheer him up." There was a lump that welled up in Mrs. Ebersmann's throat. She had more to say, but it seemed the waitress understood without the words. She hugged Mrs. Ebersmann and kissed her cheek. Mrs. Ebersmann was thinking how happy she was that this was not a hug goodbye, how she didn't have to go home and put Smoky in her jacket and then hurl herself off the George Washington Bridge. She rolled the diamond between her fingers inside her coat pocket as a cab took her home.

The first thing Mrs. Ebersmann did when she got home was call Frieda Blumbaum to make arrangements to sell the diamond. Frieda agreed to pay the retail value of the diamond minus 20 percent. Both parties were satisfied. The second call was to the vet to arrange an appointment for Smoky's operation. It was good news - Smoky would only have to wait two more days.

She heard the paperboy toss the afternoon paper on the front steps, but she was too excited to read the news. Smoky seemed to be feeling a little better. Mrs. Ebersmann sat with him on the sofa coddling him and feeding him his liver pate

.

"Soon you'll be right as rain little man, no need to call home on our own dime this time around" Mrs. Ebersmann said.

Smoky purred.

When Mrs. Ebersmann did get around to reading the paper she would find this article on its front page:

Suicidal Leap Kills Five!

A young woman jumped from the Jersey side of the George Washington Bridge and with incredible un-lucky timing landed squarely on a passing yacht below. Killed in the impact were brothers Brian and Bradley Chamberlain and two female Friends: Philomena Mahood and a woman identified only as Misty, as well as the unidentified jumper. The yacht known as The Just Bounty was cruising the Hudson River as part of a celebration to honor the business accomplishments of the Chamberlain Brothers who are well-known jewelry merchants. Witnesses aboard the yacht said Brian and Bradly were in the process of having photographs taken when the impact occurred. Philomena Mahood and Misty were onboard as models and hostesses for the evening's event and were sitting on the laps of the Brothers at the time of the incident.

Said a distraught witness, who did not want to be named: 'Out of nowhere she came through the canopy. At first I thought it was an explosion. I still don't believe it. You can't deny that young woman really went out spectacularly,'

Sargent O'Neill of the NYPD stated: "It was a simple suicide gone amiss. There was no malicious intent. From her vantage point it would have been impossible for the young lady to have known there was a yacht about to float by from under the bridge when she jumped. This was an unfortunate accident."

Mrs. Francis Ebersmann, the only surviving proprietor of the Chamberlain's New York jewelry enterprise, has not been reached for comment…

Bird Brain Experiment

Dr. Grant punched in the four digit code, opened the lab door and sang hello to her associates. "Hello my monkeys how are we today?" she serenaded. "Are we going to show off for the nice young man?" She was no doubt eccentric, but genuine, the kind of person who is always exactly themselves no matter who's around or what the situation is. I liked her from the start.

I had come to the university to do a story on Dr. Grant, the famed Zoologist, and the work she was doing in her animal behavior lab. Her published articles, suggesting that birds were actually far more intelligent than dogs, had garnered much attention in the worldwide press. Her findings had the bird people singing I told you so and the dog people barking up a storm (the cat people couldn't be bothered to care). I had come to witness and report on what her colleagues were calling her simple, elegant and crucial experiments. Dr. Grant is noted amongst her peers in animal behavioral science as being the eccentric genius of the field.

Earlier, as we walked through the halls of the university towards the labs, it was clear by the reactions of the students and other faculty, I was being shown around by someone of distinction.

"Do you always greet them with such enthusiasm," I asked, noting there wasn't any '*monkeys*' in the room only a dog and a parrot.

"Of course," said Dr. Grant, flipping her glasses up on her forehead, "they are more than lab experiments to us, they're family. They come home with me, don't you monkeys!"

The dog was a chocolate brown labradoodle named Winston. To say he was excited to see Dr. Grant would be a gross understatement. He did circles around us, prancing and galloping with his tail wagging so hard his entire hindquarters had no option but to flop back and forth as well. He was a good looking dog with bright almond shaped eyes and a mop of shaggy hair that gave me the impression he was more a cartoon character than a real dog.

The parrot was an African Grey named Gypsy. Her bluish grey coloring had the brilliance only nature can create. Her feathers gleamed softly as if they were made of silk. She looked at me sweetly and with such interest and intelligence that I couldn't help but be enamored.

"Quite a pair you have here," I said, "definitely not a bashful lot."

"Oh no," said Dr. Grant, "they get plenty of love around here. It makes them fond of people."

I looked around the room. It was as stark as one would expect within a university. There was the slight, but steady smell of Gypsy's birdcage that wasn't wholly unpleasant. An armchair sat in the corner and a sofa against the wall. A comfortable bed that was no doubt for Winston, lay on the floor. In the middle of the room was a large contraption made mostly of plexiglass and Aluminum. It was long, complicated and seemed to have many compartments.

"Mind if I sit down?" I asked.

"Oh, not at all. Use the sofa. Don't worry it's clean, Winston knows the rules, he is not allowed up there," said Dr. Grant.

I sat on the sofa and got out my notebook. Curiously the part of the sofa where I sat was warm. I looked at Winston. His tongue fell out the side of his mouth as he panted softly.

"The photographer from the magazine should be here any time now," I said. Taking out my iPhone I asked, "Do you mind if I make an audio recording of our interview?"

"Audio is fine. No video please the university doesn't allow it," The Dr. said.

Winston had come over to sit beside me. As I petted him and scratched behind his ears his warm almond eyes cheerfully appraised me.

"Oh, he likes you," Dr. Grant said. "Winston loves his chest rubbed, don't you monkey."

I gave Winston a brief chest rub and reached for my ringing cell phone. It was the photographer. As I spoke Winston put his paw on my arm and tried to force it back onto his chest. He did this with such zeal, that in order to continue my phone call I was forced to switch my phone to the other hand and continue Winston's chest rub. He gazed at me happily, panting, his long pink tongue flung to one side.

"The Photographer would like to reschedule, would that be alright?" I asked. Dr. Grant said it would be fine and reminded me once again that all photographs used in the article would need official approval by the university. This would not be a problem I assured her.

I carried on with our interview.

"One of the most wonderful things about our research," Dr. Grant said, "is the relationship Winston and Gypsy have developed. They absolutely love each other. Gypsy will do anything for Winston and Winston is so gentle and patient with her. It is a beautiful thing to witness."

"I bet," I said.

"Watch now," said Dr. Grant unlatching Gypsy's cage and opening the door. Gypsy flew over to Winston who was still lying beside me. She landed at Winston's front paws and began cooing lovingly up to him. Winston lowered his head and Gypsy began to attentively preen him. "You see she goes immediately to him," said the doctor.

It was easy to tell Gypsy and Winston adored each other. I thought about the article I would write, making a mental note to restrict delving too hard into the cliché: if a bird and a dog can get along why can't people.

"I've had fresh coffee put in the room and I've made my acclaimed cookies, of which I bet you can't eat only one," said Dr. Grant. Winston's ears perked up at the mention of cookies.

"Thanks but I've had my quotient of coffee for this morning, but I'll definitely try a cookie," I said. I got up and grabbed one from the table. "How long have you been comparing Aves intelligence to that of the Canine," I asked, sitting down again. Winston was sitting directly in front of me now, his eyes locked on my cookie. Gypsy perched on the arm of the sofa next to me. "Mind if I share my cookie with...the monkeys," I asked.

"Oh certainly. You'll see something quite extraordinary if you do," Dr. Grant said.

I gave a piece to Winston and he took it reasonably gentle from my fingers and gulped it down. He seemed to anticipate that I was going to give a piece to Gypsy and became rather eager about it. I broke off a small piece and Gypsy gingerly removed it from my fingers, her eyes blinking up at me. She then walked to the edge of the sofa arm and held her piece out to Winston, who took it gently out of her beak. I broke off more pieces and the scenario repeated .

"Wow, does Gypsy ever keep anything for herself?" I asked getting up to grab another cookie.

"She eats her bird seed," said Dr. Grant, "but anything special she gives it to Winston if he's around. She seems to enjoy giving treats to Winston much more than eating them herself."

"She's a very sweet little girl," I said, "and Winston seems to have a good thing going here." Through Gypsy I shared my second cookie with Winston. From the little bit I had tasted I thought they were very good cookies.

"Oh, he certainly does have it good here, don't you monkey?" said the Dr. "To answer your question," she continued, "this will be our sixth year doing research with Aves and Canine intelligence as you so aptly put it (I had done my research). Mostly with Gypsy and Winston, but we do use others."

I looked at the contraption on the floor. "This, if I remember correctly from your research articles, is the 'Configurable Logic Puzzle'. Is that correct?" I asked.

"Very good," she said. "Yes the CLP. It's our most succinct and demonstrable experiment so we use it for media and interviews."

"It looks quite complicated actually," I said. I was hoping she wasn't going to have me give it a try. "But isn't it a bit unfair since Winston and Gypsy have had repeated exposure to the ins and outs of the different puzzles," I asked.

"In some ways yes, but it still has value. Besides the wow factor for the media, it demonstrates the animals memory recall ability, powers of sustained concentration, learning ability over time, frustration and boredom management," Dr. Grant continued. "Think of yourself or anyone having to perform a particularly difficult task repeatedly. We learn as we go, changing tactics or possibly even making a number of complete paradigm shifts in the process."

"Interesting," I said, "are Winston and Gypsy still changing their tactics?"

She laughed. "No," she said, "they seemed to have settled on a pattern as far as the CLP is concerned; which is fine, it taught us a lot about familiarity and complacency in the animal's minds. Think of it this way, people still accidently kill or maim themselves doing something they've done repeatedly for years. An example is driving a car. It is an important aspect of psychology- why do we suddenly make mistakes.

"Enough of my babble," she said, "let us get on with it and have a demonstration. Shall we?" With this Winston's ears perked up.

"Certainly," I said.

Dr. Grant moved Gypsy back to her cage. "We'll start with Winston," she said.

"Gypsy doesn't mind her cage?" I asked.

"She's quite fine in her cage, but of course she would rather be with Winston and whoever else is around. Isn't that right Monkey," Dr. Grant said as she slipped Gypsy inside her cage. "Gypsy is quite the little escape artist though," she continued, "the majority of the time we find she has let herself out of her cage."

I looked at the locking mechanism of the cage door and it appeared inconceivable for a parrot to open it, especially from the inside.

"That's quite impressive, her opening it from the inside, seems impossible," I said.

"So far we haven't caught her in the act. One of the things on the to-do list is to add an additional camera to this room just to monitor her cage. Birds, especially Psittaciformes, the Zoological term for

Parrots, are well known for their dexterity and intelligence. They're great at getting in and out of things, solving difficult problems, as my studies have proven," Dr. Grant said. She walked to a cupboard and got a large bag of treats. "First, let's see what Winston can do."

Winston, upon seeing the bag of treats, had jumped up and sat in the middle of a one foot by one foot square on the floor outlined with yellow tape. He was eagerly watching Dr. Grant as she plopped a treat down a tube at one end of the puzzle contraption. The treat now sat in a see-through chamber, called the 'reward chamber', waiting its release down a chute into Winston's drooling jaws.

"Solve," Dr. Grant commanded, "Solve."

Winston whined a little and laid down, his chin pressed flat against the floor in a pose of capitulation.

"No Winston, solve. Solve!" Dr. Grant raised her voice. Winston lay still.

"Winston! Solve! Solve!" Shouted the doctor.

Winston lay motionless except for his eyes, which tracked his persecutor.

Dr. Grant began to pace. She had become irritated to the point that I felt uncomfortable.

Winston never budged as Dr. Grant mumbled something and reached her arm inside the Configurable Logic Puzzle and released the treat down the chute.

"There you lazy little shit!" said Dr. Grant . Winston gobbled the treat.

I felt my face blush slightly.

"He is quite capable of solving the puzzles," said Dr. Grant, still irritated. "In fact he used to be quite the expert. We're certain Gypsy picked up a trick or two from watching him. It is frustrating because what Winston demonstrated today was one of his worst scores ever."

"Scores?" I asked.

"Yes," said Dr. Grant, "each attempt at retrieving the treat is scored in categories of: attention, concentration, dexterity, speed, skill, obedience or what I call 'attitude'. Today Winston scored a big fat zero on everything but attention. He was attentive to the fact that I had put a treat in the chamber."

"But does he get points for getting the treat in the end?" I asked.

Dr. Grant seemed confused by my question. "No," she said, "Winston didn't retrieve the treat, I retrieved it for him."

I had more questions about this, but sensing Dr. Grant's frustration, I let them go.

"It's a shame," continued the Dr., "Winston's score has steadily gone down, but not just Winston's, all canines demonstrate the same downward curve in these types of experiments over time."

"Really?" I asked. "As naïve as this might sound and with all due respect, I don't see this correlating out in the real world. I don't find dogs getting more and more stupid. It seems the opposite to me."

"It's not naïve, quite the opposite and I take no offence," Dr. Grant said, "It is a very subtle thing. What I think you are noticing in the 'real world', as you say, is not 'intelligence' per say, but more the dogs ability to integrate deeper into the lives of human beings. We've shared a symbiotic relationship for at least 10 000 years. We get a lot from our canine friends, but the dog gets a lot from us as well. We give our dogs a reliable supply of food, water, warmth, a nice home safe from predators; we give them comfort and attention, not to mention medical care when needed. Most importantly and pertaining to the crux of this whole matter is we lend our brain to the dog. Compared to their wild cousins, the wolf, a dog rarely has to think for himself. An example is the simple act of us opening a gate for our dog. You can ask a chicken or sheep farmer how apt a wolf, or a fox, or a coyote is at getting past gates and fences. In laymen terms the dog's brain has become lazy."

I profess to be no doctor of animal behavior, but something about this theory didn't sit right with me.

Next it was Gypsy's turn.

Dr. Grant opened Gypsy's cage door and she flew immediately to Winston to resume preening him. Winston, who was laying on the floor, flopped on his side, closed his eyes and appeared well contented as Gypsy nuzzled his ear with her bill.

"Come along Gypsy girl," said Dr. Grant. "You have to show the nice man how you can solve puzzles."

Gypsy literally hopped to attention at the sound of Dr. Grant dropping a treat into the reward chamber of the CLP. She was in the center of the yellow square in three quick hops.

"Someone is a an eager little girl this morning," said Dr. Grant. "Now solve, solve gypsy."

I watched as Gypsy cocked her head and studied the puzzle, her little eyes flitting about. It was no more than ten seconds before she was on the move. She flew to a perch at the top CLP and pulled on a green tab which slid a tray, which allowed the treat to fall down a tube into a space in a slotted wheel. Next, she hopped onto a platform and cranked a handle, which turned the wheel until the treat was free to bounce down a peg board until it lodged between two pegs. Almost instantly she hopped down to a perch on the opposite side and pulled out one of the pegs restraining the treat. It fell onto a conveyor belt below. Next she pushed on a slider that moved the conveyor until the treat fell down on a tray below. Gypsy stopped, her head cocked to one side. For a moment she studied where the treat had fallen. She hopped down to the floor and skipped around to the other side of the

CLP. Sensing victory she let out two excited squawks and pulled on a tab that released the treat onto a tray with eight cones. The treat bounced along the edge of the cones until it fell into one of the openings. She now flew underneath to view the bottom of the cone dish, remembering which cone above her the treat was in, she pulled the corresponding slider which dropped the treat in tube and then into the receiving dish. Immediately Gypsy grabbed the treat and hurried to give it to Winston. Who had been watching with what looked like cool anticipation.

"The perches and platforms allow Gypsy to perform the tasks she needs to free the treat. Winston has no problem reaching the levers and pegs; occasionally he will plant a paw for balance if he needs to reach a bit higher. That is when he feels like doing anything at all," she said, looking at Winston with scorn.

"Does Gypsy like these treats?" I asked. "She seems to give all hers to Winston."

"She loves them. Of course she can't swallow them whole but she'll pick away at them. When she's working alone she'll hoard them in her cage for later. But, if Winston is around she much prefers giving them to him." Replied Dr. Grant.

The number of treats and cookies Winston had been given this afternoon was mounting. Quite the haul for a dog who, according to Dr. Grant, was having an off day.

While Gypsy was busy pampering Winston, Dr. Grant rearranged the puzzle compartments of the CLP. I was impressed by its sophistication and refinement, and couldn't imagine the multitude of configurations its eight compartments were capable of constructing.

"Is it really a completely new puzzle every time," I asked, "or is it possible Gypsy has memorized each individual compartment?"

"Memory certainly plays a very big part in solving the puzzles," said Dr. Grant. "but the way the Configurable Logic Puzzle is designed learning each compartment on its own won't win you the prize. The puzzles link together in unique ways. The eight compartments gives us a huge amount of combinations to test with."

Gypsy had no problem solving this new arrangement of the CLP. And just like the first time she promptly gave her reward to Winston. Who, by the look on his face, was very much enjoying all the treats he was getting, especially since he had put zero effort into getting them. I suddenly got the sense that Winston had worked out a way to 'hack' the system. I had the distinct feeling it wasn't mere laziness at work with Winston. He had figured out a way to get rewarded without lifting a paw. He simply let someone else retrieve his treats for him, Gypsy or Dr. Grant.

There was one more demonstration of Gypsy's expertise with the CLP. She seemed to struggle a little more with this third arrangement, but in the end Winston got his reward.

"Gypsy scored extremely high as usual," said Dr. Grant. "And sadly Winston is still on his steady decline. This corresponds to our overall findings: birds are just as clever and much more motivated than dogs, who seem to plateau and then decline in there aptitude. Aves are most eager and most dutiful in their perceived obligations and service to their human guardians. A place that had heretofore been awarded to canines."

"Could it be dogs had learned to turn the tables on their humans?" I asked. This question was rewarded with a blank stare from Dr. Grant. I hesitated in continuing, but I wanted to hear her opinion on what I was thinking. It would be a good angle for the article. "It seems to me that possibly dogs have gotten better at training their owners over time." I said this with a chuckle. In my mind the whole idea seemed humorous. Dr. Grant did not appear to share in the whimsy, however.

"I mean, it could be," I continued, "Winston might know exactly what he's doing. He might have figured out that to get a treat he doesn't have to complete the CLP, all he has to do is be patient."

I got the blank stare once more from Dr. Grant. She looked to be offended, which surprised me. I assumed someone in her position would have heard similar questions.

"With all due respect," she said finally, "this is a typical untrained observation. We zoologist do not make hypotheses outside the parameters of our experimentations. There is no way of reading a dog's mind. Humans can communicate through speech. We can't get into animals minds in such a way. We cannot just guess at their motivations by using our human minds to do so. We often project our humaneness onto animals. The entire Disney repertoire will back me up on this. We scientists have to judge animal motivations purely by studying their behavior, so not to taint our findings with fancies of the human imagination."

Dr. Grant began putting things away.

"Fair enough," I said. The Disney implication not being lost on me. I had to concede it was quite possible that Winston's low performance was in fact due to laziness and boredom. However, I couldn't help but wonder...

"How is Winston's score when Gypsy is not around?" I asked, "or stays locked in her cage?"

"We barely do individual training anymore," was her scant reply. She appeared more intent on putting things away than continuing with our interview. My time evidently was up.

"I want to thank you for your time," I said. "I think I have more than I need to write my article."

"It was our pleasure, wasn't it monkeys," Dr. Grant said. The kindness coming back to her voice.

We grabbed our things and headed back to Dr. Grant's office.

"Gypsy and Winston just hang out here in the room?" I asked.

"No, no. Absolutely no. We have fulltime caregivers. Soon Winston will go for his park time and Gypsy will go to her outside cage, which she loves. She can hear all the other birds sing."

"It seems they both have it made here," I said. Dr. Grant seemed pleased with my comment.

Half way to her office I realized I had forgotten my note book.

"Do you remember your way because I'm in a bit of a hurry to meet some appointments," Dr. Grant said.

"Absolutely I remember the way. But is it ok for me to go by myself?" I asked.

Dr. Grant assured me it was fine. Winston and Gypsy would be perfectly ok with me going in the room myself. She gave me the 4 digit code to the room and I headed back.

On the way back to the lab I started to think about the question I'd asked Dr. Grant: how is Winston's score when Gypsy is not around, or locked in her cage?

When I let myself back in the lab Winston was laying on the sofa, which according to Dr. Grant, was expressly forbidden. At first he seemed apprehensive and was about to jump down, but once he saw it was only me and not the Dr. Grant he relaxed again sinking back to his comfortable position. His eyes followed me as his tail wagged lazily. Gypsy had no reaction to me returning. She seemed to be half snoozing in her cage. This was no ruse. I did honestly forget my notebook. However, as long as I was here I thought I might do a quick experiment of my own. Seeing that it would do no harm and could possibly answer my question about how Winston performs by himself, without Gypsy's or Dr. Grant's help.

I went to the cupboard and grabbed a couple treats. As soon as I touched the cupboard door I had Winston's full attention. He watched as I dropped the treats down the tube into the chamber.

"Solve Winston, solve," I said.

I grabbed my note book and walked out of the lab. I stood back and watched Winston through the window of the door. He was slow to move, but finally he stood up on the sofa and stretched. Leisurely he jumped down to have a look at the treats in the CLP. He sat, looked around and yawned. Most assuredly he was full from all the treats he'd already had. Just when I decided Winston had had enough for the day and wasn't interested in my little experiment he walked to Gypsy's cage. She became instantly excited. To my surprise Winston opened her cage door with his snout in seconds, knowing exactly which ways to pull and push the locking mechanism. This solved the mystery of how Gypsy was getting out of her cage. Winston was letting her out.

Winston headed back to the sofa to resume his lounging; Gypsy wasted no time solving the CLP and getting the treats. Of course she went right over to give them to Winston, who promptly gobbled them up.

"Well played Winston," I thought. "Well played."

My last image of the pair of them was Winston's eyes closing sleepily as he lay on the forbidden sofa and Gypsy lovingly preening him.

Gypsy was certainly giving her Aves friends a good reputation by scoring high points on the CLP and other tests. But, as far as team canine was concerned, Winston had taken things to a whole new level. He was certainly no birdbrain.

Winter Patio

"Sir it's minus 20 degrees outside, your kids!" said the restaurant's hostess.

"I don't care if there's a damned blizzard out there. I'm a customer and I want a table on the patio," said the man, "and you're not supposed to argue with customers. At least not until you get their money," he snickered.

The man's wife said nothing. She stood meekly, shifting her gaze from side to side, trying to appear unconnected to the situation, like an audience member reluctantly thrust on stage to assist in a magic trick that goes horribly wrong.

The man's and woman's two children, a boy 9 and a girl 6, kept their eyes fixed on the floor. They were used to their father's scenes.

The man went on, "and besides you've got those heaters, all restaurants with patios have propane heaters."

"Yes, but for the chill of fall or spring, it's the middle of January, it's going to be absolutely freezing out there," said the hostess.

She looked to the woman hoping she might help convince the man to take a booth by the wall with the fireplace or at the big window. The woman simply tilted her head into a shrugging shoulder, resigned to be towed along like a boxcar in a crazy train. The hostess understood the woman's body language: I've given up trying to talk sense into this man.

The hostess studied the eyes of the woman. She seemed weary, frayed. For some reason the woman reminded the hostess of a screen door that had been slammed shut too many times, askew and twisted in its frame yet still performing its duty. She's hanging in there, she thought, who knows why, probably for her kids.

The hostess smiled and grabbed four menus. With the greatest kindness directed toward the woman she said, "This way please."

The man rushed ahead, impatiently pulling at the patio door.

"Just one moment sir, it's locked," the hostess said. The kindness had fallen from her voice. "I'll have to get the key from the manager."

"Ain't nowhere with good service anymore," said the man.

"Why don't we just grab a booth," the woman finally spoke, "The kids are gonna freeze."

The man scowled, "It'll toughen them up," he said. "You dote over these damn kids too much. When I was their age I wasn't pampered or spoiled, I had to take care of myself. And anyways where we're headed they're gonna have to get used to the cold."

The manager came with the keys. "I'm not certain how I feel about this," he said.

"I'm not certain I care what you're not certain about," said the man, smirking. "Just open the door. I'm hungry." He had the pleased feeling he got when he was mean and tyrannical to others; always the same thought: no dick head is gonna get the better of me.

The Manager kept his eyes forward and went on with opening the patio door. He grabbed four chairs that were stacked against the wall and set up a table, wiping the thick layer of snow off the table and chairs with the edge of a menu.

"Now you kids eat up," the man said. "I don't want to hear any whining about being hungry. We're not stopping again 'til we get up to the Canadian border."

"I hope you don't mind," the hostess had come with a tray, "I brought the kids some hot chocolate and some coffee for mom and dad - on the house."

"What do you say?" the woman prodded the children.

"Ya, what do you say kids? 'If it's free I want more!'" the man said, and laughed.

It was then the hostess noticed the man's boots. How could she not notice the way his feet were sticking out the side of the table, obstructing her. They shone the way expensive, well-oiled leather does. The man's boots and swanky leather jacket were out of place compared to the rest of the family's attire, which was clean, but beggarly. A family of mallard ducks, thought the hostess, the male all done up fancy, the female and babies plain, brown and white.

"Put your mitts around these," the hostess said, handing the kids the hot chocolate, "They'll help keep you warm."

"Thank you," said the kids, their tone soaked with weariness unsuitable for their age.

"You're most welcome," the hostess said. She noticed the boy had beautiful, but sad blue eyes and craggy hair across his forehead. The cheapest haircuts were ones given by mom, the hostess thought. The girl had long, blonde hair, which had been doted over to such a degree it glimmered.

"Look at your beautiful hair," the hostess said to the girl, "who does all that brushing?"

The girl, un-lauded, pointed to her mother. The hostess could tell the family was struggling through a meager existence. She was a mother herself and mothers are sensitive to the welfare of all children, not just their own. These kids were indeed poor, she thought, but well loved by their mom, that was evident.

"There's no sense in having a waitress freeze to death out here as well," said the hostess, "So I'll be the one braving Siberia to take your order. I'll give you a few minutes to decide and I'll be right back."

The woman mouthed the words "Thank you" to the hostess, making certain the man didn't notice.

"Are you gonna dig-up some of those heaters or what?" the man asked, like a smart ass. He had a way of smiling sometimes that made his face slant. It produced a look that could make the whole world hate him in an instant. The woman had reminded him many times of this. It was this smile he was using as he spoke. "It's freezing out here-r-r-r!" he said. He poked at his son as he pretended to shiver. The boy was not amused and as usual he ignored the man's performance. He did his best to avoid eye contact with his father. The practice had spread and he spent most of his day, even at school, averting his stare.

"I'll ask the manager again," said the hostess, tromping inside.

"Mommy my ears are cold," said the little girl.

The woman tied the girl's scarf around her head to cover her ears. She told the boy to put up the hood of his jacket.

"Up in Alaska there ain't no doctor on every street corner like around here," said the man. "So don't be getting sick on me or I'll ship you back on a greyhound bus."

"We could have just as easily sat inside," said the woman, "Honestly, I don't understand the way you think sometimes, or the way you speak to your own children."

Predictably, the deeply grooved dysfunctions of this family were starting to play out. The man and woman were settling into their ritual of squabbling at the dinner table; the children silent, amassing the emotional weight of having a mother and a father who no longer loved each other. The woman would complain about the family's decay, how things were getting worse instead of better. Her grievances would be lost on the man, dissipating like radio static into his stratospheric disinterest. He would simply, as if through a bullhorn, reaffirm what he, through his own self-interest, had decided was good for his family, whether they liked it or not.

"Adventure, is why we're out here," said the man, waving his hand in the frigid air. "Ya got to live outside the box. And don't be getting on me 'bout how I talk to my own damn kids. It's good for them I talk this way. I don't beat 'em with my belt like my old man did. Be thankful."

"Soon we'll be living inside a box, a cardboard box if all you're big plans don't work out as usual," said the woman, defiantly. Watching her children shivering had stirred her courage. "It's big talk. That's all it ever is."

"It isn't only talk," said the man, suddenly angry and defensive. He'd heard this criticism his whole life. "There is gold laying all over the place up there. Just takes a little gumption to get to it."

"Where was your gumption when you had the job at the mill?" asked the woman. "I heard all your big talk then too."

"I ain't no lunch bagger," said the man, "I got to be free to do my own thing. It's a plain fact ya can't get rich working for someone else."

"It's a plain fact you can't get rich stealing out of the employees locker room either," said the woman. She pointed to something on the menu and both kids nodded in agreement.

"Don't be spending a fortune now, it takes a lot of gas to get up to Alaska," the man said.

"Don't worry I'm not eating," said the woman, sharply. "You look frozen sweet pea," she said, taking her coat and draping it over the girl's shoulders.

"Where is that stupid woman with the heaters?" said the man.

"Why is she stupid? You're the one who wanted to eat out here," said the woman. "Let your son have your jacket."

The hostess came out to take their order.

Gruffly, the man asked, "What happen to the heaters?"

"Propane tanks are empty and stored away," the hostess said, her tone barely masking her contempt for the man. "Now what can I get you?" she asked, smiling at the kids.

"That's what I call lousy service," the man sneered, pulling the zipper of his fancy jacket firmly to his chin.

The hostess ignored the male duck and took the order of the plain mother and ducklings.

"And for him?" she asked the woman, indicating to the man with a nod of her head, but not looking at him. Without asking, the woman knew what the man would want from the menu; she pointed to it.

"Bitch," the man said, as the hostess walked away.

"Let's just eat and get out of here," said the woman. "I'm sure we'll get turned around at the border any way."

"You know I've done the time for my shitty misdemeanors. The mill and the union didn't press charges on this last one, thanks to your uncle talking em' out of it," the man said.

"Don't even mention my poor uncle," said the woman, "he went against his best judgment and got you that job at the mill and in no time you embarrassed him by breaking into lockers."

The irritating smile came back to slant the man's face. "Your uncle did a nice job convincing them to drop the charges. He told em' I had two babies and a good woman struggling back at home." The man beat the table to startle the kids, "See, you aren't useless after all." The children said nothing. Boxcars have no choice but to be towed along.

"They didn't press charges cause of that? Cause of us?" asked the woman, surprised. "Well at least it's honest what my uncle said about us struggling. He got that part right."

"Don't start up your complaining. Your life ain't boring and that's the thing. Your still here ain't ya?" said the man, with his usual acidity. He suddenly stood up - "I gotta take a piss," he announced and walked inside to find the washroom.

She watched him walk into the restaurant. She was still here, but how much of her? She used to have a lot of friends, both women and men, of all ages from all the compartments of her life: her different jobs, school, and when she was in the riding club. People liked to be around her. Her father would get mad because the phone would ring off the hook for her. Now she rarely heard from anyone, her own family included. She stopped checking her E-mails or hoping for a simple text. She couldn't blame any of them. She and the kids were seldom in one place for very long, that was part of it, people losing track of them. That wasn't the real reason, that's just what she told herself. She knew it was that she came as a package deal with him now.

No one could get her without him. A lone boxcar couldn't simply pull up somewhere without the obligatory train accompanying it.

She now looked at his foot prints his leather boots had left in the snow. He was her whole world for a time. She was 17 when she became infatuated with him, too young to know anything about anything. To her he was strangely beautiful, she couldn't look away. He was so cock sure of himself and his plans. His words fell out like solid rocks and she believed in the weight of them; it was as if he was telling the elements how to align when he spoke. "Well get in," were his first words to her, as he held the passenger door to his truck open. That was the black line in her history: her ascending world before getting into his pick-up and her declining world after. Then life had gained speed so fast she had no chance of judging in what direction she was headed, no time to do anything about it. And then the kids came.

Now she often lay awake wondering how her life might have been if she hadn't laid eyes on him, hadn't got in his truck. Recently she was plagued with bouts of sobbing. Tears came often and out of the blue. She thought she was going crazy with all the jumbled sadness she didn't understand. She pretended she didn't understand anyway. She went on ignoring what she knew was true: children or not, she wished she'd never met the man. Her regret was infinite. She felt it was killing her from within, giving her cancer or weakening blood vessels, priming her for an early death from a stroke or a heart attack.

Was this how life was, she thought, you just have to go along with everything you start. Can't someone learn and grow and see a past mistake and fix it in the present? She'd had this conversation with herself relentlessly. She knew that things weren't so simple. It wasn't like repainting the living room back to beige after a trial with powdered rose. Not that kind of mistake. People get all tangled up with each other under the surface. Lives, like roots, intertwine. There's the kids and the guilt and having no job or a place to stay and all that bookended by overwhelming fear. The crazy train was moving too damn fast now.

The poor kids, she thought, the look on their faces when she told them there would be no other kids to play with up in the middle of butt fuck, Alaska. Cooped up in a little trailer, being home schooled, it would be torture for them. What scared her was discovering her children had acquired a process in dealing with the steady stream of crap in their lives. The reactions on their angel faces when she told them they were moving once again, this time to a place bleaker than ever, the despair and weariness only showed for a second and then they suddenly disappeared, as though their unhappiness was put somewhere for later. Her kids had become swallowers. Emotions went down into their tiny tummies like driblets of molten metal, where they would digest forever.

And now the woman had begun to cry. The kids were good at ignoring her sudden out pouring of desperation, they put their minds elsewhere. The hostess appeared. The woman wiped her eyes nonchalantly, hoping she wouldn't notice her tears.

"Everything ok out here at the North Pole," the hostess asked. The boy found this funny.

"Ok, I guess," said the woman.

"You know if it wasn't for you and the kids I would have told your husband to take a hike, but I'm guessing the last thing you need is another big scene; figure you had plenty of them by now," the hostess said.

Well at least that was honest, she got that part right, the woman thought.

"He seems to get his way a lot lately on account of us," she said.

'What about you and the kids," the hostess asked, looking unequivocally at the woman, "you ever get your way?"

The Hostess caught the eyes of the woman and this time the woman didn't look away. Who can say what information is conveyed with a simple look – the fear, frustration and sorrow expressed from one side, and the reassurance, encouragement and solace offered from the other.

The man came back from the washroom. The Hostess avoided eye contact with the man and the man refused to look at her in return.

"Your food should be up shortly," she said to the woman and children, and went back into the warm restaurant.

The woman stared at the man with a chilled gaze, colder than the January air that turned her bitter breath to fog.

"What?" said the man, affronted by her glare.

"Your words are fluff," she said. "You are fluff."

"What the hell…?" said the man.

"You ooze bullshit out of every pour," the woman said.

The boy chuckled.

"Hey!" burst the man.

"I'm just as much a bull shitter as you are," the woman said softly, shifting her eyes to the deep snow on the adjacent table. She had spoken this to herself.

"Ya, damn rights you are," said the man.

"Look at us sitting out here in the cold like a family of lost souls," said the woman.

Hearing her mother describe their family this way distressed the little girl. Some words ring truth as loud as cathedral bells. The little girl began to cry.

"Well I kinda like it out here. What do ya say kids?" asked the man, playfully poking the little girl.

"Leave her alone," said the woman. "Of course they don't like it out here. What are they gonna say if someone from their school sees us out here, that their father is an idiot?"

The boy laughed.

"The kids are never gonna see this shitty town again. What the hell has gotten into you? " asked the man.

"What is wrong with eating inside the restaurant? What is wrong with you working at the mill?" the woman yelled.

"I told you…." The man started to say.

"There is no gold for you in Alaska," said the woman.

"There is plenty of gold up there," said the man.

"But not for you. Not for us."

"What the hell are you talking about?"

"Not for you. Not for a man full of bullshit and fluff," the woman said.

The vigor of his woman's insults made the man flinch as if he had been hit with physical blows.

"Any man who can't do a simple job at the mill isn't any man that can pull gold out of the frozen ground. I'm not taking the kids away from their friends again to go live in a goddamned trailer in the middle of nowhere," said the woman.

"To hell you ain't," said the man.

"To hell with you!" said the woman jumping to her feet, "To hell with every word that comes out of your mouth, to hell with your nitwit plans and to hell with your fucking truck!" Her breath shot out in the cold like steam from a piston.

The boy was still laughing, the girl made staccato inhalations as she tried her best to stop crying. She didn't want to upset her mother any more than she already was.

"What's wrong with you? What Truck? I don't got the truck no more remember? We got the van now," said the man.

"You care more about those stupid boots than you care about us," said the woman. "Those fantastic boots, your incredible boots. We're not coming with you. We're not going to Alaska." She said this with such terminality the man could only stare in return.

All the man could do was gape, his face flashing with anger and confusion.

"We're... not...going... to... Alaska?" the little girl asked, trying to catch her breath.

"No honey we're not, we're going to stay at grandpa's house for a while," said the woman. "You can take the bus to your old school."

The woman had tripped the brakes and was furiously attempting to stop the crazy train once and for all. She had tried many times before. This time, and she didn't know why, her anger was different. The kids felt the lurching of their lives once again. The woman waited for the usual quick intervention of her guilt and her fear to take her strength away, to fold her back to submissiveness. She felt only fury. This time the bonds holding the boxcars to the crazy train burst.

The kids sensed their mother's new resolution. They were cautiously hopeful. The boy had wished for a life without his father. In every way he could he had eliminated him; at school when his friends talked about their dads he talked like he didn't have one. The girl clung to her mother, glaring at her father. She would shield her mother with her small body if it came to it. She had done it many times before, a buffer against her father's aggression. He never hit, but he would press hard in to her mother with his whole body, back her against the fridge or a corner and shout, his face shoved into hers. Too see her mother tremble with fear in these instances was too much for the little girl.

The woman felt the poignancy of the moment; she was older and wiser and she had learned one decision can turn life on a dime. No matter the speed of the train now she would take the tumble.

"You know I can't go to your old man's place, we just finished up with the restraining order," grunted the man.

"I know," said the woman. "Come kids, we're leaving."

Just as the mother duck had gathered up her ducklings the hostess arrived with the food.

"Everything alright?" the hostess asked, seeing the woman and the kids were readying to leave.

"We're leaving. Can you call us a cab please?" asked the woman.

"You haven't got any money," said the man, laughing.

"I can drive you anywhere you need to go," said the hostess. She plunked the food dishes down on the table without care. She put her arm around the woman. The woman, the hostess and the kids walked into the warmth of the restaurant.

"Hey!" yelled the man. "Hey! Hey!! You can't just walk out like this."

She's walking in, the hostess thought, you're the idiot standing out here in the cold...

"You good?" the manager asked the hostess who had returned from driving the woman and her kids.

"Ya I'm good," said the hostess. "I told her she could waitress here if she needed a job, hope that's ok?"

"That's fine," said the manager, pouring the hostess a cup of coffee.

"Well, he stiffed us on the bill."

"No surprise there," said the hostess.

"But he left you a tip," said the manager.

"Ya right, good one," said the hostess.

"Go have a look," said the manager, pointing towards the patio.

The hostess stepped out onto the winter patio and saw the man's fancy boots stiffened by the cold sitting next to his chair in the snow.

The Crooked Bank Robber

"Make your choice, adventurous Stranger,

Strike the bell and bide the danger,

Or wonder, till it drives you mad,

What would have followed if you had."

— C.S. Lewis, The Magician's Nephew

What follows is my experience ringing C.S. Lewis' miserable bell.

To start, my lawyer wants me to point out this does not intend to be a confession of any kind. What follows is strictly for entertainment

213

purposes only. I pay him a lot of money to tell me these kinds of things and I've learned to do as he suggests.

It began with me tuning into a podcast over the internet, one I'd listened to many times before. A program that ran quirky stories about quirky people, called 'This F'd Up Life of Mine'. To give you an idea what the program was like, one of the stories they had done in a past episode was about a teenage girl who somehow became Noriega's pen pal. She ended up going to visit him in Panama, but then the bastard kidnapped her, wouldn't let her go home, using their 'friendship' for photo ops and propaganda purposes. U.S. Marines had to extract her. Another was a story about a grandma who was responsible for getting her nine year old grandson and a few of his nine year old friends addicted to heroin. Of course she claimed it was all an innocent mistake.

This particular day's episode was about some guy known as the 'Potluck Bandit'. Here was a guy who broke into people's houses merely to eat. He would make himself a sandwich or microwave pizza pockets or make popcorn or barbecue steak, whatever happened to be in the fridge that day that struck his fancy. He never touched any valuables or stole anything. He even cleaned up after himself, scrubbing dishes and wiping down counters. Part of his M.O was sharing what he prepared with family pets if there were any.

This story got my attention not because of how weird it was, but because of the way the public had seemingly warmed up to this guy.

Although the show never actually interviewed the Potluck Bandit himself, they interviewed a lot of his victims. These people talked as if they were special for having their refrigerators raided by this guy. It set them apart from their neighbors, made them feel exclusive. Here was a common thief being talked about like he was some magical elf from the North Pole or folk hero, some modern day Robin Hood. It was the law of novelty in full effect - oddball, but harmless.

The podcast interviewed the detective assigned to the case and it was clear, even though it was now ten years later, he hadn't gotten over his frustration with the way the public and media had embraced someone he was trying to incarcerate. Then they played a recording of an interview the detective did at the time it was all happening. The detective's voice was surly: "Sure he only made a salad today, but who's stopping him from raping your daughter tomorrow."

The podcast host stopped the ten year old interview, "Those are pretty strong words," she said to the detective, "especially since in the end we know he didn't rape or harm anyone, he only ate food and fed pets."

"Ya, well what put me over the top," answered the detective defending his frustration at the time, "was when people started leaving food on their back porches enticing him to come by, even though clearly the guy had mental issues."

"I think after all this time a lot of people can understand your frustration," said the interviewer. "You being the detective in charge of the case at the time, what did you do about it - these people leaving food out?"

The detective hesitated before answering, "Myself and my fellow officers," he said sheepishly, "carried out a strategic plan to eat as much of the food as possible in an attempt to head off the bandit - so to speak."

"Seems a bit unorthodox," said the interviewer.

"Ya, well I personally gained ten pounds," said the detective, "But I don't believe in wasting food. We couldn't just throw it all away."

So I'm listening and the story went on. Turns out they caught the 'Potluck Bandit' and he was convicted and went to jail. The detective had since retired and apparently put himself on a diet. But that story stuck with me. It planted a seed in some dark orchard in my brain and it gestated there, soon to bare its bitter fruit.

While I was turning the Potluck Bandit's story over in my brain my own story took a lousy turn. I was one of those people hopelessly stuck in the wrong vocation. Why the hell I chose to be an Industrial Mechanic god only knows. It had something to do with not having a rudder on my ship and having said ship, which is of course a metaphor for my life, crash head-on into Shit Island. In other words I never chose anything in life, I fell into things. I fell into this Industrial Mechanics course and then into an apprenticeship and on to being a Journeyman. I found out after I had invested a lot of time and money and bought a shit load of expensive tools that I was absolutely no good at being an Industrial Mechanic, or being any kind of mechanic for that matter. I couldn't even fix my own bicycle when I was a kid. But, I was too far down that rabbit hole to consider doing anything else.

I'd worn out my welcome at most of the factories in town and now I was getting grief at my current job. I was taking it hard from the foreman and co-workers at the industrial plant I was working at about my performance. Finally one day the guy from the union came by and told me to take a walk with him. Seems I was costing the company money and they had enough shit on me to can my ass directly. It was just a matter of a little paperwork. But, he'd done me a favor and worked out a deal: if I got the hell out of the trade I could remain an employee if I'd take a position as late shift janitor. They'd even give me fair price for my tools. So that, as they say, was that. You can't be too particular about the kind of rope someone throws you when you're sinking in the shit.

The problem was the pay was naturally less. When I say less I mean a lot less. Every week the money screw turned and I felt its squeeze. As it says in the Bible somewhere: Out of want comes scams and schemes. Possibly I made that up, but it should say it in the Bible. Considering, it was my want for more money that brought all the thinking and scheming I'd done about the Potluck Bandit to the surface.

What stuck in my head about that story, I finally realized, was 'The Potluck Bandit' (whether he knew what he was doing or was simply a full on nut job) hit upon a few new twists to the age old craft of thievery: 1) the nature of his crime was novel, stealing only food. He didn't take anything of real value, which went a long way in keeping the masses from wanting his head on one of his own skewers. 2) He managed to get the sympathy of his victims, as well as the public, by cleaning up after himself and feeding dogs and cats and Chinchillas and whatever the hell else people had as pets in those days.

So just for fun (that's what I told myself anyway) I started thinking of other ways to reinvent thievery. The only part I didn't like about old Potluck's version was the not stealing anything valuable part. No point then, why go to jail for hotdogs and leftover spaghetti? Forget that.

I came up with a few half-baked and very ill advised ideas. To give you an understanding of my state of mind at the time, one of my plans was to break and enter and leave monopoly money in place of the things I'd steal. I would be known as the 'Monopoly Bandit' and people would admire the novelty of it and kind of hope I'd hit their house when they were at work or whatever and they could show all their friends the monopoly money I left. The colored paper would be a keepsake and they could tell their grandchildren about the 'Monopoly Bandit'. Proudly showing their little colored money mementos, saying: 'this is what was left the time your grandfather's Rolex was stolen. You know they never did catch the Monopoly Bandit. Oh to hell they didn't Grandma, they caught him buying fifteen Monopoly games at Wall Mart!

Then I had a really twisted idea that made me worry about my sanity altogether. It involved kidnapping a child, preferably a girl around 8 to 11 years old, and strapping a pretend bomb on her, but she wouldn't know it was pretend. I'd send her into a bank with a note: 'this is a robbery.... I have a bomb strapped to my body... a man has the remote...I'm terrified...please help me...put the money in the bag!" All the while I would be outside with the fake remote detonator. I know you think I'm evil even imagining this. It was the pressure I think. I'd gone nuts from the strain of losing an acceptable paycheck. I mean forget about the psychological damage it would do to the kid, I'd get it worse than her in the end. Kidnapping is felony- one, along with the bank robbing I'd go to prison for a hundred years! I realize now it was my subconscious nudging me in the direction of an ever evolving scheme, but at the time I believed I was ever so slowly losing my mind.

So for sanity sakes, I tried to forget everything about the Potluck bandit and anything to do with robbing or stealing. It was all just fantasizing anyway; at least that's what I told myself. I'd put my mind towards trying to be a reasonable janitor and looking for a second job.

Then I woke up one morning and there it was - what my subconscious had been working on since I'd first heard about the Potluck bandit, a scintillatingly brilliant scheme just sitting there in my head, complete and beautiful like a fine jewel. For days I tried to ignore it, but it kept twinkling at me from the corner of my psyche. Guardedly I started poking at the idea, refining a detail here, tweaking a concept there. I say guardedly, but once I started thinking about it I couldn't stop. It became an obsession. I made myself believe it was only fantasizing, nothing real, mere entertainment. I had (honestly at first) no intentions of carrying out such a thing; no matter how great it seemed or how sure I was I would be able to pull it off.

As bad fortune would have it my financial situation was headed more south than I initially thought. Every pay check I ended up $187.00 in the hole. That's $374.00 every month if you are counting. And I was counting. I tried everything I could to cut costs. I stopped driving, parked the car, bought baloney instead of steak and cancelled the cable because I'd sold the TV anyway. In general I made life not worth living and still the money hole kept devouring my future and wellbeing.

And then something snapped in my brain. It's hard to say why it finally happened. It's like I had been forever struggling to build a ladder to the moon and one morning I woke up and I had no idea why the hell I wanted to get to the moon in the first place. That's how it felt anyway – fuck the moon. I couldn't remember why anything was worth caring about. Maybe that's all a fancy way of saying I'd given up.

A nice thing happens when you actually, authentically give up (even though for me it was only temporary and came at the worst possible time): you stop resisting, stop fighting things. A lot of what

220

you thought was important shit, all the things you believed you were required to care about, instantly becomes meaningless. I didn't care anymore about my money hole or my job or what happened to me in the future. It was as though I'd lost all fear. And I figured my life was shit anyway. I couldn't really make it worse. What would be the harm in taking a chance, pushing a boundary here or there?

So I stopped pretending I didn't have a diamond mine of a scheme sitting, like a golden elephant, in my head. What the hell, I figured, if I'm going to slip out of this tight squeeze I better do some wriggling. If it worked even once there'd be enough money to pull me out of the hole and set me up so I could keep my head above water and live half decently again. Pull it off twice, and shit, I'd be laughing. Fail and I'd go to jail, but like I said I didn't seem to care what happened to me anymore (later I found out that is easy to say when you're not actually in jail).

Now, with the intent of genuinely carrying out my plan, I started going over and over it in my mind again. I'm sure, at this point, you are wondering what this great criminal master plan is, or more correctly, was. And how great could it have been if I got caught?

The idea was that I didn't need to kidnap a child, or anyone for that matter. I only needed to kidnap myself. I would be the kidnapper and the kidnapped. I would be the 'victim' with a bomb strapped to his body and the invisible perpetrator somewhere with the remote waiting to detonate if I didn't bring back a bag of cash to myself. The genius part of the plan was that if I got caught I could maintain that I had been kidnapped and I believed the bomb to be real. I would cooperate fully with the law to help bring the kidnapping, bomb strapping, foreigners (of course I would make them foreigners) to justice.

See what I mean the plan was pretty damn good, and simple which is the most important ingredient in the greatest plans. And to the best of my knowledge it was pretty damn original as well. I'd never heard of anything like it before or since. Although I'm sure now there will be copycats, people who will continue to push the envelope. But I was the first. I was the one who broke the 4 minute mile of bank robbing, the first in the underworld to bench press 500lbs so to speak. Now everyone will be doing it.

The plan was definitely simple, but daunting. I got to work dividing the operation into three tactical phases: 1) Planning and preparation. 2) Execution. 3) Asset management and security (or more correctly avoid getting caught).

As much as I thought I was beyond worrying about consequences I became jumpy once I'd decided I was going to actually do it. I kept telling myself there was no shame in backing out. Somehow I knew I was going to go through with it. Every cell in my body confirmed it as well. You know how some things you just know. I could visualize myself doing it, everything in minute detail, like I'd already done it. The planning and preparation was easy compared to the execution and avoiding getting caught phases. The first thing was to go to the bank and take out another credit card (my two existing cards were both maxed out). Funny how easy it is to get a credit card in this country, all you need is any sorry job and anything better than 'disaster' for a credit score. Anyway, I needed it to buy supplies I would need. Now don't think I was dumb enough to use the card directly. This is all pretty much 'crime 101' kind of stuff. I would take cash out on the card at local ATM machines. Not that I was buying anything outrageous like an Uzi, but I was worried about the things I'd need being traced back. You never know when you might make a simple mistake like dropping something, an article of clothing for example, a sweater say. The cops are smart these days; they can trace shit all the way back to where it was made (so inevitably right back to China). With cash there is no paper trail, no signatures. Cards present a risk. The cops might very well show up at the Gap or wherever and say 'We would like to talk to the staff about this sweater which was purchased here at this location sometime last month,' and the response would no doubt be 'nobody from last month still works here, sir.' The cops naturally question everyone, watch security video and check the records, they always check records. If you paid with debit or a credit card for the sweater bingo there's a record. But, cash means no paper trails, no records.

The next thing in my preparations was to find a safe house. Somewhere I could go after the heist, lie low for a few days, or disappear fast if I felt the cops were hot on my trail. It was easy to find one. This city is crawling with slum lords with disgusting, vile places for rent for a couple hundred bucks a month, all on the sly. I also needed a stash for the anticipated loot I'd bring in. Crime 101 again:

you never want to get caught with loads of cash on you. A suitable stash spot was harder to find. I found some reasonable places, but I couldn't help but imagine some bum or kid getting lucky and making off with my hard earned cash. I finally settled for a broken pipe in the condemned building next door to the safe house I had rented.

Next, for part of the evasion aspect of the plan, I bought some rope and duct tape at the local hardware store. The kid behind the counter asked if I wanted to sign up for their credit card and get a discount. I told him I only use cash. 'What's wrong, don't want to leave a paper trail?' the kid said, smirking. I know he was joking but it unnerved me.

Back at the safe house I made the rope into a loop that I could slip on over my feet and cinch up tight. I did the same with a stretch of duct tape, making a loop with enough room to just get my hands through and back out. The tricky part was the back out. I practiced hog tying myself repeatedly until I could do it in less than forty seconds. First slapping a strip of duct tape across my mouth, next cinching the rope around my feet and lastly my hands duct taped behind my back. I'd practiced screaming through the duct tape and the 'thank god you found me officer' speech until I couldn't keep from laughing and adding stupid stuff like: 'all this duct tape reminds me of the last time I saw your wife officer'. I could joke then, but I wouldn't be joking if I had to do it for real. It would mean the police were coming for me. I'd have to carry out the ruse of being a victim in the whole thing, forced against my will to participate in a crime I could never commit on my own initiative. I hoped it wouldn't come to that. It was the weakest part of my plan. I was doubtful my victim story would seem plausible for very long, although I had worked it out extensively. Cops have a way of getting to the bottom of things; it's their job, they can afford to be patient.

I didn't let myself worry too much. I stayed focused and active, going over every detail, rehearsing where I could. I'd take the subway to point A, then a bus to point B, changing clothes and discarding old garb in trash (didn't actually do this part in rehearsals –not rich yet), taking subway back to point A to throw off any followers, then a different bus to point C, then the subway to near safe house, then long zig zag walk home. I did the whole routine on my days off, twice in the morning - quick nap, lunch and one more time in the late afternoon. It pains me to wonder why I didn't put this much effort into trying to be a good mechanic. Not much art of craft for me in being a mechanic I guess.

I'd prepared as much as I could, even got to the point of over preparing. I didn't care. I wasn't going to fall into the trap of being over confident and cause myself to get complacent. I put a big red x on the following Wednesday on the calendar in my mind (real calendars with x's on them are evidence). When Monday came I called in sick at work. I did it kind of huffy like, out of breath and talking like I was possibly under duress. I said I'd be off at least a couple of days. I don't think the bitch of a receptionist gave a damn! All I got was a couple of 'ya's' and the smacking of her chewing gum.

I slept at the safe house Monday night amidst the background of constant sirens. Tuesday morning I got my hair buzzed as close as I could get without technically being bald. Then I hung out all day back at the safe house, relaxing amongst the sirens and cockroaches. It was a shithole nestled in the shithole part of town but it fit the plan perfectly.

Tuesday night came and I slept adequately. I wasn't nervous because I had done my homework: dotted every i and crossed every t. I made sure I triple checked everything twice. It was, as they say, go time.

I woke at 4:37 am, two hours before the alarm. It took a while to figure out where the hell I was and what day it was. I laid there for a moment in the dark with my eyes open. Then I remembered. Suddenly, I felt frantic energy surge through my nerves and form into a vortex in the pit of my stomach. It was the first time I felt uneasy about my plan in weeks. My nervousness grew into hysteria. Abort! - I thought – I must be fucking nuts! I closed my eyes and took deep breaths. Soon it came back to me: the meaninglessness my life held in its current form and the fact if I didn't do something about it, it would only get worse. The plan was solid, even a little genius. It would be a gigantic waste not to give it a try.

"Fuck them all!" I yelled to the stained ceiling. I regained my nerve. Somewhere a siren wailed.

I got up and took a cold shower. The horrid state of the bathroom - rusted tub, mold and filth - reinforced my resolve for action. What was the worst that could happen? I could go to prison, which, without exaggeration, I thought could be an improvement over my current situation.

I got dressed and walked the few blocks to the Denny's. I had the Grand Slam breakfast along with four cups of coffee; I would need the reserve of energy only a hearty breakfast could provide. As I walked back, the streetlights turned themselves off; the city was filling with morning light.

Back at the safe house I began my preparations. I changed into the two sets of clothes that I had laid out ahead of time. First the pants: jeans with belt worn over a light sport pant with draw string. Then two t-shirts: bright yellow over beige. I put on the attention drawing red tennis shoes and stuffed the non-conspicuous black hi-tops in a back pack. Over the t-shirts I put on the bomb vest which I had spent a fair bit of money and time making look authentic. On top of all of that came the reversible overcoat. Next I put on one of the wigs I had purchased. They were all long hair wigs which I tied in a ponytail. Over that I wore a baseball cap on backwards. I looked legitimately seedy after I added the black frame glasses. I stood in front of the cracked mirror and examined myself. My goal was to provide almost a cartoon character which was easy to remember and therefore easy to describe to the police. Judging by the mirror, I had undoubtedly succeeded. I left the safe house and took the subway to point A.

The financial district was beginning to bustle. I grabbed a cup of coffee and pretended to read a paper across the street from the target bank.

At my last gulp of coffee I felt a gritty resolve come over me. I threw the paper and the styrofoam cup into the bin on the corner and dogged it across the street towards the bank. I took deep breathes as I walked up the concrete steps and through the heavy brass and glass doors. I blocked out all thinking and strode right up to the first teller on the left. There were only two early bird customers occupying the teller windows to my right.

"How can I help you today?" said the teller yawning, a women in her late forties. "Oh excuse me," pardoning herself for the yawn. Then she must have sensed something strange in my appearance or movements as she suddenly looked at me uncertainly.

"Yes....well...you could probably save my life today," I said. She jumped in alarm. "Listen," I said, "for god sakes they'll kill us all." I opened my overcoat revealing the vest of wires and white blocks stuffed into eight specialized pockets all connecting up to a cell phone that was clipped to the center.

"..a..bomb?" the woman asked, warily. Her eyes were the size of garbage can lids.

"Yes," I said, "and a big one. There are people out there with a remote detonator." I could feel beads of sweat dripping down my face, which made my act all the more convincing. "They're expecting me to walk out of here and hand them this bag full of money." I handed her a yellow, plastic shopping bag.

"How much should I put in it?" the lady asked. She was trembling now.

"Whatever you think my life is worth," I said. She started putting bundles of cash from a lower drawer into the bag. "And for the love of god no dye pack or they'll kill me!" I said it as a precaution, because I was watching and was sure she hadn't put one in, but sure enough she removed one from the bag.

"Here," she said handing me the bag.

"Thanks," I said. "Now if you hear a loud explosion in the next ten minutes or so please pray for my soul." She swallowed hard. "Please, I beg of you no alarms. I don't want to die. I have six kids." I said. She slowly put both hands flat on her desk and nodded.

"May God be with you," she said. The words sounded strange and mocking coming from this particular woman.

I turned and walked towards the door. The security guard moved to meet me. I was ready to throw back my overcoat and display the bomb, but he simply opened the door for me. Seemingly lost in his own myriad of life's problems and without looking at me he said flatly, mechanically, "Have a pleasant day sir."

I took the bus to point B and trying to act as casual as possible despite the fact that I was dazed with panic. I got off the bus and walked into a large shopping center. In a stall in the public washroom, as rehearsed, I removed my top pants and top t-shirt and changed my shoes. The cap, wig and glasses came off as well. Everything went into the empty backpack, which I left on the floor near the trash container. Knowing someone would steal it within minutes. This would virtually erase the evidence. Who would hand over clothes from a back pack if you stole the back pack in the first place? Lastly I reversed the overcoat. I still had the bomb vest as it was my only leverage if the cops caught me. I would maintain that I was scared to death about having a bomb strapped to my chest, that I was a pawn in some unknown criminal syndicate's game. If or when the cops finally discovered the bomb was a fake I would act all relieved as if I really hadn't known. I would also maintain that I was ordered, under the threat of death, to do all the activities up to that point – starting with renting the safe house, etc. But, as I reminded myself, the goal was not to get caught.

Now, as I had rehearsed, I took the subway back to point A-which was near the bank. On the street there was chaos. I asked a guy what was going on.

"Something about a bomb at a bank," he said, "they have the whole area blocked off."

"Hmm," I said, as casually as I could, but my stomach was doing back flips. Then I suddenly realized a massive error in my plan. How the hell could I have missed it?! I was carrying the bright yellow plastic bag from 'The Phone Mart' full of cash right out in the open. Jesus could I have picked a more conspicuous bag! It was quite conceivable that the lady from the bank could raise the alarm over such a bright recognizable bag if she spotted it. She could be anywhere in the crowd. I'm sure she had given that detail to the police with her description. I folded it and tucked it under my arm. I high- tailed it to the bus stop to catch a bus back to the subway station, as rehearsed. On the bus I realized it was better to just carry the bag full of cash folded under my arm rather than try to hide it under my overcoat as that looked completely suspicious. I took the subway to the station nearest the safe house. Then I walked the rest of the way in a crisscrossing pattern, being sure I wasn't followed. All as I'd practiced.

Once at the cache I pushed the bag of cash and the bomb vest as far up the large pipe as I could then hurried to the safe house where I needed to empty my bowels. I was a nervous wreck. I could hear dozens of distant sirens that all seemed to be getting louder, heading in my direction. I had a sickening feeling the entire city was in an uproar over what I had done, that every cop in the state was coming for me. I imagined Taser spikes hitting my chest and volts upon volts running through my body, my head caved in with batons, bullets shattering my spine and exploding my spleen.

Trembling, my legs weak, I pulled myself up off the toilet with the help of the sink. Then I labored to hog tie myself, fumbling as if the hours I had spent practicing were only a dream. What seemed an eternity later I finally lay quivering on the grimy floor with a strip of duct tape over my mouth until, utterly exhausted, I fell asleep to the sound of sirens that I was sure were for me.

Just after 6 p.m. I woke again wondering where the hell I was for a brief, calm moment. I like these moments because it's as though I'd fallen through a crack in the world, like I didn't exist. When you don't remember who you are for 30 or 40 seconds you don't own your problems for 30 or 40 seconds either; and that's a good feeling. Then everything came back and I had to stay down there for a while to let the reality of what I'd done sink in. A sense of foreboding came over me almost immediately I regretted what I'd done. If I could have gone back and undone everything I would have, but the bell had been tolled.

My hunger finally drove me off the floor and out of the duct tape and gag. I walked down to a nearby burger joint I'd been eating at while I stayed at the safe house. The place seemed half assed clean and friendly. A lot of my jitters had gone, but I still expected to be jumped any minute by S.W.A.T. - flash grenades and Tasers and all that lovely stuff. To my amazement I made it to the diner without being tackled and hand cuffed. "What's the news," I said, as I sat at my regular place at the counter and ordered my usual cheeseburger, fries and coke, trying to act as if I weren't a boiling stew of nerves.

"News?" the cook said.

"Ya," I said, "some trouble at a bank I thought I heard."

"Oh you mean that bomb thing. That's old news. The latest is some crazy fuck is running around the subway whacking people with a hatchet."

To hear that made me feel immensely better (twisted I know). "No shit," I said.

"By tomorrow even that'll be old news," said the cook, "something worse will come along ... always does."

What he said was true and it made me feel better. Outside, a cop car screamed past and finally I let myself believe the sirens weren't for me. I was going to be alright. I ate my cheeseburger in relative calm, while the cook and I talked about all the nut jobs in the city.

The next day I went back to my apartment in the suburbs. I called into work and told them I was feeling better and I'd be into work on Monday. I had to tell the receptionist twice who I was. How nice I thought, they didn't give a rats ass about my whereabouts or if I was sick or dead or worse. That got me finally appreciating my situation again and what I'd done. By the time I'd hung up the phone I'd stopped regretting the bank job.

The weekend was rough. I was broke as hell. I thought of all that money at the stash as I ate dehydrated soup from a coffee cup and boiled potatoes. But, I didn't dare touch the stash money, not yet. On Monday I went into work. Nothing had changed. The security guard didn't even look up at me from his guard house as he pushed the button to open the gate. In the hallway outside the changing room I saw the Russian lady who cleaned the offices. She and I had never bothered to get each other's name or for that matter spoken to each other. I doubted she spoke English. She looked at me and started shaking her head and waving her finger accusingly. It scared the shit out of me. Had she put the timing of my absence together with the incident at the bank? Did she know? How the hell could she know anything? Then she pointed to her own head and then to my head. Shaking her head saying "No no no." I realized she disapproved of my new buzz cut. Jesus, I thought, I've got to get a hold of myself.

"Ya, well it will grow back," I said.

"No no no," she said followed by something that sounded ridiculing in Russian.

"Maybe when I go get my stash I'll buy you a mink coat," I said sarcastically. Not understanding a word of English she simply looked at me with confused disdain.

"Bitch," I added. This she seemed to understand.

234

I spent the next few days looking for anything in the paper about my handy work. There wasn't much. The gist of the few measly articles I'd found was that it was an ongoing investigation with no leads. This I didn't entirely believe. I think the cops often say that when they don't want suspects knowing they are hot on the trail, hoping they'll drop their guard. This thought got me wondering about my own guard? Was it up or down? I couldn't tell.

Later in the week, when I got my pay check and seen how dismal it was from missing all those days and having limited sick benefits, I knew it was time to retrieve the money.

Taking public transit with a bag full of stolen cash is hard on the nerves I can attest to that, especially when there is only a thin film of plastic insulating the truth from the whole world. Finally back in my apartment I had to take a few moments to compose myself with some deep breaths. Once I stopped sweating I opened the bag and counted the money: $67 609.00. That bitch! I thought. That was all my life was worth to a goddam bank teller?! After lamenting for a few minutes about how society had broken down to the point where a man's life wasn't even worth seventy grand anymore. I cooled myself by thinking of all the ways even this humble amount could get me off the treadmill to Shitsville.

I started buying as many things as I could with cash. All food items from groceries to fast food were purchased with cash. I got the car back on the road again and paid the entire years insurance in one shot. 'That's a lot of cash' the insurance woman said, 'I sold my boat' was my answer, 'I see,' she said. I sold my boat or my motorcycle was my answer to anyone suspicious of raw cash. Sometimes when I went to the bank to put a wad down on what I owed the credit cards the bank teller would raise an eye brow, but the sale of my 'boat' was enough to pacify suspicions. I started to realize cold hard cash had long gone out of style.

I sold a lot of boats and motorcycles, if you get my meaning, and bought a lot of real stuff: some nice but, well used furniture, new HD TV, awesome sound system, some cool duds, really expensive Spanish cowboy boots and a bit of bling - namely a really beautiful Swiss watch, but nothing that would attract any real attention, like an expensive car (not that my haul was large enough anyway). A janitor that drives a fancy car raises a lot of red flags. I bought nothing any idiot couldn't get on credit. I got my parents roof fixed and gave my sister five grand for my nieces college fund. At a family dinner they tried to pull an intervention and asked me if I had started selling drugs. 'No no,' I said, 'I sold my boat.' 'Ah', they said, their suspicions eased even though I had never previously mentioned owning a boat.

My booty had dwindled considerably as I was quite aware it would, but I was better set up and could now live a meager yet semi-comfortable life with my janitorial wages. I'd have to stop eating out and buying fancy duds, but life was reasonable again, for a while at least.

So why did I start thinking of putting my hand back into the cookie jar? At first it was just fantasy as before. Thinking of ways I could do it better and imagining how well I could live with a wad of cash now that my debts were paid off. I could pace myself and make the money last a hell of a lot longer. I struggled with myself over the idea, going back and forth between the pros and cons. The pros eventually won. Then I realized that deep down inside I had intended to go back all along. Why had I hung on to the safe house? Why did I still have the bomb vest?

I waited seven weeks and then the time felt right. Preparations were simpler this go around. I bought a new back pack, set of spare clothes and put together a new disguise. This time I had curly red hair and wore a sun visor. I kept the glasses and added a convincing beer gut using foam as padding. I called in sick at work again, eliminating the melodramatics as no one there seemed to give a shit one way or another.

I went back to the stash and retrieved the bomb vest. After not seeing it for a while I had to stop and admired my work; it looked convincing as hell. If someone had found it they would have cordoned off ten city blocks and got the bomb squad in with their robots to deal with it. I spent that night at the safe house and this time I slept relatively soundly, the sirens serenading me.

I got up early the next morning. Part of my plan was to hit the bank early in the morning for the simple reason that the cops are in the middle of changing shifts and this puts them at a slight disadvantage. Of course traffic is also still chaotic from the early rush and a lot of people haven't had their second cup of coffee yet; this all adds up to give a slight edge to a guy like me who wants to get in and out and then disappear.

I stood across the street from the bank until I saw the security guard open the doors. By the time I crossed and entered two other people had beat me inside, which was fine because for some reason it calmed my nerves to have at least a few other customers inside. I zig zagged my way through the empty rope maze. The fella at the open teller window waved me over.

"Good Morning," I said, almost forgetting to look worried.

"Good morning sir. How can I help you?" The man said flatly. I guessed he hadn't had his second cup of coffee.

"Listen," I said, "please remain calm." I opened my coat and showed him the bomb vest. "Some very cruel and unscrupulous men have strapped a bomb to my chest. I don't want to die today, do you?"

His face was disturbingly calm. He stared at me for what seemed to be an ice age. Slowly, with his eyes locked on mine, he started to move his hand under the counter.

"Stop!" I said. "Maybe you don't quite get the situation here. There is enough Semtex strapped to my body to destroy the whole city block. I don't have the remote, someone who is a safe distance from the bomb blast does. Pushing that alarm button under there is not going to get anyone anything but dead." He remained fish eyed and motionless. Jesus Christ! I've picked a bloody suicidal maniac for a bank teller, I thought.

"Ok," he said finally, "what do you require?"

I handed him a plain, beige generic shopping bag and told him to fill it. I also gave him the warning about what an exploding dye pack would mean to the people in and around the bank when the Semtex went off shortly thereafter. He returned the shopping bag full of money.

"Now if you are a praying man," I said, "please pray that I get out of this in one piece (the humor of that line was not lost on me). I have four young children and I'd like to see them again."

"Just go," he said pointing to the door - so much for sympathy and compassion from a fellow human being.

I turned and as I walked towards the door I noticed the security guard approaching, looking suspicious. I was a second away from opening my vest and giving him the bomb spiel when the bank teller shouted, "He's fine, he's fine let him by!" The security guard's body stopped, but his eyes continued following me. I beat it for the door; I knew the bastard behind the counter would hit the silent alarm as soon as I got outside. I didn't stick around to find out.

My escape plan was the same except for one detail: I didn't circle all the way back to the crime zone as I did last time. Reviewing everything from the first time I realized this was an unnecessary risk and instead of throwing off the police, which was my initial reasoning, it could actually get me caught. For instance someone from the bank may recognize some nuance about me that went beyond any disguise, like the way I walked. More likely a police dog tracking my sent might by chance get near me. With or without a disguise I still smell like me. The dog would have no problem pointing this out to its handler. Besides, I would be laying down another fresh sent for a dog to follow by showing up too near the crime scene again.

I went to the mall, changed, discarded the disguise and went straight to the safe house. I stashed the bag of cash and bomb vest in the pipe and then took a long hot shower. To distract myself I spent the rest of the afternoon attempting to clean the place. When I finished I couldn't detect much difference. Maybe a wrecking ball was needed for this kind of clean up. I went to the burger joint for diner, wanting to watch the evening news while I ate. To my surprise it wasn't even one of the lead stories; it was the fifth or sixth story, I'd lost count. It came after a long block of advertising.

"...police are reluctant to link today's brazen bank robbery with a similar incident a few weeks ago. In both cases a man with a bomb strapped to his body claiming to be there against his will demanded that a shopping bag be filled with money. In both cases the man with the bomb declared someone with a remote detonator would explode the bomb if his orders were not carried out. Police are denying that there is a general threat to the public and urged anyone being approached by a man wearing a bomb strapped to his chest to cooperate fully…"

No shit, I thought, yes cooperate fully. Immediately following the story there was a brief weather update and the cheeky son- of-a- bitch weatherman says: "Really, against his will…isn't it what they all say." The cook, who was bringing me my coke, chuckled. Fucking weather people, I thought, always the smart asses.

I finished my lunch and went back to the safe house. There was one close call where a multitude of sirens howled up and stopped somewhere very nearby. Panicking, I grabbed the duct tape ready to gag myself and waited, sweat dripping down my face. I waited twenty minutes when it appeared I was in the clear. Then more sirens wailed by. Screw this, I thought, I can't take these sirens another minute. I took the bus back to my apartment in the suburbs.

I went to work on Monday evening and everything was as usual. I decided not to wait a week to retrieve the money this time. I went the following day. I spent an hour walking around the stash, casing it, making sure the cops didn't have it staked out. I went in quickly and grabbed the money, making sure the vest was as concealed as possible. I took transit home. A man, dressed in a square three piece suit and really playing up that he was something special, sat beside me on one of the busses. He was one of these haughty, look-at-me types, which is foolish when you have to take public transit. I had a strong impulse to say: "Hey, can you guess what's in my shopping bag and then open it just enough to for him to have a peak at the bundle of cash. That would be stupid of course, so I settled for telling him that I hoped he made it to the suit rentals before they closed or they might charge him an extra day. To this he first looked stunned then settled into embarrassed anger. Walking from the bus stop to my apartment with a bag of cash under my coat made me feel it was all worthwhile. I dare say I even felt a bit of pride.

'All that cash' turned out to be $211 000.00. I was stunned. I expected half that amount or less. This put me in a very nice financial position to say the least. If I were to spend a thousand dollars a month, which would make life very comfortable, it would last more than seventeen and a half years.

So why did I immediately start thinking of going back for a third time.

I'm no psychologist and I don't pretend to be. I can only make guesses as to why I felt the need to hit another bank; it wasn't the money, I was never the type that needed a shit load of money. Maybe my life in contrast seemed a bit too dull when I wasn't robbing banks. I actually enjoyed being a janitor. I never missed a day of work except to rob banks. I did my work with earphones in, music playing. As long as the urinals were clean I answered to nobody. The day to day tug-o-war with work when I was a mechanic was gone and the extra cash from the heists made it all the more easy. So it is possible I was just plain bored and needed the excitement. At the deepest level, I honestly think I was simply proud of my plan and how well my strategies were working. I felt ownership in the detail and preparation of my 'enterprise'. If only I had felt satisfied enough with what I'd already accomplished- if only... if only.

Everything was basically the same as the time before. The only thing different was my mustache gimmick. I had tried various fake mustaches and beards and they looked overwhelming phony. I discovered that I could grow a mustache and shave it off with a beard trimmer in not more than 40 seconds. Sure it wasn't the best shave but it was enough to thwart any witnesses' description coming over an all-points bulletin. I'd go into the washroom at the mall with a mustache and the rest of my disguise and come out without one. I practiced this a few times by growing a mustache, which took about two weeks for a convincing one. Then I clipped it off with the trimmer as fast as I could. I got plenty of disapproving finger shakes from the Russian cleaning lady. Apparently she didn't like mustaches.

Other than the mustache the sequence was pretty much the same. This time I would be sure to act more frightened. The last time I was a bit too cavalier with the teller, I needed more of a reaction similar to the first teller. I needed to generate as much sympathy as possible; this was an essential part of the whole scheme. So if possible I would try to approach a female teller.

I went with 'laid back contractor type' for a disguise: blonde wig under a Yankees baseball cap, fake belly and black rim glasses. The mustache was four weeks in, so it was somewhat bushy, something that would be noticed and included in a description to police.

I called into work, but this time I didn't pretend to be ill. I was to take care of my sick mother. Some part of me knew I'd eventually be going for number four and five and possible more, so I wanted to root out and break up any patterns that might invite suspicion. I rented a different 'safe house', very close to the old one, but on a different block.

When the day came I awoke early, had a big breakfast, and then took public transit to the financial district. I had chosen a bank a fair distance from the previous banks. I didn't want to be predictable in anyway. I stood across the street as usual until the security guard opened up. There were a few customers already waiting at the doors. Half the teller windows were occupied. I had to settle for the dark haired, dark complexioned young lady who was smiling at me, her first customer of the day. I noticed her name tag said Noor.

"Good morning sir," she said. She must have read my body language because her smile quickly faded as I approached.

"I need your help Noor," I said with as much tension and fear in my voice as I could manage. "My life and yours and everyone's in this bank is, this very minute, hanging in the balance. I need you to remain calm or we are all going to die." I showed her the bomb strapped to my chest.

"No, no …oh no," she whispered. She looked absolutely terrified, so much so that I wished I'd picked a different teller. I thought this might be too much on the poor girl, she might become unpredictable.

"Everything will be fine ….Noor are you listening? I said. She seemed frozen and possibly about to faint.

"Noor?!"

"Yes," she whispered, her enormous, fearful brown eyes fixated on the bomb.

"Everything will be just fine if you do as I say. They won't explode the bomb if they get their money. Now please fill this plastic bag with as much money as you can and no dye packs. Act easy and natural, we don't want to alert anyone in the bank who will press the alarm button," I said. She finally looked at me and I gave her a half re-assuring smile. Her demeanor suddenly changed. She began to study me. I actually felt her eyes infiltrate my disguise. A wave of panic swept up my spine…

"You're faking," Noor said, almost vacantly.

I felt sick. My legs began to tremble.

"Listen, fill the bag please, before they level this building," I said. "This is taking too long."

"You're a bloody, fucking faker," she shouted throwing the bag back at me.

It was my turn to have enormous, fearful eyes. I turned quickly and noticed everyone in the bank staring. I walked quickly towards the door. The security guard and another man, probably the bank manager, headed me off and stood in front me in the middle of the large, marble lobby. The security guard had his hand extended, palm out motioning me to stop.

"What seems to be the problem here sir," he said, forcefully.

I had no other choice but to open my coat and show them the bomb. Fear enveloped their faces.

"Now, now," the manager said, "let's not do anything crazy." His hands were moving up and down, motioning me to stay calm.

"The only crazy thing happening right now is you guys blocking me from leaving," I said, "I don't have the remote for this bloody thing and I also don't have a bag of money and that is going to make the people who do have the remote very angry. If they think the robbery is a bust they'd rather detonate than leave any evidence."

Both men's eyes grew huge with fear over something happening directly behind me.

"No don't!" the security guard screamed.

I was about to turn to see what the hell was happening when I felt a hard, sharp blow on the back of my head. I hit the floor like dead weight and the last thing I remember was Noor standing over me with an old cast iron three- hole paper punch.

I wasn't out for very long. There was pandemonium all around me. Noor was still standing over me; another woman was screaming her head off close by. I was trying to get to my feet the way a boxer does after he's been hit with a knockout blow – but there was no referee to wave the match over. I needed to get the hell out of there. Everything had gone black and white and grey. There was a large pool of what looked like black oil on the marble floor. I realized through my haze it was my blood. It startled me how large the puddle was. Somewhere in the back of my mind the Pot-Luck-Bandit was saying: 'Sir, I don't approve of your technique'. I put my hand to the back of my head and I felt it oozing through the fibers of the wig. With one awkward sweep I pulled off the wig and baseball cap.

"Everybody out!" Someone was yelling, "We have a bomb situation, everybody out!"

"It's not a real bomb!" Noor was yelling, "He's a fake!"

I had lost vision completely in my right eye now and there was a strange tingling in my legs. I felt at the wound in the back of my head. There was a large flap of my scalp detached from my skull, this I could easily feel, and when my fingers touched, where my skull should have been, I felt a strange and powerful tingle go down my spine. Christ! I'm dying, I thought.

"Someone else has the remote," a man's voice yelled, "We're all in danger. Now let's move it!"

Then it struck me: I needed immediate medical attention and that was not likely to happen with a bomb strapped to my chest. I'd assumed I'd probably bleed to death or die from blunt trauma to the brain before anyone would get within two city blocks of me.

"She's right," I yelled as loudly as I could. I noticed my speech was waning and the bank walls appeared askew. "It's a fake...It's a fake...there is no remote...now for Christ sakes call an ambulance!" I said, fumbling to get the vest off and ripping the wires out of the fake receiver. "It's fake," I screamed again, "please get me to a fucking hospital."

"You used a fake bomb to scare the shit out of everyone," said the woman who had been screaming, "Just so you could rob the bank. Ooh... that's crooked!"

I looked up at Noor. "How did you know?" I asked.

"Because I've had a real bomb strapped to my chest," she said.

If only I had picked a different teller, a different bank...if only...if only.

I passed out.

My lawyer was laughing. "You see," he said, "this is where your story becomes implausible."

We were watching the bank's security video, again. The lawyer seemed to enjoy it. I could hardly stomach it: Noor nearly jumping off the ground when she lambasted me with the hole punch, blood everywhere - my blood - and me stumbling in it, that stupid cow screaming and screaming.

"The part where you ripped out the wires and threw off the bomb vest, screaming, admitting it was a fake, that's the part that makes your story implausible," he says, for the two hundredth time.

"If I were you," he said, "I'd forget your story and plead guilty. We can negotiate a lower sentence. I'll make a special appeal noting your decision to come clean, saving the taxpayers a lot of expense and resources; saving the police a search for kidnappers and bomb makers that don't exist."

So that's what I did: I pleaded guilty. With good behavior I'll be out in seven years. The Judge said the only thing that kept me from a twenty five year sentence was essentially I had no weapon and that in reality no one could have been injured. I guess he didn't count my concussion and the twenty five staples it took to put my skull back together.

I'm doing alright in prison. I help out with the maintenance and sanitation where I can and keep my nose clean. This afternoon a couple of guards came to tell me some media people were here to interview me. I met them in the visitation room. Two guys came in, one with some recording equipment. "Hi," the other one said, "we're with an internet podcast show called 'This F'd Up Life of Mine'. We'd like to do a story on you."

Still the bell tolls.

The Scarf

By the end of the party I was blunderingly drunk and angry as hell. The result of nearly trading away my soul. I guess there's a new low waiting around every corner if you don't watch yourself.

I arrived at the party with anticipations of hooking up with a girl named Katya, whom I'd met two days before. I know the name sounds Russian or something, but she was definitely American. My friend said she was originally from California, which might explain a lot. Anyway, we ran into her at a sandwich shop uptown. My friend and Katya were old acquaintances. While eating a vegan sandwich Katya explained she recently graduated from University with a Masters in literature. The literature part tweaked my interest. She informed us she was burned out and was taking the summer to let loose. She invited us to a party in the Village. It seemed a friendly gesture so I took the opportunity to confess I was a poet and wondered if she would like to hear one or two of my poems and give her Masters in literature, opinion. By the end of my little spiel I was doing a self-conscious shuffle. My friend eyed me suspiciously, which made me even more self-conscious. There was something about Katya that made me nervous.

'Sure,' she said. She had finished her sandwich and was trotting off in a hurry, "bring them to the party."

I was shocked when my friend told me he and Katya had dated a few years back.

"Not for very long," he said, "she's a narcissist."

"I think she's hot as hell," I said.

"Ya, you made that pretty obvious," my friend snickered.

I couldn't get her out of my mind. I kept imagining hooking up with her at the party. I picked out the poems I wanted to read her. When the evening of the party had arrived I selected a folky knitted scarf and looped it, beatnik style, around my neck. I wanted to play up the role of the dark, brooding artist. I'd selected what I thought were my most philosophical and weighty poems, the ones I hoped would appeal to someone just out of a literature program.

'Seriously dude?' My friend said, looking woefully at the scarf as we left for the village.

"I can't just show up in a bloody t-shirt," I said, "not with a girl like Katya."

"What's wrong with dressing like yourself?" my friend asked. "She's not worth it, I'm telling you."

Soon we were sitting in lawn chairs at a courtyard party in Greenwich Village. Katya was sitting so close her boozy breath infiltrated my nostrils. It mixed with the perfume she'd sprayed with abandon across her half bare and bra-less chest. I liked it. The mixture of smells I mean. I had slammed back a few Long Island Ice teas myself- to bolster my nerves. The DJ was playing Miles Davis, alternating with Bob Marley and it was a nice fit for a Saturday evening in late August.

Now, many drinks into the party, I shifted nervously in my lawn chair, the scarf making itchy red welts on my neck, while Katya breathed her boozy breath on me and talked about herself. I brought out my poems. I tried to channel my personal heroes: Charles Bukowski and James Joyce, hoping this would, at the last minute, give me some aplomb; it did not. I noticed my hand was shaking as I held the papers. I suddenly became severely aware that I had never read my poetry to a real person before, only my mother and a few friends who knew I wouldn't take criticism well, even though I'd assured them I wanted their honest opinions. So like shoving off across dark seas in a boat that had never known water, I launched into my poem.

Do we move towards death?

Or does death move towards us?

"Ah…see, to me…it's a bad start," Katya said, immediately.

"Wait, are you going to go line by line?" I asked, "I'd thought I'd finish and then…," I was half yelling because I was drunk and nervous and because the music had got very loud.

"Line by line," she shouted back. "There's gonna be too much for me to remember if I wait 'til the end I can just tell."

"You don't like it already?" I sulked. It wasn't quite the response I had expected and what did she mean - 'there's gonna be too much' ?

"In a way it's total bullshit," she said, "because death is only the byproduct of aging, the replication of our cells breaking down.

You've personified death and I don't like that. I hate poetic bullshit like that."

I could tell she was drunk. "Well, this is a poem," I said, a bit red in the face. Her eyes disengaged mine and scanned the party.

If I hadn't wanted her so badly, I would have stopped everything right there, grabbed another drink, been polite and moved on. But I'd always felt my poetry had the potential to be my thing when it came to women. I'd even had sex dreams wherein I'd read my poetry at some point during the process. I imagined Katya opening like a flower for me, captivated by the acumen of my words. Besides, Kurt Vonnegut had said he never met a writer who didn't have a hot wife. His definition of writer, I was certain, included poets. I didn't stop everything... I went on:

In the depths of my fearful heart

Would I or should I make a fuss

If death, wearing a mask of my shame

Dumps its heathen water or' my flame

She started to laugh. "Dude that's fucked up," she said, "You don't know how to say what you really mean do you? Put it in a way I can see it. If I can't visualize it then it is meaningless to me. If you're afraid of death just tell me. "

"Like… tell you now, or like… in the poem?" I said.

"What?" she said.

"The thing about telling you - you just said." I said.

We were both drunk and the party was very loud. A little awkwardness and miscommunication was alright, I told myself.

Katya sat looking bugged by our exchange and it was clear to me I was in love with her. The alcohol in my blood served to consolidate this.

Katya's face wasn't beautiful in the classic sense. Possibly a line askew somewhere. If you isolated and analyzed her individual features they were less than exceptional, but together, in sum, it all added up gorgeously. Her body was ravishing and hard, steeped in feminine muscularity, the type that makes men's subconscious procreation indicators go off the charts. The molecules of her skin had obviously aligned themselves in a pattern of extraordinary, tanned perfection. From the contours of her jutting, intoxicating collar bones, her skin shone like a beacon of health and sexuality. It reminded me somehow of soft creamy chocolate and it served as counter point to her sleek muscular frame. A half unbuttoned blouse revealed breasts, slightly less than a handful, but sculpted as if by Michelangelo himself. Glimpses of her cuspate nipples were like little rewards for peaking partygoers all evening. Everyone at the party, including women, had been checking her out all evening. Katya wore extremely tight jeans, which for some reason didn't make her look slutty, only more elegant.

I continued reading:

Thus, I wrote a letter of warning and

mailed it

to the deepest part of myself

"No! No! No!" she shouted.

Katya has unusual grace in the way she moves. I noticed this the first seconds I laid eyes on her. It's as if a company of Russian ballerinas were spliced into her nervous system, choreographing her movements. Her attributes kept piling up like those late night TV offers: 'What would you give to have sex with this woman? Don't answer yet because we are also including incredibly shapely, sexy upper arms and an enchanting, seductive way of talking…'

"Oh my god," she was yelling now over the party music, "that is just so much bullshit. When is the last time you actually wrote a letter and mailed it?"

"I mailed a check to the cable company the other day," I said, my voice feeble.

"You got to be fucking joking'" she said. "What's wrong with email?"

"I didn't know you could e-mail a check…."

"No, you idiot! In poetry!" she said. "Why aren't poets talking more about texting and email and YouTube and STD's. You know modern stuff?"

I guess she had a point. So I read the lines again.

I wrote a letter of warning and E-mailed it

to the deepest part of myself

To me it had lost its ring.

"Oh, just go on," Katya said, looking around the party as if she had entirely lost interest in being near me.

Warning of the tide of time

and it's taking but not giving

How it would pound the shores of my dreams

"For fuck sakes," Katya said, with a kind of brutality in her eyes, "if Hemingway was here right now he'd punch you right in your face. You've got to develop a bullshit detector man. I mean really, you lose everyone in the flowery, bullshit language you choose."

With only slight hyperbole I can say she was the most beautiful woman I'd ever seen in real life. Even the way she had positioned herself in the white plastic lawn chair made it impossible for me to resist staring (not with disrespect) at the two lines commencing from her pubic bone, traversing her inner thighs into her hip bones, and the mini landscape of mounds and crevices between those lines. It was nothing short of Mother Nature herself, disguised in revealing denim, calling to me, saying: come forth- fornicate - multiply.

As I was about to read the last few lines I looked down at my words and it suddenly struck me how much I had toiled over this particular poem, how much I cared for it. It's always a struggle when I write; as I imagine (and hope) it is for all poets and writers. I remembered going back and forth between using the words buttresses and fortresses and ink and blood on this particular poem for days as I read it out loud hundreds of times to myself. It came to me then, drunk as I was, how draining it had been to make micro adjustments each and every one of the times I read it to myself, often only to change it back to the way it was the next time I read it. I thought about how upsetting it was when I finally felt it was finished and I read it one last time and it seemed flat and hollow. I had to put it away for a long time before I could read it again and not think it was a barnacle stuck on a whale's ass.

I read on:

As I know death will one day ruckus my shore

I will not alter my course or flatten my sail

Instead dance with the time I have now

Enjoying this ink until I can write no more

"The end," I said.

"Thank god" Katya said. She went to take a drink but her glass had been empty for a while. "I heard the beginning of a rhyme scheme and then you abandoned it," she said. Her voice sounded detached. She looked around the party as if she was missing out on something more important. Then turning to me she added, "Sorry, but it actually made me want to hurt you …hit you or something," she said, laughing. It was not a congenial laugh. "Listen, I'm going to be nice… no kind to you," she said, as if digging as deeply as she could for some suitable charity. "You should give this poetry shit up and find a different hobby."

The word hobby flew out of Katya's mouth like a roundhouse kick to my testicles. Suddenly she appeared different to me. Where previously she'd been electrified she now seemed drunk and uncouth. It was as if a drunken partygoer had tripped over her power cable, abruptly unplugging her. I stood up, unwinding my scarf and throwing it down on the lawn chair.

"Why don't you go get something you wrote Miss M.F.A in literature. That is if you can walk without splitting your jeans."

"Easy," my friend said. He had grabbed my drink off the table and held it out to me. "Take it easy. Have a drink."

"I'd like to see that misaligned face of yours stick its neck out and read me something you wrote." I fumed. By this time I was loud and drunk as hell and people were staring. "On second thought," I yelled with a conviction that surprised even myself, "why don't you shove your M.F.A up your ass!"

I stomped away with my poems to get another drink. The night air felt cool on the red, itchy welts on my neck. My friend sidled up to me and put his arm over my shoulders.

"Dude, no lie...it was awesome," he said.

He was as drunk as I was, if not more. I noticed my discarded scarf sticking half out of his pocket.

I never saw Katya again.

Google It!

It should have all ended with the arrival of the internet and Google, but my twenty five year battle with my friend turned brother-in-law, Trevon, over facts, big and small, important and trivial, continued right to the bitter end. Who recorded the song 'Dreaming' for instance, ABBA or Blondie, should have been easy to settle once and for all by simply Googling it (checking a Cd jacket was for whatever reason out of the question). Or finding out whether the largest fish in the world is the Whale Shark or the Blue Whale, the answer is as close as a couple of taps on the keyboard. I know for most of us these trivial questions are no brainers, but not for Trevon. Trevon swore up and down for years that it was Abba and the Blue whale. I'd say, 'Trevon a Blue Whale is not a fucking fish!' But in his mind he was always right; so he didn't bother checking facts and I didn't bother following up on convincing him. When someone says, I'm pretty sure you are wrong about that? I, like most people, go home and check my facts, look on the internet or look it up in some book or check a god damn album cover. I just can't see how someone as bravely verbose as Trevon was, and be called out (most of the time by me) on so many of his proclamations and not, secretly at least, fact check. I think Trevon felt if he admitted he was wrong it meant he lost at some secret contest vitally important to his self-esteem, like his ranking on some cosmic leader board would go down a notch. Being right all the time meant too much to him. And the fact he was wrong most of the time was a recipe for disasters big and small. In fact it turned out worse than I ever could have imagined.

I admit fact finding was a lot harder before the internet and search engines such as Google. When Trevon and I became friends there was no such thing as a smart phone. It was the early 80's, a time when bullshit was at one of its glorious apexes. It was the start of the 'ME' generation, a time to tell personal glory stories and talk shit to make it seem you've been everywhere, knew everything. For a lot of people not knowing something was merely a license to make shit up. Especially at a time before facts could so easily be checked.

Personal computers were few and far between in the early and mid 80's, but we had libraries brimming with books filled with unmitigated certainties. Trevon's own parents had a big set of encyclopedias moldering away in their basement; I saw them with my own eyes. So there is no real excuse, if you were determined enough, you could always check facts no matter the decade.

So in a way I blame myself for what happened in the end. I let Trevon carry on too long with his artificial facts. I should have rubbed his nose in reality more often. I should have followed up every one of our arguments, trivial as they mostly were, with details, numbers and certainties. I should have made a conscious effort to nip his abuse of reality in the bud. At least try to break his habit of believing his own bullshit. But, the thing was, it was just his way. People around him mostly accepted him for it. It was merely a bunch of harmless, trivial squabbling over nonsense most of the time. Let's face it, unless you are completely anal or insecure, a person's misrepresentation of the facts, really shouldn't be that big of a thing to bother about. Or so I thought. My mistake was not seeing it was an accumulative thing, how his constant defamation of facts was amassing and wearing on me. I was not aware of the rift that was growing between Trevon and myself, all because of these constant squabbles over trivialities.

I do place a lot of the blame on myself. Years ago, in his parent's basement, I could have taken out one of those moldy encyclopedia and shown him that the Whale Shark was indeed the largest fish in the world, made him realize there was value in the truth of things, dignity in wielding the sword of factual data, put it in his head if he didn't know something there was nothing to be gained by blatantly making shit up and then forever believing it himself, like he'd heard it from a reliable source. But, in those days, back in the 80's, down in his parent's basement, Trevon and I were usually arguing about girls, music or sports. There were so many opportunities to defend the truth while we listened to the new wave bands of the 80's we were so fond of, The Talking Heads, U2 and the Police, getting drunk on whatever we could get our hands on. I guess I got tired of arguing. Or just maybe, knowing I was right and he was wrong, made me feel superior. It's possible on some Freudian level I didn't want him to change.

We are all aware of the 'Trevon's' in our lives: the archetypal person who believes the truth is something you make up as you go along. There was the time he laughed at me when I said Egypt was in Africa. I mean I used to think how can it be he was educated in the same school system as me? How could he not know about Egypt and Blue fucking Whales! 'Ok where the hell is Egypt then smart ass', I'd ask? 'It's in the Middle-East brainiac', he'd say. 'That's not a continent, it's a subcontinent'. I would always let him under my skin and get pissed off and start yelling. 'And you're a sub-continental idiot' he'd say, laughing his smug laugh. If I hadn't been in love with his sister I would have punched his face.

'He's always been like that', Trevon's sister, and eventually my wife, Gina, would say. 'Don't let him bother you'.

'But, he never checks anything and he's wrong 99% of the time,' I would say. 'Do you think he has been pretending to be a dick all these years, just to get under my skin', I'd ask? At times I actually wondered if he was putting me on. It would explain his stubborn, almost absurd divergence from reality? Gina would keep saying 'Only if my dad has also been pretending to be a dick, because they are two peas in a pod'. To which I'd say, 'I don't recall your Father being such an annoying ass'.

'Well why don't you ask yourself why the hell you are friends with Trevon in the first place?' Gina would ask that every time I bitched about him. It was a very good question I have to admit.

To tell the truth I stopped considering him a friend after a certain point. And it wasn't just his refusal to use Google or any other means of fact checking. He turned into kind of a dick in every sense of the word. He treated his girlfriends horribly. Gina once took a Budgie he was given as a gift away from him because he annoyed the poor bird to the point of it being actual animal abuse. Trevon would do shit like constantly asking me, 'would I or wouldn't I?', about a woman at some party we were at or at the grocery store; meaning would I or wouldn't I have sex with them. I'd have to keep reminding him I was going with his sister. 'You pussy', he'd say.

Trevon never liked that I went with and eventually ended up marrying Gina. 'It violated the male ethical code,' he'd say. 'Real men don't do that to each other. Would you like it if I'd married your sister?' He'd asked. I would always thank god I didn't have a sister. "If you did have a sister,' he'd say, 'I'd be banging her. I'd do her right here on your balcony in front of you'.

I'd go into a rant about why my sister would never be caught dead with the likes of him; I'd get really worked up. 'Relax dude,' he'd say, 'you don't even have a sister'. Then he'd laugh that sinister, cruel laugh of his. I'd want to punch his face again.

Trevon did have a few good attributes, if you can believe it after how I've just gone on about him, but nothing redeeming enough to compensate for all his bullshit. He made a lot more money than I did and he never really had a job. He simply did that thing where if you stick with what you love and not worry about money, the money eventually comes. For him money came pretty easy. Trevon's thing was classic cars, he lived for them (well I'd actually argue that he lived to annoy me). He bought, refurbished and resold old cars. He was well known all over the country as a reliable American classic car expert and consultant. He was a walking search engine when it came to all things auto. He went on and on about cars, but in a way that was interesting. This was the Trevon I liked. This was the Trevon that everybody liked. This was the main reason he'd had so many girlfriends, plus he was a good looking guy; Trevon and Gina came from good stock. He talked very thoughtfully and even eloquently about cars, how they were a fusion of art and engineering. He was a poet when he talked about cars. And he did not let anyone pass one morsel of bullshit by him about anything to do with cars. He couldn't see this glaring contradiction within himself.

Another sign of the good in Trevon (although it might have been an isolated incident) was the time he called up Gina crying and all upset, going on about how he didn't like himself and wanted to change. Amen to that I thought. I asked Gina if he was drunk. 'Just a little', was his answer when she relayed my question to him. Gina put her hand over the receiver so Trevon couldn't hear and said he was crying. He was upset because he missed one of his old girl friends, Sara. He realized he'd been a prick and wanted to change, wanted her back, wanted to marry her. Fat chance in hell, I thought, the way he treated her, the way he ended it with her. He'd probably turned her into a lesbian. But, let's face it, kudo's for anyone seeing the error of their ways and at least talks about changing. Even though the next time I saw Trevon and asked if he'd talked to Sara he said, 'Why the hell would I talk to that bitch?'

So, given these few extenuating traits, feeble as they were, it wasn't totally outrageous that I would turn to Trevon for support when Gina and I broke up. She had had an affair and the guilt was eating her alive so she confessed one evening. It broke my heart. To make matters worse I knew the guy. I moved in with Trevon the next day. He told me, that as much as he would rather have me staying with him than Gina, he thought that I should have kicked her out, since she was the one who had the affair. In fact Gina did offer to move out, but I just couldn't be in that house without her, it would have been miserable.

Trevon did his best to pick my spirits up, almost to the point of irritating the crap out of me. I started thinking it was a mistake not getting my own place or renting a motel room for a few weeks. Repeatedly I told Trevon I needed a few down weeks, but he was dead set on taking me out and getting me laid. He kept saying 'Don't you waste this ticket dude, don't you waste this get out of jail free card! You and Gina might get back together and this window is going to close. If you act now it's technically not cheating!' Finally I convinced him that for now I would rather settle for getting wasted at his place and crying in my beer. The way I felt I probably wouldn't be able to have sex anyway. 'Jesus man,' Trevon said, 'this is why I'll never get married…it turns you into a god damn pussy. Plus, I don't trust these modern women, they're all liberated, they may as well come right out and say they think men are always the asshole in every situation'.

I'd say what I'd always say, 'you do know we are talking about your sister right, my wife?' He'd always reply, 'don't you start that shit again man, don't you even start! I love her, she's my sister, but they're all the same.'

In late November I really hit the blues. All those damn Christmas decorations come up so early and they are everywhere

270

these days. It just served to make me miss Gina and my old life even more. Trevon had the idea that we should get the hell out of Dodge, so to speak, go somewhere for a holiday; change the scenery. At first I wasn't interested in the idea. Getting drunk as hell and sunburnt somewhere down in Mexico wasn't my idea of a healing retreat. But he started talking about the south island of New Zealand and the Cook Islands, places like that. When I come to think of it this was so Trevon: he's the kind of guy that would rather get lost in some remote desert than lay on a beach in Maui. We narrowed it down to, Khoa Lak in Thailand about 50 miles north of Phuket. We could relax and do some scuba diving. I started to really get into the idea. I had loads of unused holidays at work, so we started planning to go for an entire month. That was until my work told me that they couldn't give me the time off.

"Well that is complete bullshit," said Trevon, "even after you told them about what's going on with you and Gina?" I couldn't believe my ears. "Are you nuts?' I said, 'I'm not about to tell them what's actually going on. I've got some pride you know." Trevon started shaking his head, "Oh you poor bastard," he said, "this isn't about your pride man, it's about honesty. (Hearing this from Trevon I actually laughed out loud) You don't have to tell everyone just call a meeting with your boss and your bosses boss and tell them the truth. Tell them you need some time, that you're about to crack. Your boss's boss will play the big sensitive, understanding, generous, caring boss. He'll jump at the chance to be the fucking hero. Because he doesn't actually have to worry about the implications of you fucking off for a month at Christmas. It's your immediate boss that will have to deal with that. And your immediate boss won't say shit. He won't want to ruin his boss's grand act of generosity. Just tell them you want to keep this whole thing quiet, by law they can't say a word. Besides they know something's up anyway, the way you mope around all day like you lost your dog or something."

"Or maybe like I lost my wife," I snapped.

So that's what I did and Trevon was exactly right, right down to my boss's boss acting like he was Mother fucking Theresa. He even predicated correctly my immediate boss's cold shoulder and contempt after the meeting. 'You do remember how crazy it is around here at Christmas don't you?' He said as he walked me back to my desk after our meeting. 'I'm sorry I just can't concentrate,' I said, which was in fact true. 'I'll have to arrange it with payroll," my boss said looking at me with cold, un-festive eyes. "Merry fucking Christmas," he said.

So that was it, Trevon and I were off to Thailand. On the flight over to Phuket Trevon got into an argument with the lady sitting behind us; her obnoxious, hyperactive kids kept banging the back of our seats. To make things worse Trevon was already drunk, so our side of the dispute had no credibility with the other passengers or flight crew. Having consensus on your side is important in these kinds of travel altercations. It got so serious the co-pilot came back and told us if we didn't all settle down the plane would be making an emergency U-turn and landing in San Francisco and we could deal with the police. That little announcement got more than an angry reaction from the rest of the passengers. Finally I suggested someone trade seats with us. We moved to the front of the plane as the woman with the kids kept shooting her mouth off. Finally a stewardess flipped out on her and the lady shut up and sat down. I told Trevon not to even so much as look at the woman or I'd poke his eyes out. He just kept telling me to relax. He thought it was all very funny until he went to order another drink and the Stewardess informed him he was not only cut off for the rest of this flight, but was now on the airlines 'do not serve alcohol list… forever. 'That's bullshit, we're switching airlines for the trip home,' Trevon said. "You are. I'm not. I would have cut you off a long time ago!' I said.

Eventually things settled down and I thought I'd try to have a nap. I laid my head against the window which felt cool. I closed my eyes and listened to the humming of the engines. 'It's amazing these things can even fly,' Trevon said. "Hmmm,' I said faintly, trying to make it known I was trying to sleep. 'Nothing aerodynamic about these big bastards, yet we fly,' he said. I knew that wasn't true, but I let it go. 'Scientists say these jets shouldn't even be able make it off the ground, yet here we are at 3500 feet.' I tried to ignore him, which you must admit is hard to do when you know someone is completely erroneous in what they are saying, like they're a bloody child or something. 'You mean 35000 feet,' I murmured with my eyes still closed, 'and that's the bumblebee.' I could feel Trevon glaring at me. 'What the hell you on about – what ya mean bumblebee?' 'Come on man give me a break,' I said turning deeper into the window. 'No seriously dude you said it now I want to know. You perked my interest,' Trevon said. 'It's piqued,' I said. 'What?' Trevon said. Which I replied, 'Forget it man, let me sleep'. Trevon was getting angry. 'Don't be a douche bag,' he said. 'Look, are you shitting me right now or what?' I asked, sitting up and looking at him. He had that excited look he gets when he's about to try and defend one of his abstracted versions of reality. 'Trevon, scientists don't know how the bumblebee flies. They know exactly how a jetliner flies,' I said. Trevon snickered, 'Oh my god here we go… bumblebee. You're crazy man,' he said. I was about to get mad, but instead I looked him straight in the eyes and said, 'Trevon, are you fucking with me right now? Is this your way of pissing me off? All these years you have just been fucking with me haven't you?' The way Trevon erupted at this I knew it wasn't an act. I would have thrown him right out of the plane if he had said yes, for decades he'd been merely fucking with me. He would have had to be the greatest actor on earth.

'I've got a Popular Mechanics magazine at home,' he shouted, 'it talks about how they don't know why jetliners can fly and they didn't say anything about fucking bumblebees. You know,' Trevon continued, somewhat calmer, 'you are not always right all the time. You don't know everything. I mean you are a smart guy I'll give you that, but you are not always right.'

To this I didn't know what to say. All these years I'd been busting Trevon's balls about his shit, I never once thought about how I must have looked to him. I felt like an uptight ass all of a sudden. 'Your right,' I said, 'I could be wrong. Show me the article in Popular Mechanics when we get home. I'm gonna have a nap,' I said, turning back towards the window. Of course Trevon got all self-righteous. 'Damn right you're wrong... Fucking bumblebees... Man you crack me up, you really do,' he said. Again, I fought my urge to punch his smug face. 'Can I get a bourbon?' he asked the stewardess as she passed. 'Nooo- yooo- maaaay- naaaahhht,' she sang, as she buzzed by us down the aisle.

The plane landed hard which won a reward of smattering applause. I think we were all happy to have the long flight over with. Trevon had sobered up and was miserable. We waited for the carousel to roll out our bags and then we walked out into the warm wet air of Phuket. We had dinner and got drunk at a place near the airport before we caught a bus to Khoa Lak. We stayed at an out of the way, not too touristy, resort. The place was stunning. I could already feel this trip was going to be good for me - one way or another.

'What do you mean one way or the other?' Trevon asked when I told him that at the resort's swimming pool the next day.

'What do you mean what do I mean?' I said. 'I don't mean anything. I'm saying it's gonna be good for me no matter what ends up happening,' I said. 'What ends up happening?' He asked. Incredulously he said. 'You're not thinking of going back to her are you? I didn't take you out here so you could decide to go back to Gina for fuck sakes —She cheated on you. It's over.' This got me absolutely hot. 'Listen,' I said, 'let's get a few things straight right now. You didn't take me anywhere asshole; you are not my fucking dad – ok. And I'll do whatever I see fit. If I feel like going back to Gina then that's exactly what I'm gonna do. I know she fucking cheated on me I'm trying to come to terms with it. But I also know, as you should know, she's a good person. She's a lot to lose.'

Suddenly I felt like crying. It was the first time I'd said it out loud, the part about a lot to lose. When I heard those words come out of my mouth it made it real. It was the end of my inner negotiations with reality; I had to accept that Gina and I could be losing each other. I let out a strange overwrought, staggered sigh. I could feel hot tears flowing down my cheeks. Trevon sat down at the end of my lounger shoving my feet over to make room. 'I know bro, I know. Settle down. I'm just saying it wasn't like it was one time. She had a relationship going with this guy.' Those words made me wince. I laid my head back on my towel squeezing my eyes hard to stop the tears. I let the Thai sun fill the inside of my eyelids with brilliant orange. If I choose to go back then I'll damn well go back, I said to myself. Deciding it could be as simple as that.

I felt Trevon get up and a few seconds later there was a splash in the pool. 'I know what we'll do,' he said, popping up at the edge and resting his forearms on the rim of the pool, 'we'll have his legs broke, we'll Guido the mother fucker.' This made me laugh. 'Ya sure,' Trevon said, 'I'm half Italian didn't you know?' 'Ya, let's break his legs! Why the hell not?' I said, as I plunged my sorry, whining ass into the pool.

So December of 2004 Trevon and I vacationed on the beaches of the Indian Ocean. We scuba dived every day. Trevon partied and I soul searched, he saw every sunset and I every sunrise. It was a hell of a time. The weather was spectacular. Just when we were getting sick of the sun a torrential rainfall would come and give us a needed break from the heat.

'Look around,' Trevon would say continually, 'lots of opportunity. Don't let it all slip by you. You might not get this chance again.' He was talking about women of course. There were lots of partying vacationers about. At night the bars were full. There were plenty of locals to engage with as well. I became friends with a local girl, Nurul. She had moved to Thailand from Indonesia. We spent a lot of time talking at nights in a local bar called the 'Banana Leaf'. All the while Trevon was boogying up a storm on the dance floor. I told Nurul my story one night over drinks and she said, 'You know it's just my luck that I start to like a guy and it turns out he's heartbroken over his wife. Does she want you back?' she asked. I told Nurul that Gina had said her affair was over, she hoped I wanted to work things out. 'All you have to do,' Nurul said, 'is keep your manly pride out of it. You guys will be fine, you'll see.' Hearing that was the turning point, I think. Not of me deciding to go back, I'd already made up my mind to go back, but of me not beating myself up over my decision, as if going back was somehow shameful.

Of course, with all the time we were spending together, Trevon and I didn't escape having an argument or two. The worst one being the time he was drunk as hell and told Nurul and I and his date for the evening, that we were all going to go skinny dipping in the ocean. 'No…no,' his date said, a local girl whose name I don't think I ever got. She could barely speak English. 'No…no' she said when Nurul explained to her in Thai what Trevon wanted to do. Apparently it was far too dangerous to swim at night because of sea snakes and puffer fish and Thai box jelly fish, which you wouldn't be able to see to avoid and which were all extremely deadly according to Nurul and the local girl. 'That's a complete load of crap,' Trevon said combatively. 'Listen Trevon skinny dip in the pool,' I said, trying to calm him down, 'it's a hell of a lot safer.' 'It's a load of crap,' Trevon stood, scowling in my face. 'They don't want Americans to spend their money here, he shouted. They want us all to go to Hawaii.' I stood up and pushed him back. 'Get the fuck out of my face you prick,' I yelled. Nurul grabbed my arm, 'He's drunk,' she said. 'He's always fucking drunk,' I said.

'You don't want to go skinny dipping 'cause my penis is bigger than yours! Google it...' He turned to the girls, 'Ha...why don't he fucking Google that!' he yelled.

This got the attention of the bar's proprietor who promptly came over. He was a small guy, but he looked tough and mean as hell. It was clear he wasn't there to mess around. 'You,' he said to Trevon in broken English, 'you too drunk ...too loud...you leave.' I thought Trevon was gonna start something with the guy. 'Trevon, so help me god if you don't leave right now we're through. I'll leave tomorrow, I swear to god,' I said. By this point I was yelling myself. Nurul kept pulling my arm to sit me back down. Then out came Trevon's opportune charm. 'Everyone just relax', Trevon said smiling, 'we're all good here, we're all nice. My lady and I were just leaving. Off to the pool where we'll strip down and howl at the moon.' Nurul and I sat in the bar for about twenty minutes before my cell rang. It was Trevon. 'Do you have any idea what this call is gonna cost you, you fool?' I asked. 'Relax man,' Trevon said, 'we're at the pool. I'm showing the girl my blue whale.' I laughed. 'Anyway, come on - come skinny dippin' with us,' Trevon said. 'I'm not so sure Trevon,' I said. 'Come on man, I was really hoping to see Nurul naked,' he said. 'You're such a prick,' I said.

Christmas Eve I called home and talked to Gina. I told her I missed her and I was still in love with her and I was willing to work things out if she was. She cried and said she was more than willing and that this had been the worst Christmas of her life. I told her we'd make up for it.

In the evening Nurul took Trevon and I to Christmas Eve Mass at the small local Catholic Church and to my surprise it appeared Trevon enjoyed it. Although after the mass he gave a whole load of crap story about how the Catholics had tried to get the Communist into Thailand, but the Buddhists were the ones that kept them out. I think he was trying to impress Nurul. She was about to correct him, but I waved her off. I think by the way I rolled my eyes she got the idea it wasn't worth the effort. But it did irritate her. So much so she made a point of telling Trevon it wasn't easy being a minority Catholic, here in Thailand or back home in Indonesia. And people making up ridiculous stories didn't help matters.

Christmas Day we had a picnic on the beach. Nurul brought a lot of food and Trevon brought his date from the previous night. We all got drunk. I missed Gina and tried not to talk about her; the more I drank the harder that was. Trevon, for the most part, was his charming self and we all had a good time. The girls had bought us gifts. Trevon's girlfriend gave him florescent, lime green speedos. Of course Trevon put them on right then and there in front of us. Nurul got me a bottle of champagne. 'It's for you and your wife to celebrate when you get home,' she said. Trevon shot me a condemning look, 'I knew, I knew it –you pussy.' he sneered. Nurul gave him a suitable retaliatory punch in the arm.

Towards evening Trevon and his date wandered off somewhere and I walked Nurul back to her place. I thanked her for the champagne. We hugged and ended up hesitantly and awkwardly necking for a few minutes. Nurul eventually pushed me away and we wished each other a Merry Christmas. I walked drunkenly back to my room.

The next morning Trevon woke me up early by jumping on my bed. 'What bloody time is it?' I asked. 'It's early,' Trevon said, 'we've got some diving to do'. I had forgotten about our plans for a Boxing Day dive. 'I was dreaming,' I said. 'About who,' Trevon asked, 'Gina or Nurul?' and he started moaning and humping the spare pillow on my bed. 'Ohhh Gina- Ohhh Nurul,' he groaned, simulating sexual intercourse with an unsettling amount of fervor. In between his juvenile thrusts I noticed an odd and different frequency of pulsation move through the bed. 'Trevon stop,' I yelled. He kept at his thrusts, 'Ohhh Gina,' he moaned. 'Trevon for fuck sakes stop!' I screamed. His eyes lit wide open when he did stop and the room continued to shake in deep undulations. 'Earthquake,' he said, sounding stunned. I looked at the clock on the nightstand; it was 7:58 am. The tremoring subsided. 'Well,' said Trevon 'wasn't that a bit of fun.'

We met our scuba guide and boat operator, Gustavo, down at the beach restaurant for breakfast. 'You guys feel the earthquake,' he asked. 'Sure did,' Trevon said. 'My girl asked if I was that good or did the earth actually move. I said it was all me baby.' Gustavo laughed. We sat at our usual table on the roof top patio, ordered the sea food breakfast and watched as the sea seemed to retreat further and further. 'Wow, the tide is really out this morning,' I said. Gustavo said he'd never seen it like this before. The boats at the docks where all pitched over in dry sand. We ate our breakfast and watched the birds dive down at the smorgasbord of stranded sea life.

We drank coffee and waited. It was now about 9:30am local time. 'Looks like it will be a while before we can take the boat out gents,' Gustavo said. 'I can't even see the water it's so far out,' I said.

'I wonder if this has something to do with the earthquake this morning,' Gustavo asked. 'Ya maybe it made a big crack and the water is draining into the center of the earth,' Trevon said, laughing. No one else found this funny.

There was a strange eerie silence about; the birds had finished their feast and were absent; in fact all the birds were uncommonly silent now. 'I don't know, I just don't like it,' Gustavo said. 'Nah,' said Trevon, 'I tell you what fellas, I'm gonna go get lunch.' He motioned towards where the ocean should have been. 'Trevon wait,' I said. Gustavo and I spotted an English fellow we had become acquainted with walking up the beach from where his boat leaned in the sand. He looked pale and irritated. 'Jackson!' shouted Gustavo. Jackson came over. 'Listen,' he said immediately, 'I just talked to a local and he thinks this is what happens right before a tsunami. The ocean recedes like this.' My heart jumped in my throat. 'The earth quake we felt earlier must have had its center out in the ocean. Everybody needs to get off the beach and up to higher ground!'

It's a strange thing when you hear something, no matter how horrible it is, and know in your bones that it's true. I saw the reality of Jackson's words slap a terror stricken look on Gustavo's face. I was sure he and I shared the same expression. 'Trevon we got to get the hell off the beach,' I yelled. 'What are you guys all panicking about for fuck sakes,' he said. 'Trevon,' I said, 'it must be what is happening. The ocean receding like this must be because a tsunami is coming.' 'This isn't even a tsunami zone for shit sakes,' Trevon said, insolently. 'It's just an extreme tide, probably because of the earthquake.'

'We've got to move Trevon,' I shouted, 'Quit pissing around'. Gustavo and Jackson had already left the restaurant and had started moving up the pathway to the road. I could still see them from the patio. 'You're not always right man; you don't know everything,' yelled Trevon. He turned and walked towards the ocean. Incredibly Trevon wasn't the only one walking out onto the barren sea floor. Some couldn't resist the enticement of this rare opportunity to walk so far out onto the sea bed. 'Trevon!' I yelled. What he did next will be burnt in my mind forever: Trevon, with his back to me walking towards the open ocean, raised his hand and flipped me the bird. 'It's the Blue fucking Whale,' I'm sure I heard him shout. 'Trevon get back here,' I shouted, 'The Blue Whale is not a fucking fish, now get back here.'

The inhabitants of the beach that morning seemed to be split between raw panic and leisurely curiosity. I saw a young couple leave the beach gear they had just set up a minute ago, someone had convinced them of the approaching danger, now they were running in blind panic. They passed along the way to higher ground a family with two young children going the opposite way, eagerly headed towards the mystery of an ocean without water. Myself I fell altogether on the side of panic. I wanted to tackle Trevon to the ground and drag his ass up the path to the road and get to the upper floors of the Horizon hotel where Gustavo and Jackson were already headed, but my instinct to save my own ass took over and I fled, leaving Trevon.

I met up with Jackson and Gustavo on the patio of the third floor restaurant of the hotel. The staff and patrons of the hotel seemed to be confused about all the commotion outside. Gustavo was doing his best to explain the approaching danger to the manager (even though no one was sure the Tsunami theory was actually correct). From the restaurant patio there was a clear view of the beach. There were two sets of observation binoculars mounted on fixed tripods that were for the use of hotel patrons. Jackson was on one and Gustavo manned the second. "Jesus merciful lord!' Jackson said in a low stunned voice. Then both he and Gustavo erupted into shouts to the people below, warning them to get to higher ground, Gustavo in his primitive Thai and Jackson in English. My heart jumped out of my mouth. I looked through the observation binoculars and after getting my bearings and fumbling with the focus I saw it: a twenty five foot wall of water. I knew it wasn't merely a large wave heading for shore, but the ocean itself, skulking back to contentiously reclaim its rightful position and more; much more. The waters had gathered itself, all throughout the Indian Ocean, pushed up from the large movement of the sea floor by the earthquake an hour and a half before. It was now going to assert itself as far inland as its extra twenty five feet of amplitude would allow.

I could see the wall of water coming, convulsing with deadly force and I could see the smattering of people, looking miniscule by comparison, poking around on the sand before it. I was afraid for Nurul all of a sudden and wondered where she might be, but there was nothing I could do to find her. I hoped she was on high ground, or far enough inland. I searched for Trevon's blue shirt. I thought I spotted him amongst the people farthest out. I thought about my next call home and what I would say to Gina. Without thinking I pulled my cell phone out of my pocket and flipped it open and dialed his number. 'We're sorry the cellular customer you are trying to reach is unavailable,' said the recorded message. I hung up and immediately tried again, this time it rang. I looked through binoculars at who I thought was Trevon. Jackson and Gustavo were still shouting at the people below to come up to the higher floors. I wondered if Trevon and the others out there on the ocean floor could see the wall of water approaching; they must hear it I thought. I wondered because no one out there was trying to run. It would have been futile at that point anyway. For their last minutes on earth they would have to live with the mistake of being beguiled by the allure of a deserted ocean floor.

Through the binoculars I saw the man in the blue shirt reach in his pocket and pull something out and put it up to his face.

'Hello,' came Trevon's voice.

'Trevon!' I screamed.

'Ya, I know. I know,' he said.

Main Street

Henry rested his chin on his hands and gazed down the long, wooden table. This way he could see clear down his miniature replica of Main Street, circa 1949. He searched his memory for anything he may have over looked. For the thousandth time he referenced the old black and white photos pinned on the wall. He studied the fences and trees, the mail box and fire hydrant. He took care to see that the Christmas lights and decorations were exactly right. Everything was in perfect placement and scale.

The one thing that bothered him was Buddy the black lab frozen on his back legs as if caught in the middle of a playful leap.

This miniature version of Buddy was far too frisky. The real Buddy, as Henry could not forget, was tempered and mellow, but he could not find a model in the proper scale and look that mimicked Buddy's actual demeanor. The man at the hobby shop brought out some catalogs and offered to special order a more appropriate Buddy, but Henry confessed he hadn't the time to wait. Besides, Henry thought, this problem could be fixed with a little imagination: Buddy was merely leaping for a low flying bird and once time started moving again he would quickly regain his low-key disposition.

Once time started moving again other things would correct themselves as well. Henry had always had an odd opinion about the workings of time. He couldn't explain it in words so he seldom talked about it. But he knew time was in no way fixed. He saw in the way minutes ticked by slowly during the week and flew by during the weekend, how one minute his daughter was in diapers and the next she was graduating college. To Henry time could be worked with, it was malleable.

Yes, once time started moving again little errors in his model would correct themselves. There was, for instance, no felt hat on Mr. Philips head as he sat on the bench outside the barber shop smoking his pipe. The reason for this was the hobby shop didn't have a miniature Mr. Philips with a felt hat. Henry had to settle for the model which was the spitting image of Mr. Philips: a pipe, paunch belly, a blue shirt and suspenders. It was only the felt hat that was missing. Henry was ok with these minor inconsistencies, they would correct themselves. It would soon be revealed that Mr. Philips' hat was at the haberdashery getting its silk band replaced.

Overall the accuracy was stunning. This was Main Street, 1949. No mistaking it. Henry could even hear the whistle blowing from the textile mill. He checked his watch: 1:37pm. No, he thought, that's not right. Then he realized it wasn't the whistle from the textile mill at all. It was the kettle from the kitchen. He had forgotten he had put it on. Henry went to make himself a pot of tea.

On the counter next to the stove the message machine flashed - 17 messages. There was also now a note taped to the outside of the back door facing in through the window. The message written with a red felt pen said: *Lois call your daughter, she's been trying to get a hold of you and Henry. You guys alright in there? - Sandy.* Sandy had been Henry's and Lois' neighbor for forty years. Henry knew his daughter would be worried and she had called Sandy to come by and peak through the windows and check up on him and Lois.

But sticking the note on the kitchen door had been Sandy's idea; Henry was certain of this. He had heard Sandy's knocks and calls at the front door and then the back door and then the front door again. Henry had always known Sandy to be a determined and patient woman so the relentlessness of her knocking was no surprise. He had ignored her rapping and shouting, while he installed the last of the wires to the miniature street lights. He was grateful that Sandy had either forgotten she had a key or she'd misplaced it. Lois had given her a key to the house twenty six years ago so she could water their plants and generally keep an eye on the place while she and Henry and their daughter were off on a holiday in Europe.

Presently, in the kitchen, the phone rang again. Henry ignored it and poured the hot water into the teapot and placed it along with two cups and two saucers onto a carrying tray.

"It won't be long now Lo," Henry hollered down the hall towards their bedroom.

The answering machine took the call.

Henry carried the tray past the spare room where the model of Main Street awaited its final touches, and stood outside the closed bedroom door.

"It won't be long now my dear," Henry said again, softly. "It's all looking as beautiful as it did back then. I'm just waiting for a delivery from Lupton's hobby shop. Snow! Lo can you believe it, model snow. I didn't know there was such a thing. This stuff is from Germany and of the highest quality. It's supposed to sparkle like the real stuff. Do you remember how it snowed Lois, on this day back in 49', the day we met? Boy how it snowed that day. Now you rest dear and don't mind the phone or the knocking." Henry didn't seem to notice the rank odor coming from the bedroom or that it had permeated the house.

He carried his tray into the spare room, sat down and studied his creation. He had worked on it for 16 months. The only thing taking priority over his model Main Street was his doting over Lois. In the beginning he didn't know why he had such a drive to build an exact model of Main Street in December, 1949. The idea just popped in his head on the drive back from Lois's doctor. Lois was talking about not worrying, saying everything was going to be fine, that the newer treatments were effective. All the while he was imagining a miniature Main Street. As soon as they got back to the house he started sketching and planning, gathering up old photos and calling hobby shops.

Model railroad products proved to be a blessing. Their catalogs had all the necessary sizes and types of buildings and scenery. Cars, people, street lights and landscapes. You name it and it could be ordered. Even trees and bushes of differing types and shapes could be obtained with relative ease. Best of all everything was scaled and worked accordant with each other.

Now, he paid particular attention to the miniature hardware store at the end of the street. After all this time it was a pleasure to focus this much attention on such a fine memory as Ray's Hardware, which held a paramount place in Henry's childhood. It was his first real job and he found it himself, much to his father's surprise. It was the first time Henry had felt truly proud. He threw his heart and soul into Ray's Hardware store. Getting paid to be there was merely a bonus.

Years prior his father had got him on as an Altar Boy at St. Mary's Holy Church and he considered it a chore or to be more accurate, torture. Now, Henry couldn't wait until the evening service was over on Sunday so he could go to Ray's and sweep the floor again. The store was closed on Sundays, but old Ray had given young Henry the key. He turned the radio on loud. The Jazz station came in crystal clear at night and he listened to Duke Ellington and Ray Mercer as he dusted and straightened the shelves until every corner of every box was plumb and level, and every shelf dust free. He remembered walking home those winter evenings, his feet making the crunching noise in the snow, with only the moon and Buddy the Lab keeping him company. Back then he had the feeling he was king of the world and having the key to Ray's Hardware store in his pocket was proof he was.

It was there at Ray's store on this very date back in 49' that he first laid eyes on Lois. Back then Henry and his young pals had many times talked over plans of seeing the world and in the process enjoying a plethora of exotic girlfriends. One look at Lois and for Henry that plan had gone directly into his dust bin along with the afternoon sweepings. The first thing he noticed about the young woman as she entered the store was the chroma of blue in her eyes; he had never seen a crystal sea in a girl's eyes before. As he watched her stroll up and down the aisles of hardware goods he could have sworn he knew her from somewhere. The feeling of recognition was so intense he had to fight his first instinct, which was to hug her and say he'd missed her. Finally he gathered courage enough to ask if he could help her find something. She explained, all without looking up from the shelves, her family had just moved to the area and her father had sent her for a door hinge. Henry inquired what type, that there were many. Lois looked up and when she saw Henry's face her mouth stopped in mid- word. 'I guess… I'm not certain', she said falteringly when finally she spoke again. Then she said: 'Do I know you? Have we met before somewhere?'

Henry got permission from old man Ray to walk Lois back to her home to inquire about the door hinge. There and back they walked through the swirling snow. As often as possible, but disguised as an accident, Henry made the back of his hand touch the back of Lois's hand. Unbeknownst to him she was feeling the jolts of warm electricity from the contact as much as he was. They laughed when they simultaneously told each other they were glad it was snowing. And then Lois put her arm in Henrys and told him he was a gentleman for making sure her father got the proper hinge. From then on they were inseparable, spending every day together for the next 66 years.

They got married, bought a home and had a child. They settled into a splendid, contented life. Together they watched all the changes to the world. These last six months when Lois's hair began to fall out Henry kissed her as much as he had done when she was young and ravishing and beautiful. When her treatments made her so sick she lay bed-ridden for days, Henry laid with her for hours upon hours, rubbing her back or stomach. When she finally slept he worked on his model of Main Street.

Now Henry sipped his tea and tried the street lights and Christmas lights. They all came to life in a flawless array of scaled-down grandeur. He rested his chin on his hands again and took another long gaze down his past. By the memories leaping up from his mind and the feeling of nostalgia pulling at his heart he knew he had captured the essence of the original.

For some reason it made him remember the day old man Ray had him help Mrs. Wilkinson look for her missing cat instead of working in the store. Ray was like that, paying him a whole day's wages to look for a neighbor's cat. It was well past quitting time when Henry climbed the treehouse behind the Flanagan's house to find nine year old Wendy Flanagan stroking Mrs. Wilkinson's cat who was sleeping next to a child's tea set and a large and empty bottle of cream. 'You're not going to tell are you Henry?' asked a tearful Wendy. Later, when Lois asked Henry how his day was, and he told her about Wendy Flanagan kidnapping Mrs. Wilkinson's cat and admitted he'd kept Wendy's secret he was rewarded with a marvelous kiss from Lois. It was these simple memories that had the power to stand un-eroded by time.

That was more than sixty years ago. Yet, it was as present in Henry's mind as if it were only yesterday. Even smells were coming back. His nose filled with the faint, familiar scent of spent kerosene from the textile mill's large engines. It mixed with the cool crisp scent of freshly falling snow. Sounds too, he could hear a train blowing its whistle as it approached the Main Street crossing and the roar of Nash 600's and Buick Roadmasters racing to beat it. The tones met his ear as fresh as if it were all happening right outside his window. That's how Main Street smelled and sounded back then. It was exactly what Henry wished for from his model: the ambience, the feeling of physically being there, a conduit. He wanted to be spellbound, detached from the present moment, adrift in that place, in that time. People say you can never go back, but Henry had his own ideas about time.

He was still afloat in his reflections when a pounding at the front door snapped him back to the present. He knew it wasn't Sandy this time because the knocking was different; it had a serious, business cadence.

"Ah, the snow my dearest, the snow has arrived!" Henry shouted to the next room.

Henry opened the front door. He was pleased to find that snow had come in two ways: a delivery truck had come to deliver the facsimile and the real stuff had come via the gray, December sky. He had been expecting both. A new white blanket had accumulated on roads and sidewalks that had been plowed and shoveled only days before.

"Sorry to be so late sir, the roads are a bit treacherous," said the delivery man. "Yours is the last delivery. After this I'm calling it quits. Snows too heavy and the roads are too slick and they don't pay me enough…"

"Beautiful," said Henry, dreamily, indicating the fresh falling snow.

"Ahh, ya," said the delivery man. "A bit treacherous," he repeated, somewhat dismayed at the lack of sensitivity to his complaints.

"You're not late, you're just in time," Henry said.

The delivery man stepped forward to hand Henry the parcel. His nose at once perceived a faint yet rancid odor. His face wrinkled into a grimace. Henry took the parcel. The delivery man retreated a few steps. He held out a clipboard for Henry to sign and tried to remove his attention from the odd smell.

"Everything alright in there, sir?" the delivery man asked.

"Why my good man, everything is as right as freshly falling snow."

To this the delivery man only shrugged. Henry signed his name and handed back the clip board.

"Here you are my good man," Henry said, slipping the man something. The Delivery man took it without looking to see what it was.

"Sir it's not necessary, really," said the delivery man, trying to hand whatever it was back.

"No, no you can't begin to imagine what this parcel means to me," Henry said. Looking only at the package in his hands, he said, absently, "Please Drive safely, now," and closed the door.

The delivery man walked almost to his truck before he reluctantly looked at what was in his hand. He preferred not to be tipped, especially by the elderly, who he knew to be stuck in a golden era where a quarter held much more dominion then it did presently. Usually his tip never added up to much more than an insult. Looking down now he was shocked. Abraham Lincoln's face peered up at him. It was a 1949 silver dollar, worth a tidy sum.

The house was dark inside except for one sparse light in the room down the hall to the right, where Henry's replica awaited him.

"Snow my dear, the snow has arrived," Henry pronounced from the hallway. "Snow outside and snow inside, snow like the day we met. Soon Main Street will be glistening the way it did all those years ago. You'll see Lois. It won't be long now."

There was a sticker slapped haphazardly across the front of the package of imitation snow with instructions translated from German into English. It advised: to achieve an authentic look apply by sprinkling from a distance of approximately eighteen inches above project. It was more pleasurable than Henry could have imagined, playing the hand of God, making it snow over Buddy and Mr. Philips, the sidewalks and the trees, the Christmas decorations and the cars, the houses and factories. The most pleasure came from sprinkling snow on and around Ray's Hardware store, as if he was sprinkling joy back on the days of his youth.

He stood back and looked at his handy work. It was more stunning than he ever thought possible. The fine silicate of the model snow twinkled and shone with as much richness and splendor as the real snow outside. He turned the room's small light off and when he turned the switch to activate all the lights interspersed throughout his replica of Main Street, he had to sit down. His heart filled with heavy nostalgia and sorrow. He thought about all those years with Lois. He began to weep, his jaw quivered with inconsolable heartbreak. It didn't make any sense that he and Lois should ever have to say goodbye to each other. It was impossible for Henry to be without Lois. He simply would not accept that she was gone, irretrievably gone. Such emptiness shouldn't have any place among the order of things. Such a void puts a tear in nature, a rift in the fabric of the universe itself, a crack in time.

"Lo, oh Lo, wait 'til you see the Christmas lights, it's a miracle, it truly is," Henry whispered, his voice broken with grief.

There was heaviness in his chest. A pain shot up through his jaw. A wave of fatigue far more intense than he had ever felt before engulfed him. It forced his head back down on his hands. It took all the effort he had to keep his eye lids open so he could stare down Main Street. He concentrated on the lights and the twinkling snow as the pressure in his chest turned into terrorizing pain.

Old memories surged up from the snowy street:

He was watching Lois march past the Christmas carolers outside of the department store. She was ten paces in front of him, boiling with anger. He couldn't remember why she was angry, but he knew it was something he'd done or hadn't done. 'Alright Lo,' he remembered saying, 'go on then I'm not about to chase after you.' He'd turned his back to her. There came a hard impact of a snow ball in the back of his head and Lois's laughter. He turned and Lo was smiling, forming in her mitted hands another cold, hard projectile. He spread himself out like a crucifix. 'Ok Lois, 'I'll give you one more free one, just don't hit me in the...' The snow ball walloped him square in the face. He remembered seeing stars and tasting blood from his split upper lip. He was momentarily blinded and stunned. Then Lois's warm hands, mittens removed, placed on either side of his face. And her kiss on his bloody lips. 'Let's get you home,' she said, 'I'll make you some warm soup and we'll talk this through. There is nothing we can't grow through, Henry.' He remembered she'd said grow…grow through.

"Grow through," whispered Henry. The words Lois spoke with such poise so long ago, could barely leave Henry's lips now.

There was a loud bang at the back door and the sound of breaking glass; it all sounded very far away. He thought he heard the voice of his daughter and that of a man.

"Oh my god," his daughter's voice was frantic, "something is wrong."

Henry heard rushed footsteps down the hall towards the bedroom and a hysterical scream.

"Mother, oh lord Mom."

Henry heard his daughter's cries from the next room. Behind him the door opened. And then a policeman was standing beside him with a handkerchief over his mouth and nose saying, "Sir, are you in need of medical assistance?" Then his daughter vaulted into the room.

"Dad, dad!?" she cried.

There was no more pain in Henry's chest.

Time had started moving again. Henry was walking down Main Street. Buddy had just finished leaping after a swooping Blue Jay and was now content to walk placidly, as he always did with Henry, all the way to Ray's Hardware Store. It had snowed during the night and it looked as if it would snow again. As Henry passed the barber shop he said good morning to Mr. Philips.

Henry opened Ray's Hardware and began his day like so many Saturdays before, happy there was no school or church. The day was all his.

The first thing he noticed about the young woman who had just then entered the store was the chroma of blue in her eyes. He had never seen a crystal sea in a girl's eyes before.

ABOUT THE AUTHOR

Kevin Habekost is a machinist and author. He lives with his wife Marita - and their dog Jackson in New Westminster, British Columbia. He is currently working on more short story anthologies and an alternate history novel.

All of these stories were written sometime between 2015 and 2019.

If you enjoyed this novel please give a favorable review to a friend or on line (Amazon, Goodreads etc.). Thank you.

Comments are welcomed at:

kghwords@gmail.com

Made in the USA
Columbia, SC
17 June 2021